D0340031

# AS YOU
# WALK
# ON BY

## ALSO BY JULIAN WINTERS

# AS YOU WALK ON BY

## JULIAN WINTERS

VIKING

VIKING
An imprint of Penguin Random House LLC, New York

First published in the United States of America by Viking,
an imprint of Penguin Random House LLC, 2023

Copyright © 2023 by Julian Winters

Penguin supports copyright. Copyright fuels creativity, encourages diverse voices,
promotes free speech, and creates a vibrant culture. Thank you for buying an authorized
edition of this book and for complying with copyright laws by not reproducing, scanning,
or distributing any part of it in any form without permission. You are supporting writers
and allowing Penguin to continue to publish books for every reader.

Viking & colophon are registered trademarks of Penguin Random House LLC.

Visit us online at penguinrandomhouse.com.

Library of Congress Cataloging-in-Publication Data is available.

Printed in the United States of America

ISBN 9780593206508

10  9  8  7  6  5  4  3  2  1

BVG

Design by Monique Sterling

Text set in Cheltenham

This book is a work of fiction. Any references to historical events, real people, or real
places are used fictitiously. Other names, characters, places, and events are products of
the author's imagination, and any resemblance to actual events or places or persons,
living or dead, is entirely coincidental.

The publisher does not have any control over and does not assume any responsibility for
author or third-party websites or their content.

# FOR ALL THOSE

who are too afraid to dream big—
I dare you to believe in yourself.
Win when the world expects you to lose.

# THE RULES OF A DARE

**Rule number one** to accepting any dare: never agree to something you're not 99.5 percent positive you can complete.

It's the easiest rule to honor.

Never ask a random peer an invasive question if they look like they've had a bad day and could potentially murder you on the spot. Don't agree to eat a ghost pepper if you have a low tolerance for spicy foods. Absolutely no streaking in a neighbor's yard if you can't outrun their usually playful but extremely protective Akita.

On second thought, no streaking. Period.

I know all this by heart. I also know the second Jay Scott opens his mouth to say, "Theooooooo, you're up!" at the beginning of lunch, I'm doomed. As if this never-ending week of studying and exhausting track practices weren't enough.

Now it's a Dare Day too.

Since freshman year, Friday dares have been a staple for me

and my two besties, Jay and Darren. Back then, we were awkward, hormonal nobodies. The self-appointed TNT—The Nameless Trio. As juniors, we're a tight, debatably corny crew who've become the heart and soul of the boys' varsity track-and-field team. But the dares were the gateway to breaking out of our shells here at Brook-Oak.

Jay started it all. On an arbitrary Friday in November, he crowed, "Someone dare me to do something!" It's as if he knew we were all tired of trying and failing to find our footing in a new environment. Out of the three of us, he's always been the most outgoing. Ready to jump into a fire without looking.

So I did.

"I dare you to run around the quad three times, as fast as you can . . . shirtless."

Not my most creative effort. What can I say? I'm not my best when put on the spot. He did it anyway because, of course. It's Jay.

A month later, he dared Darren to eat three packets of sriracha with no water. Then Darren dared me to propose to Brianna Matthews using only Taylor Swift lyrics. Once a month, on a Friday during lunch, Dare Day rolls around. It's an established tradition. And no matter how much we've grown out of it, none of us have the heart to disrupt the status quo. Least of all me.

There are some unspoken rules to this: Nothing illegal. Nothing that'll cause *too much* bodily harm. Only things that'll earn us weird looks or gauche laughs. Oh, and the occasional after-school detention after jumping on one of the quad's tables to sing Mariah Carey's classic "Always Be My Baby" for all to witness.

Not bragging, but I *nailed* that performance. Even added a little falsetto at the end to noisy applause.

That's another bonus: the attention from other students. I can genuinely say I've made several acquaintances—authentic friends too—from the stunts Jay or Darren have challenged me to do.

The dares solidified our group. We find ways to get in trouble together so no one takes the fall alone. All for one, one for all or whatever. Like last month when Darren had to reenact a scene from *Magic Mike* . . . shirtless.

(Seminudity is a recurring theme.)

Anyway, Jay and I stood shoulder to shoulder with him as we all got scolded by Vice Principal Clarke for disrupting the lunch period.

But none of our history prepares me for Jay's challenge.

"I dare you to ask Christian Harris to prom."

"Oh. Shit."

In my periphery, Darren's thick eyebrows shoot up his forehead.

We're outside. Early April in Louisville means the weather hasn't turned violently hot yet, but my face is on fire. My breath catches uncomfortably in my throat.

It's not an unreasonable dare. Public humiliation is very on brand for us.

It's just that . . .

Okay, I swear I'm not a serial crusher. *Anymore.* But briefly, I was a seasonal crusher. Fall of freshmen year, I was all about Jonah and his football-camp calves. Post-winter-break, it was nothing but Danesh and his sweater obsession.

Then came sophomore year and Christian Harris.

Brook-Oak is a magnet school. Christian's enrolled in the Young Performers of Tomorrow program. I'm in the High School

University program. But all general academic classes are taken in the main building. That year, I randomly selected the desk behind his in language arts.

Fine, it wasn't coincidental.

Christian was one of the rare out kids in our grade. I was too. It's not always the wisest thing to crush on the *first* queer person around your age you meet, but I couldn't help it. My strategic desk choices resulted in us being partners on a mock trial project. I still daydream about his radiant expression whenever I misquoted a passage or asked for his help.

Even now, my eyes are drawn right to him.

The body count in the quad is scarce today. It's the Friday before spring break. Most students are either holed up in our school's glass-enclosed cafeteria or the library, studying for last-minute quizzes.

Christian's surrounded by his usual cartel of band geeks, talking animatedly with his hands. There's this old song—"Brown Skin" by India.Arie—that my pops loves. It reminds me of Christian. Warm sepia complexion. Baby-faced with a wide smile, crinkled eyes when he laughs. It's not just the thirst talking either. He's genuinely friendly to everyone.

A true prom prince in the making.

"Well?"

Across from me, Jay patiently sips on a glacier cherry Gatorade, smirking. He's got a severe case of Confident White Boy Syndrome. Blond topknot, gray-blue eyes, mostly clear skin.

I chew the inside of my cheek.

Why did I ever mention my crush on Christian?

On my left, Darren says, "Give him time to think, bro." He stuffs a handful of spicy cheese puffs in his mouth. Luckily, Coach Devers isn't on lunch duty today. She'd annihilate him for breaking diet.

I'm not one to talk since I smashed an entire cup of soft pretzel bites ten minutes ago.

Darren chases his food with his own Gatorade. Jay always brings a six-pack from home for us on Fridays.

"What're your terms?" he asks Jay. "What's the reward?"

Another implicit stipulation of the dares—incentives. Little rewards. Since Darren and I aren't typically as . . . *bold* as Jay, he's found ways to encourage us to play along. Free iced coffees for a week. An extra pizza pie after a track meet. New cleats spikes.

"Glad you asked." Jay unlocks his phone before scooting it across the stone table. The open tab is our school's prom page.

This year's theme: When You Wish Upon a Fairy Tale.

Cheesy? Yes. Is every junior and senior making a big deal about it? Hell yeah.

"If you pull it off, I'll front your whole prom experience, Theo. Tickets. Car service. Dinner. Suit and shoes. All of it." Jay reaches over to brush nonexistent lint off my shoulder. "Can't have my boy looking weak when he scores a date with his dream partner."

I roll my eyes.

First off, Jay's family has that old money wealth. As in Scott Boulevard is named after his great-great-grandfather's contributions to the city. They could afford our squad's prom package, plus a fresh SUV just for Jay's *shoes* to arrive in. I'm not hating— his mom and my pops go way back to their days at this very high school. It's just facts.

Second . . . "dream partner"? Really?

Jay's levels of trying too hard are infinite.

"Think about it, bro," says Darren, nudging my elbow. "Picking up Christian wearing a sick Gucci suit for the night of your life."

I know Darren's overselling the idea because he's dying to witness another wild dare. But he doesn't have to.

Something my best friends don't know is, I want this. Badly. I'm not as economically blessed as Jay, Darren, or 75 percent of the Brook-Oak students. Prom is a barely attainable goal for me. I've found an off-brand tux online. New shoes don't even enter the equation. Dad volunteered his semi-dented, two-door Civic for the night. Dinner wouldn't be more than a trip to a cheap, inauthentic Italian restaurant with stale breadsticks at best.

Between that and tickets, Dad would have to work a week's worth of overtime. He refuses to let me get a job before I'm eighteen, which isn't until November. I can't stomach him doing all of that just for *junior* prom. Not with college app fees on the horizon.

Selfishly, though, I can't stop thinking about prom night. Getting dressed up. All the selfies. Kissing a boy in the middle of a dance floor. After prom . . .

I want it all.

Using some of that Scott family money to fund my dream is high-key incentive enough.

"Wait." I tilt my head. "What happens if I fail?"

At worst, a failed dare has included detention and being shamed by the group. Sometimes, one of us is the latest victim of #BOHSFail on Instagram. The hashtag has its own unique following—mostly Brook-Oak theater kids, students from nearby schools. None of us have ever opted out of a dare.

But the prize has never been this large either.

Jay's mouth curls up on the left side, the way it does when he knows he's about to win at a round of Mario Kart.

"If you fail, then you have to wear MV High gear to our first practice after spring break."

My spine locks, shoulders pulled up to my ears.

Mountainview High is our rival. An equally competitive college prep school on the other side of Wilder Park. We're pretty much neck and neck in academic achievements. It's athletics where things are imbalanced. MVH owns us in football, softball and baseball, and soccer while we continuously destroy them in basketball, swimming, volleyball, and cheerleading.

The sport that could tip the scales: track-and-field.

In two weeks, we meet in the conference finals.

Coach Devers unapologetically despises our rivals. Since her days as a track star at BOHS. Four straight years of finishing second to Mountainview in all the major events.

Not a single W against them.

If I'm caught wearing their apparel at a practice, she'll bench me. "Support whoever you want *outside* of *my* lanes," she tells us every year. Coach is strict about her rules. If dress code is broken, that means no conference finals, where a dozen or so college scouts will be in the stands. As the anchor of our 4x400 relay team, this is my chance to stand out. Senior season is too late to chase scholarships from the top colleges. I'd be missing an opportunity to hit an asterisk on Dad's plans.

I can hear his voice in my head: *All we have to do is follow*

*The Plan. Stay focused. Your bright, unstoppable future is right there . . .*

"Damn!" Darren's howl pulls me back to the moment. "That's . . . harsh."

Jay shrugs listlessly. "Our boy Theo can handle it."

I purse my lips. We're both good at this—ego-boosting. While playing video games, during practices, before a dare.

"Coach will slaughter him," Darren notes.

*Yes, thanks for confirming my worst fears, D.* In our group, he's the Jiminy Cricket. Our conscience. The "hold up, this might get us arrested" voice of reason.

Every squad needs one.

"She'll think it's a *joke*," Jay insists, laughing. "Wearing MVH gear right before we crush them at finals? She'll send pictures to that dick-breath Mountainview coach." He turns back to me. "Besides, how hard is it to ask a guy to prom?"

*Very, actually*, a concept Jay will never comprehend.

My eyes flicker over to Christian.

Despite being out since I was fourteen, I've never *approached* a crush before. But something about the way the sun brightens the brown of Christian's eyes, I'm certain of this:

I want him to be the first.

I want his laughter against my lips as we kiss at prom.

"I'm in," I say.

Darren nearly flails out of his seat. Jay's eyebrows rise slowly like he's simultaneously shocked and impressed. I don't know why. Making bad choices is in my genes.

Exhibit A: Theodore Jamal Wright, my full government name.

For seventeen years I've lived with the knowledge that my name's an amalgam of Dad's favorite childhood TV character—Theodore Huxtable—and the actor who portrayed him—Malcolm-Jamal Warner. Clearly, tragic decision-making is inherited.

"Just . . ." I whisper, feeling the adrenaline tripling in my system. "Gimme a sec."

"Sure," says Jay. "Take all eight minutes you have left."

"What?"

Darren, all smooth light-brown skin and undercut showing off his sharp jawline, holds up his phone to indicate the time.

12:52 p.m.

Fuck.

Another rule: all dares must be completed before the end of lunch. Since we've rarely shared classes at BOHS, a built-in pre-requisite to prevent cheating was needed: *At least one member of the squad must be present to witness the dare.*

Scrambling, I open my selfie camera.

Overall, I don't look like a complete disaster. My sponge twists could use a touch-up. Glowing brown skin with gold undertones. No leftover pretzel mustard around my mouth. Plain black T-shirt and matching joggers. An old pair of Jordan 1 Retros in Smoke Grey.

Simple and classy.

"Ticktock, TJ," sings Jay.

I lower my phone to give him an unobstructed view of my middle finger. I don't do nicknames. Surviving years of teasing from my elementary school classmates—*hello, Theodore Roosevelt!*

*Ted! Teddy Bear!*—earned me that right. Only Dad is permitted to call me TJ now.

"I'm going, *Jayson*," I shoot back with an equally taunting grin.

Jay's face reddens. Only his mom calls him that.

As I'm leaving, Darren narrates, "This is really happening. Way to lean into your confidence, Theo. Get yours. Step right into that big, bright, romantic—"

"Added commentary not helping, D."

Darren throws a hand over his mouth, nodding.

When Jay's eyes meet mine, he lifts a brow as if to say, *Well? Are you gonna punk out?*

Nah, I'm not. I'm Theo Wright, soon to be conference champion in the 4x400 relay. Christian Harris's future prom date.

Across the quad, Christian and his friends are packing up. They toss their trash in the proper bins. Other students pivot toward the main building. I cut through a pack of senior cheerleaders, nearly knocking Makayla Lawrence over.

"Sorry, sorry," I mutter, quickly helping her reorient.

As far as cheerleaders go, Makayla's harmless. She's pretty much sociable with everyone at Brook-Oak. According to rumors, she's *extra* friendly with the guys.

"Be careful," she says with a sigh, running to catch up with her friends.

*Right. Find your chill, Theo.*

How can I when Christian slings his canvas messenger bag over his chest? He beams at the short, curvy Black girl beside him. They turn in the direction of the stairs. He's leaving, along with all my prom dreams.

I hop, swerve, and wiggle through another group of students.

I'm close enough to hear Christian's cool voice among the noise.

"Whatever, Keyona." He snorts. "Don't get mad at me 'cause I have better plans than mainlining *Gilmore Girls* with you this weekend."

The girl, Keyona, tosses fruit snacks into his messy, dark curls.

"Like what? Masturbate?"

Christian's light-brown cheeks instantly go dark red. I almost choke. Suddenly, my joggers are much tighter.

"No," Christian blurts. "Studying."

"Lies!"

"Practicing the new Lizzo song for spring tryouts?"

"More deception." Keyona tosses another fruit snack at him. "You know that song better than anyone on the drumline."

It's true. Christian is the star of our school's marching band. All eyes are on the way he goes *in* while playing the snare drums.

"A party," Christian finally concedes.

"I knew it!" Keyona swats his hip. "You're gonna be all over—"

Christian shushes her before she can finish.

I pause. *All over* . . . who?

Thing is, Christian, as charming as he is, hasn't ever dated anyone at Brook-Oak. Our school is far from ground zero for homophobia. The ZERO TOLERANCE and BROOK-OAK WELCOMES ALL signs posted around the halls say so. We even have a QSA—sixteen members deep, not that I'm one of them. Still, our small, openly out queer community seldomly does the whole hand-holding, kissing-between-classes thing.

But most people know Christian's gay and available.

I just need to make a move.

Beyond Christian's group I spot Aleah Bird. Her head is lowered, body curled inward as an impatient Coach Hollingsworth talks to her. My stomach flips. I keep waiting for Aleah to look up, scowl my way. Thankfully, it doesn't happen. Instead, she walks in the opposite direction.

It takes a beat to clear the last ten seconds from my brain.

Then I see Christian is five feet away. I lick my lips, willing confidence into my gait and—

*WHAM!*

I collide with another student. It's a slow-motion disaster. Papers fly. Index cards spill across the pavement. My arms flap wildly before we both thud against the ground.

The first "Ooooh" is the worst. Gasps and high-pitched laughter follow. A small crowd forms around us as I roll to my side. *Please don't let Christian be one of them*. Phones are out, even while Coach Hollingsworth threatens confiscation and suspension as she intercepts the crowd.

It's too late, though.

#TeddyBearEatsCement is probably already trending.

"Are you—"

Before I can fully ask the person I smashed into if they're hurt, I hear a clipped "I'm fine." The other student adjusts crooked glasses, scrambling to collect the items I sent airborne across the quad. All I see is the back of a shaggy, copper-brown head. Woven bracelets running up a forearm. A collage of anime stickers on a backpack before they're lost in the wave of people fleeing to the main building.

Christian and his friends are gone too.

"You okay, Theo?" Darren asks between chuckles.

He and Jay stand over me. Without meeting his eyes, I give two thumbs-up. It's all I can do with the weight of failure pressing on all my limbs.

"That deserves a do-over," says Jay, reaching to help me up.

Once I'm standing, he slides an arm around my sagging shoulders. He leads me back toward the building. Darren falls into step next to us.

"How am I gonna get another chance?" I mumble.

The lunch rule was established for a reason. We won't see each other again until after school. Chances of me being in the same space as Christian on the Friday before spring break are also slim to none.

"Trust me," says Jay, his grin at Cartoon Network–villain levels of mischief, "I'll think of a plan."

# 2

# PROMPOSAL GONE WRONG

**"Chloe Campbell's Spring** Break Bash."

Brook-Oak's north wing hall is eternally crowded. Students collide in every direction trying to get to their next class. I almost don't hear Jay over the after-lunch rush.

"Huh?" I ask, head mostly buried in my locker.

The walls and lockers are striped cerulean, gold, and ivory, our school's colors. Please don't refer to them as blue-green, amber, or white unless you want to face the wrath of alumni donors or a barrage of *The Devil Wears Prada* memes.

I pluck out my beat-up copy of *The Catcher in the Rye* for Mr. London's class. Not my favorite book. At least he's letting us pair it with *Aristotle and Dante Discover the Secrets of the Universe*, which I'm loving. I stuff the paperback into my JanSport before shouldering my door closed, pivoting to face Jay.

"Second chance!" he announces. "Tomorrow night."

"At Chloe's party?"

"Yes!"

"Sounds like a scam," Darren says before I can, sidling up to us.

"It's happening, my dudes," Jay insists.

"How?" I ask.

He tightens his topknot, then beams as if he's not just insinuated we waltz into a party hosted by the senior captain of the girls' varsity basketball team.

Brook-Oak isn't as cliquey as it appears on the surface. From the beginning of freshman year, students are divvied up into our respective programs: High School University; Science, Math, and Technology; Journalism/Media; Visionary Arts; and Young Performers of Tomorrow. Yearly, hundreds of kids from across Jefferson County apply. Acceptance for the first three programs is decided by your academic performance in middle school, plus testing in. Auditions are required for the VA and YPT programs.

After that, everyone's in survival mode. Magnet schools are competitive. You tend to figure out who your people are after seeing the same faces for a minimum of 180 days a year. Drama kids socialize with other YPT kids. STEM students chill with other science-y, tech-y, engineer-y, and math-y students. Band kids are tight-knit. Athletes befriend other athletes.

Chloe's never hovered in TNT's little social hemisphere, though. And I avoid the basketball team for . . . reasons.

"It doesn't matter how," says Jay. "We're in!"

"That means Jayla's involved," teases Darren.

Jay doesn't deny it.

"Perfect," I sigh.

Jayla Owens is a junior on the cheer squad. She's pretty with pale brown eyes almost the same color as her complexion. Flocks of guys have been thirsting over her since forever. How she ended up with Jay is beyond me.

Especially since Jayla and I briefly dated.

I mean, what's dating in sixth grade other than a kiss on the cheek at a school dance, then a "Check yes if you like me" note passed around the following Monday morning?

Anyway, our tweenmance didn't end amicably.

I broke things off. Every day was nausea-inducing, knowing I didn't *like-like* her back. Guilt is so exhausting. After I told her, she shoved me in the chest, and I cried behind the jungle gym at recess. Two understandable, if not dramatic, reactions.

A year later, I came out.

I've heard that's why she's not my biggest fan. We haven't talked much, despite her dating my best friend.

"Tomorrow night. The dare's still on," Jay says, unearthing two energy bars from his backpack. He passes both to me. "You can't maintain proper energy off just pretzel bites, bro."

"Thanks." I tear into a bar. Peanut butter caramel, my favorite. Damn, Jay's always looking out for me.

Between bites, I say, "You sure we're not gonna have any trouble getting in?"

Chloe's parties are labeled as "exclusive to seniors and close friends only." Without an invite, you're likely to suffer extreme harassment from drunk seniors. Sometimes worse.

"It's a done deal," Jay confirms.

He shows us a string of texts from Jayla that are largely

inappropriate emoji usage or over-the-top love declarations. Neither Darren nor I signed up for another episode of *J & J: Sext City*.

Oh yeah. *J & J*—Jay and Jayla. They're *that* couple at BOHS, according to the underclassmen who idolize them.

#RelationshipGoals. #BaeForLife. #ImNotAHaterButThisIsGross.

As disgustingly cheesy as Jay and Jayla are, the thing I'll never say out loud is I want a version of that.

The lactose-free kind, of course.

For the longest time, it almost felt too dangerous to dream about. To give myself that kind of hope. Another boy's fingers laced with mine as we walk the halls. Being late for extracurriculars because we're too busy making out in an empty classroom. Maybe it's because the visual representation at Brook-Oak is severely lacking.

Having two straight best friends—plus a host of teammates regularly sipping from the heteronormative cup—isn't . . . easy.

When I came out, Darren was exceptionally chill. He hugged me tightly. Hasn't once asked an insensitive question about my sexuality. Jay, however, was overly enthusiastic about it. Captioned a photo of us as kids on Instagram with: #MyBestBroIsGayWhatOfIt. Rainbow emojis included. Later that night, over pizza, he added an unsolicited "My cousin Jenny's a lesbian. So, I get you."

Back then, I lacked the vocabulary to explain how association by proxy doesn't give you the slightest range to what it's like to be *inside* that community. I still struggle with that. It feels weird to think about calling out my own best friend for the sometimes-problematic shit that slips out of his mouth.

Jay and Darren are clueless when it comes to being queer

and crushing on someone, even if that other person is out of the closet. The asking-someone-out thing isn't the same. Neither is dating when, at any moment, you could be risking your safety or theirs. Homophobic assholes can be anywhere. As progressive as Brook-Oak—Louisville as a whole—is, it's still a *lot* being gay here.

Lockers slam around us. Sneakers squeak on the vinyl tile. A group argues about song lyrics as they pass.

A new set of texts flashes across Jay's screen.

"It's your mom," Darren informs him.

"Shit." Jay quickly turns his phone around. He scowls while reading, thumbs smashing out a reply. "It's like she fucking forgets I'm at *school*."

I smile empathetically. Dad's the reason I leave my phone in my locker between classes. He's always sending me words of encouragement or checking to see how I did on a test. It's sweet but distracting.

"She says to tell her golden boy hello," Jay grumbles to me.

My face wrinkles. Another unwanted nickname.

"Anyway." Jay locks his phone, pocketing it. "Chloe's party? We're going, right?"

Darren's eyes dance between us.

"Okay." I finally exhale. "Let's do this."

Jay fist-pumps the air.

"We're gonna get kicked out," Darren comments, laughing.

"*You're* gonna get kicked out if you try break dancing while buzzed again," Jay says with mock admonishment.

I grin, looking around.

Brook-Oak's design is breathtaking from the exterior, but not the easiest to navigate once inside. It's a three-story, Gothic-lite structure—think Westminster Abbey, but modern and cooler—filled with over a thousand talented, genius, and/or privileged students.

Getting here was step one in Dad's Plan. It's all he talks about. A guaranteed strategy for me, a young, economically average Black kid, raised by a single parent, landing at a top college outside of Kentucky.

Brook-Oak's admissions committee was exceptionally clear that I scored in the bottom third of applicants. That I was "lucky."

Frankly, luck had nothing to do with it. I studied my ass off. Jay helped a lot too. We'd spend weekends at his house in the East End going over problem sets and science terms.

Now I'm here. Shoulder to shoulder with my best friends. One step closer to the future.

Jay and Darren part ways with me at the end of the hall. Darren's in the Journalism/Media program while Jay's a STEM student. I chuck a peace sign their way. "See y'all on the other side!"

Jay shoots me an uneven smile, nodding.

By tomorrow night, he'll be saying peace to half his trust fund after I ask Christian to prom.


The pressure to keep up with my classmates is very real. I test decently. I can fake a passable answer when called on. My papers are flawless. But remembering concepts taught in class has always been a battle. My handwriting is shit so my pops bought me a refurbished tablet to take notes on. It saves me the hassle of teachers yelling about using my phone during class.

Now my tablet's the reason I'm about to be late to American Lit with Mr. London.

The warning bell pierces my eardrums as I book it back to my locker.

Two-a-day practices are really paying off. I easily dodge the east wing slackers. Cut a corner like I'm trying to break a world record. Nothing's in my way . . .

Except Brad Jennings and Gracie Abbot having a last-minute make-out sesh by my locker.

Usually, I'd give them a pass for being in the genesis of hormonal overload. You love to see freshmen with priorities. But not today.

I clear my throat loudly until they part like startled squirrels.

Once I'm done, I almost trip over a sophomore dropping her backpack in my path. Darren's the hurdles champ in our trio. Still, I hit a respectable landing before I'm stopped again, five doors from Mr. London's class.

Luca Ramírez paces the hallway. He's whispering to himself, reading something off his phone. I don't think I've ever seen him this stressed. To be fair, Luca and I mostly socialize in passing. This isn't one of those times, though.

He looks ready to vom without one of our all-gender bathrooms in sight.

The roses-and-ivy pattern on his T-shirt is a nice contrast to his gold-brown skin. His hand skims over the top of his deep umber hair. It's styled like the crest of a wave.

I toss him a casual what's-up nod, then realize his eyes are still on his screen.

"Hey, Luca."

His head jerks up just as his phone slips from his hands.

"Whoa, whoa," I say, scrambling to swipe the device out of its midair plummet. Another reason I run track instead of playing other sports: *no catching skills necessary*. The phone bounces on its side, then lands facedown on the floor.

Luca groans defeatedly.

"My bad!" I kneel to pick it up. "I kind of came out of nowhere with that greeting."

"Oh, right," he says. "I forgot politeness is to blame for all phone casualties."

Still on one knee, I snort loudly. Luca's expression is softer, less puke-worthy. I ignore the late bell ringing. We're the only ones in the silent hall.

That doesn't last long.

Behind me, I hear . . . singing? Luca pales, lips parting. Whatever he says is drowned out by the Rolling Tones, our school's competition-winning a cappella group.

Soon, I'm surrounded by a harmony of vocals and choreography and cheery faces. Two of the bass singers hold up a bright-blue banner. *PROM?* is dusted in gold glitter.

It hits me: *This is a promposal.*

Also, I'm on bended knee in front of Luca, raising his phone toward him like a freaking engagement ring.

Luca flails his arms around. He tries to stop the beautiful swell of voices singing . . . Hold up. Is that One Direction? Seriously? Luca Ramírez is promposing to someone with a decade-old boy band song?

You hate to see it.

"Stop!" he pleads, finally destroying what I realize is his promposal-ready hairstyle.

One by one, the Rolling Tones go quiet, mouths scrunched as they look around at each other.

Amanda Cox, the group's leader, stomps between Luca and me. "What's the prob, Ramírez?" She taps an impatient ballet flat on the floor. "You agreed to *pay* us to be here after lunch for a promposal. We even got special permission from Mr. Murphy to miss the beginning of class for this."

"Not for *him*!"

Maintaining a neutral expression at the sharpness of Luca's voice takes tremendous effort. As if I'm unworthy of being serenaded by a sweet but poorly chosen One Direction song. Like it'd be offensive to take *me* to prom.

Luca's eyes momentarily meet mine. His cheeks pinken. But his attention is quickly drawn back to Amanda when she starts snapping her fingers.

*Yeah, no need to apologize.*

"I told you, Amanda, this is for—"

Before Luca can finish, someone parts through the Rolling Tones.

"Luca?" Devya Anand stands dressed out in her phys ed gear, black hair tied up in a sloppy ponytail. The hallway lights glint off the tiny stone in her left nostril and the confusion in her almost-black eyes. "What's going on?"

Luca rushes toward her, shouting, "Now! Now!" He drops to one knee, cupping Devya's left hand.

On Amanda's order, the Rolling Tones restart their performance. It's even cornier the second time around.

I shrink backward. Heat prickles under my skin. It's not because I've been embarrassed *again* by a clumsy disaster. I've had my fair share of trips to the top of the #BOHSFail pile—thank you, Mariah Carey. Attention like that fades as quickly as it comes in high school. Someone's always right behind you, ready to fall flat on their face and catch all that shame you were just suffering through.

I'm anxious because, for a fleeting moment, I got a taste of what it's like to be Jay and Jayla. Like all that swoon-worthy shit in rom-coms isn't strictly meant for the straight kids.

My eyes scan back to Devya. Her expression is . . . definitely not the way I'd look if, say, Christian was promposing to me.

In fact, last I heard, Devya and Luca broke up during winter break. Darren made it a Thing at lunch one day. They were another *J & J* at Brook-Oak: posting couple-y photos using the cutest animal filters on Insta. Repeat hand-holding-in-the-middle-of-the-hallway offenders. Legitimate prom court contenders.

If this is Luca's take-me-back encore, things aren't going as planned.

"Luca, I—" Out of nowhere, Devya's face goes from apprehensive to euphoric. Peter Vasquez, another junior with great hair—and Devya's rumored new boyfriend—shamelessly slides on his knees into the Rolling Tones circle, shoulder-checking Luca aside.

"Dev, babe. I wanted to do this differently, but . . . me and you? Prom?" Peter says it so casual, so *easy*, unlike Luca, who was stuttering out an entire speech ninety seconds ago.

"Ohmygod, hells yes!" Devya shouts.

I wince as Luca collapses on his ass. Devya squeals happily while Peter lifts her into the air. The Rolling Tones don't miss a beat, shifting into a Harry Styles song like this was all by design.

A cold feeling sinks into my bones. I kind of want to help Luca off the floor. But a familiar boom of thunder cracks through the hall, one I'm used to hearing on the track, not when I'm late to class.

Coach Devers might be only five foot six, but her presence feels like seven foot two. She nudges into the circle with a repeated "Excuse you" while clapping.

I jump back. When a Black woman claps like that, it means *Move*.

Coach clocks every face in the area, including mine. No one speaks.

"Another one of these, huh?" She signals toward the prom banner. "I don't get you kids' obsession with making everything a cinematic spectacle." Her eyes squint at three of the Tones filming everything. They immediately lower their phones. "Can we please keep it to non-class time? You're here to *learn*, not gain YouTube followers."

"I'm just trying to get verified," whispers one of the Tones.

I frown. *Not the time, dude.*

"Get to class," demands Coach, "before I start handing out in-school suspension like Kangol bucket hats at a LL Cool J concert."

"LL who?" asks Zain Ahmed, a senior Tone.

"Now!"

The Tones scatter like cockroaches. Everyone except Amanda,

who glowers over a still-in-shock Luca. "Don't forget to Cash App me our agreed fee," she says. "I won't charge extra for the encore. This time."

If Rachel Berry from *Glee* and a made-for-Netflix mob boss had a child, it'd be Amanda.

"Ms. Cox?" Coach tilts her head. "Are you collecting personal funds for a school-sponsored club's performance?"

"At a discounted rate," Amanda mumbles, tipping her chin up defiantly.

"Care to discuss *my* discounted rates for Saturday detentions after school?" They're almost the same height, but that might be because Amanda's facade is starting to wilt. Coach adds, "Trust me, I give better deals than Amazon."

Amanda takes two cautious steps back.

"No, ma'am."

"Good."

Amanda throws one last stink eye at Luca on her way to class. Thoughts and prayers for whatever teacher has her for the next ninety minutes.

"You too, Ramírez. Show's over," barks Coach.

Watching Luca collect himself is beyond tragic. He doesn't attempt to hide the ache on his face as Devya and Peter, hands clasped, walk away. He pauses in front of me.

"Oh, hey." I grin so hard my cheeks feel permanently inflated. "What's up, Luca? Are you good? Need some water?"

What the hell is wrong with me? Yes, that's what everyone needs in the face of public—and videoed—humiliation: to stay hydrated.

"No." He exhales. "Can I have my phone back?"

I forgot I'm still holding it, despite the edges of a freshly cracked screen digging into my palm.

Luca mutters a half-assed "thanks" when I hand it to him. He drifts down the hall without another word.

"So." I know that tone in Coach's voice. Disappointment followed by a speech. "Is this how you spend your time when you're not preparing to destroy MVH at finals?"

I chuckle quietly. Inside the halls and on the track, Coach is usually all business. School Faculty 101. But on occasion, she lets out her sense of humor. She isn't afraid to scream at you to pick up the pace while also roasting your poor form.

"No, Coach."

"I hope not." Her mouth trembles like she's suppressing a smirk. "Can't have VP Clarke catching you cutting—"

"I wasn't—"

The twitch in her right eye says not to interrupt her. "You had your meeting with Dr. Bernard last week, right? About Duke?"

I bite down on the inside of my cheek, nodding.

"You're working on getting that recommendation letter?" Coach lifts an eyebrow.

"I am, Coach."

It's a lie. I've been low-key avoiding thinking about the letter ever since Dr. Bernard suggested it. She made it sound so simple. *Just ask him*, she'd said with a Colgate-bright smile. *You're best friends with his son. Should be no problem!*

As if she knew what it's like to ask Jay's dad for anything.

"That's what I like to hear, Wright! Always making your dad

proud." Absently, she fixes her dreads, smiling at the wall behind me. "By the way, how is Miles? Still . . . happily unattached?"

I wish I could say the shy glint in her eyes was at all shocking. That this was the first time an adult *hinted* at my pops's romantic status. But it's not.

Dad and Coach—and everyone else who hasn't moved past their glory days in this part of Old Louisville—attended Brook-Oak together. They might've dated? I can't keep up with the multitude of folks Dad still acknowledges with an authentic smile everywhere we go.

I swallow my annoyance.

"He's . . . good."

"I'll have to text him sometime." Even with her dark skin, Coach looks flushed. "Maybe I'll Facebook him."

"Uh, sure," I say, desperate to get away from the conversation. "I'm gonna head to Mr. London's class now."

"Smart. We can't have Miles Wright's son missing finals!"

Of course not.

The privilege of being the son of the great Miles Wright never, ever ends.

# 3

# IS THIS A PEP TALK?

**Darren and I** have a tradition.

Every other Friday, we hop in his car after school and head to the Highlands for haircuts. Jay wore the same buzzcut all the way up until high school. These days, he settles for a touch-up every now and again. I refuse to go that long without a fresh cut. While Darren and I are at the barbershop, Jay has mandatory family time with his parents and younger brother, Jasper.

Jess Scott, Jay's mom, and my pops were tight in high school. Shared classes. Had the same friend group. According to Dad, she even helped him write his college admissions essay. When he found out Mrs. Scott was moving back to Louisville after attending college in Boston and marrying a lawyer, they immediately reconnected.

Jay was my first real friend. More like a sibling since I'm an only child. Darren came into the fold around middle school. Something about his chill attitude created the perfect buffer between Jay's intensity and my stubbornness. It was weird at first, a duo turning into a trio, but I won't lie—I've stopped feeling guilty about enjoying moments with just Darren around.

We vibe on another wavelength.

After haircuts, we grab our favorite corner table at a cozy, family-owned ramen bar off Baxter Avenue. Once we've ordered, Darren hangs on to the menu, scanning the back page.

"You're thinking about getting the mochi ice cream, aren't you?" I tease.

"No!" The corners of his mouth tick upward. "You don't know me, bro."

Oh, but I do.

In sixth grade, Darren and I found ourselves hanging at the same end of a lunch table, ignoring the other kids. Me because of the nicknames. Him because of the ignorant "WHERE ARE YOUR PARENTS *FROM*?" questions. Tweens can be cruel. Our interactions started casually: trading chocolate milks and juice pouches over square pizzas, eventually falling into loud, obnoxious conversations about our favorite cartoons or foods.

So, yeah, Darren wants the mochi ice cream. He'll convince me to share. And I won't hesitate to grab that second spoon.

"Noticed you gave DeAndre some special instructions while getting your cut," Darren comments when our food arrives. "Looking mighty clean!"

Thank goodness for that extra melanin in my system. Otherwise, Darren would be witness to the deplorable amounts of blush kissing my cheeks.

"It's nothing," I lie.

I most certainly asked Dre to put some additional craftsmanship into today's look. It took him another thirty minutes, but . . . worth it. Sides tight, temples faded. My twists are conditioned, springy from the curl sponge. My wannabe mustache is darker, well defined.

"Is this for anyone in particular?" Darren smirks as he slurps a spoonful of broth. "Perhaps the little drummer boy?"

"I don't know whom you speak of."

I dive into my chicken ramen. Jay was right—the soft pretzels and energy bars weren't enough to sustain me through my last two classes. My eyes water at a whiff of the red chili oil in Darren's tonkotsu ramen. Spicy foods are a hard no for me.

Darren inherited his iron stomach from his mom.

I really love his parents. Professor Jacobs, Darren's dad, heads the African American and Africana Studies department at the University of Kentucky. His mom, Mrs. Jacobs (née Ishikawa), is a retired book illustrator. They both have this dry humor that I appreciate. Also, they're a family of success stories. Even Darren's younger sister, Connie, is a district spelling bee champ. She's eight.

"What about you?" I point at his haircut, deflecting like a pro. "Who're you trying to impress?"

"Oh, go to hell." He laughs, cheeks rosy.

Darren's fully focused on two things: school and track. By choice, not from parental pressure like Jay and me. But another commonality we share sans Jay is our ability to crush and not date.

I mean, I've *had* relationships. There's Jayla. And I made out with a boy from an opposing track team under the bleachers once. Okay, twice. Great kisser, even better at ghosting me when we finished.

Darren's never had a girlfriend. He's still a virgin, which isn't bad by any means. I'm still one too.

Jay practically texted us *during* his first time. He spared no details when we finally saw him in person.

"I'm not trying to impress her," Darren admits, chugging his glass of water.

The *her* is senior cheerleader Makayla.

"Jay's been on me to ask her out," he continues, staring into his steaming bowl. "To finally . . . *you know.*"

*Get laid?* I don't need to say it. Jay's always playing wingman for Darren. His pep talks usually involve one of Jayla's friends and sex. "It's the best, D, I swear," he'll say, an arm around Darren's shoulders. "Just try it."

That's the kind of person Jay is—someone who, once they've found something they like, wants everyone in their life to love it too. It's worked on us before. *Fortnite*, pizza with ranch dressing, James Cameron movies.

But the sex thing . . . I don't know.

I *want* to. My phone has enough incognito tabs open to confirm I'd probably enjoy it. Thing is, Jay's never tried to persuade me the way he does Darren. Sometimes, I wonder why it's like that. Why he never asks about boys I like. It's not until after I've volunteered the information that we discuss it.

But I'm not supposed to wish he'd ask about my sex life, right? To treat me like he does Darren? It's just the way guys talk sometimes. No big deal. Jay's not purposefully leaving me out . . . is he?

"You don't have to go through with it if you don't want to," says Darren as he spoons up more ramen. "The dare."

Ah, shit. Being caught up in my own head gave him the upper hand.

I shrug.

None of us have ever reneged on a dare. Even the gross ones. I can't be the first.

"I want to go to prom with Christian." I shake my head with a tiny smile. "It's just that . . ."

Darren leans on his elbows, waiting. I almost tell him. The words tickle the roof of my mouth. Darren's the same guy who, on the way here, offered me his notes on the Cold War for my US History 2 class because he took that course last semester. Who, just last week, told me about the time he cried over his favorite Disney Channel star getting engaged. We're thoughtful dorks like that.

I want to discuss how hard it is being the only queer dude in our trio. How the prom thing would make me feel *normal*. Then I think about Darren's reaction when he realizes I've kept this secret from him. That I second-guessed our friendship. I didn't trust him with this part of me.

"It'd be really nice," I whisper instead of explaining, barely holding on to my smile.

"Definitely." Darren looks like he might ask more but doesn't. "If you fail, we'll have your back. Whenever one of us crashes and burns, we all take the fall. We'll be right there with you at practice, MVH gear and all. TNT forever."

It's true. This is us. Maybe Jay's right. If we all show up in MVH apparel, Coach'll think it's a joke. She wouldn't bench three of her star runners.

Sure, she came close to beating Mountainview her senior year.

Rumor has it, at that final meet, an MVH student trashed Brook-Oak's locker room, tagging the benches with some choice (see: racist, classist) words in black spray paint. Mentally, it took Coach Devers out of the competition. She tripped during the hurdles finals, finishing fourth. But that's the past.

Maybe she's forgotten all that?

Darren offers me a fist bump. "Always here for you, Theo."

"Th-thanks," I choke out, tapping his fist. We share a grin. "But I'm going to prom on Jay's dime."

After we've finished our bowls, Darren *finally* orders the mochi ice cream. Weak-minded, that one. I tense up a little when he tells the waitress to bring one bill. The Jacobs household of overachievers isn't quite on the level of financially gifted as the Scotts, but they're doing really well.

The proof: Darren has a family credit card.

Jay and Darren never flaunt their wealth to me. They're both good at making it seem like it's merely returning a favor. As if my friendship is enough. They'll pay for food or a movie ticket. "Because you're my boy," they say.

But in moments like this, when Darren won't meet my eyes while signing the receipt and pocketing that gold AmEx card, I'm reminded where they're coming from and where I'm at.

As we wait on the ice cream, I study the new customers coming through the front door. Anything to avoid that weird sensation swirling in my stomach. Someone's kid runs around singing "The Pee Song" with zero fucks given. A young woman struts in like she's on a mission.

The bell above the door chimes one more time.

My heart climbs to the center of my throat. I'm light-headed watching a man I recognize stroll in.

*Mario.*

It's like staring at a ghost. He looks mostly the same. Deep-brown complexion. Tall and built. Streaks of silver fleck his dark goatee. He's a little less bouncy than I remember. Subdued, but still smiley like he knows the world will always embrace him.

I haven't seen him since he moved to Texas years ago, crushing Dad's heart. The aftershocks of their fallout led me to do one of the worst things ever.

It's the reason Aleah Bird hates my guts.

"Dude, have you been on Jayla's Insta?" Darren asks, shaking me from my daze.

I sink down in my chair, hoping Mario doesn't see me. He *can't* know I'm here.

"Theo?"

Darren's foot kicks mine under the table. I jolt. He shoots me a curious stare, trying to track my focal point. If he looks at Mario, then Mario might glance our way, and—

"What about Jayla?" I ask, panicked.

"She posted a cryptic message about backstabbing friends." He lays his phone faceup on the table before excitedly rubbing his hands together. Darren loves gossip. A career at TMZ is in his future. "The comments are on fire. Everyone's speculating it's about what went down with the Ballers at state."

Seriously, F my whole life.

The Ballers, Brook-Oak's girls' varsity basketball team. The one Aleah's on.

"Really?" I fake interest, not even reading Jayla's caption.

"It's a shit show."

Darren unloads all the details. His sources are suspect. Anyway, for a month, the whisper networks have been buzzing about the unexpected end of what was a record-breaking winning season for the Ballers. The two stars and besties—point guard, Aleah, and power forward, Lexi Johnson—imploded off the court. No confirmation on what happened two nights before the championship game, but the following Monday morning, all hell broke loose.

Lexi and her longtime boyfriend, Derek Miller, a senior on the boys' team, called it quits.

Aleah wasn't sitting with the Ballers at lunch anymore.

By the end of the day, someone had filled Aleah's locker with crumpled paper, browned banana peels, and unwrapped condoms. Written on the outside in Sharpie: *TRASH!* Word is Derek cheated on Lexi with Aleah.

No one on the team is talking.

"We should go," I say once Darren's done ranting. "I need to— uh, you know. Rehearse what I'm gonna say to Christian tomorrow."

"How about 'I like you. Wanna go to prom?'"

*"Psssh."* An almost genuine laugh escapes my lips.

I notice Mario seated on the other side of the restaurant. "I'm capable of far better game than that," I say while scooting out of our booth.

"Are you?"

"Ouch, dude." I lightly punch his shoulder. He doesn't even flinch. The guy's all muscle. "Great pep talk."

"Whatever." He smiles while rolling his eyes. "I'll tell the waitress we're getting the mochi to go."

Before I exit, I can't help peeking over to Mario's corner. His head's down, eyes on his phone. He looks so much like his niece, Aleah. A recognizable feeling aches in my stomach.

This is one thing I'm always too slow to run from: Aleah was my first *best friend*. Not like Jay, Darren, and me. She was pre-TNT. A separate reality.

I've never been able to outrun the memory of how quickly I ditched her once Dad and Mario broke up.

# 4

# THE MILES WRIGHT FACTOR

**The next morning,** sweat itches against my temple as I finish my Saturday run. It's only nine a.m. and slowly warming up outside, but I've been pushing myself lately.

3:13.51 versus 3:13.56 looks like a small gap on paper, but it's huge to me.

That's Mountainview's best time in the 4x400 versus ours.

I unlock the front door. We live in a two-story, single-family home off Willow Avenue in the South End. It's a three-bedroom, two-bathroom with a porch and a deck in the back. Ideal for Dad and me. The second I tug out my earbuds, my phone pings with multiple messages.

TNT's WhatsApp group chat is busy early for a weekend.

Last summer, the Jacobses vacationed in Osaka, visiting Darren's mom's family. We spent hella time texting while he was gone. Jay suggested we move our messages over to WhatsApp before Mr. Jacob confiscated Darren's phone because of the senseless international rates. After Darren got back, we maintained this group chat. Creatures of habit.

## TODAY

**Jay**
big day! scooping up D then T @ 5ish
9:01 A.M.

**Darren**
5? Isn't the party later?
9:02 A.M.

**Jay**
pregame baby! 🎉 🍾 🏢
9:02 A.M.

**Darren**
Theo won't be ready at 5. 😬
9:03 A.M.

I roll my eyes while toeing off my sneakers by the door. Dad will freak out if I dirty up the new area rug that covers most of the living room's hardwood. I fire off a quick middle-finger emoji in response to Darren's last text. Just because he's right doesn't mean I need to co-sign. Besides, I'm asking a boy—*my first boy*—to prom later. That kind of prep work needs time.

As a polite gesture to Jay doing his ceremonial wingman duties, I confirm I'll be ready.

Ready-*ish*.

I'm midway through my post-run cooldown when I hear a familiar gasp, followed by an "Oh, shit!" coming from the kitchen. I grin to myself.

"Dad! I'm back!"

No response.

I should've expected that. Saturdays are dedicated to Dad catching up on his crime dramas. I do a couple of quad stretches, savoring the tightness exiting my muscles, before heading toward the kitchen.

On the way, I pause at the wall outside the entryway. The Louvre of Wright Family History. Old portraits in discounted frames. It starts with a yellowing photo of my G'Pa and Granny on their wedding day then shifts chronologically all the way to me and Dad, last year, laughing outside of Friday Night Film Fest. My favorite picture is of Granny and me hugging at Kentucky Pride. I was only nine then. We were there supporting Dad. Anytime I look at this photo, I imagine Granny knew she was there for Dad *and* me, even though I hadn't come out yet.

I didn't even know then.

She died when I was twelve.

The picture reminds me that sometimes people can love you even before you know who you really are.

I kiss the tip of my index finger, tapping Granny's cheek before stepping into the kitchen.

Dad's at the table, invested in his usual routine: watching *SVUNCISWhatever* on his phone while sipping orange juice and crunching on turkey bacon. He's a computer systems administrator who's essentially on call all the time. Thankfully, it's a remote job now. Still, it doesn't leave much time for mindless TV marathons.

"Morning, Dad!"

Without looking, he flaps a hand at me, signaling I'm interrupting a crucial moment.

"Miles Davis Wright . . ." I start, putting on my best Granny voice, waiting for his head to snap up.

"Watch it, TJ," he replies, his scowl on level ten. "G'morning."

Yep, Dad's another victim of the celebrity first-and-middle-name game permeating throughout the Wright bloodline. At least he's named after a famous musician, not a TV character who didn't even get a spin-off series.

He grew up in a ranch-style house in the West End. A lot of that area has changed since then. The government calls it "revitalization," a nice SAT alternative to gentrification. But Dad's "people" are all over Louisville. Same friends, same enemies, same *everything* since graduating from Brook-Oak.

Granny's shown me numerous photos from Dad's high school days. To put it lightly, he was quite popular. Homecoming Prince. Senior class vice president. Prom court. Co-captain of the soccer team. Voted *Most Likely to Succeed*.

I call it the Michael B. Jordan factor. Dad's always had acne-free, smooth brown skin, a handsome, round face, winning smile. *All the girls wanted him*, Granny used to tell me. *Different dates all the time. Then the boys came around and watch out!*

He's got double the number of followers I have on all social media apps.

"Good run?" Dad asks during an ad break.

"Eh." I shrug.

"'Eh' won't win conference finals," he reminds me.

As if I needed it.

Track has been a part of my life since before winter break of freshman year. It was all Jay's idea. Another way for the three of us to hang out more. At first, I agreed because it's what my boys wanted to do. Then I fell in love with running. Moving faster than my brain could think. Being the reason everyone else around me won.

Dad loved it too. Not only because I excelled at it. Track eliminated one or two steps from The Plan.

Colleges adore a star athlete.

"It was good for a Saturday. Almost got my time down by two seconds," I amend, ducking my head into the fridge.

"Impressive!"

I locate a Gatorade on a shelf crammed with takeout boxes and a Tupperware of chili Dad made a week ago. We're not a family of cookers. Not since Granny died. My heartbeat triples when I almost knock over Dad's pitcher of homemade cold brew. The last time I did that, he was furious. I'd left the mess for him to clean up. I chose to endure Dad's wrath rather than Darren's for being late meeting him outside my house.

Since he lives in the southeastern side of the city too, Darren's cool enough to give me a ride to Brook-Oak on mornings Dad has early meetings. Our school's only ten minutes from my house by car. Otherwise, it's a forty-minute ride via public transportation, not counting the time it takes to walk to the nearest pickup stop.

I flop down across from Dad. He's deeply engrossed in his phone again. I sneak a piece of his bacon, grimacing at its coldness.

"I saw that."

I guzzle half my Gatorade. "Dad, at least eat the bacon when it's warm!"

He shakes his head, laughing.

We share a lot of the same physical traits—almost six feet tall, the wide Wright forehead, eternal baby face—but there are parts of me I know aren't his. Ones I got from my biological mother.

At the ripe age of thirty, Dad had one unfulfilled dream: being a father. Cue the lengthy process of finding an egg donor, a surrogate, extensive testing, getting a *second job* to counter the new debt he was amassing, and then . . . me.

Theodore Jamal Wright, conceived via in vitro fertilization.

I've never met the surrogate who carried me. Never asked to either. Granny swears she was a wonderful woman. I was satisfied with the family unit I had—Dad, Granny, and me. Later, just Dad and me, though that's taken longer to adjust to.

"You need more than that," Dad comments, nodding toward my bottle and the second strip of cold bacon I just swiped.

"M'good," I mumble while chewing. "This is all a growing boy needs: meat and electrolytes."

"How did I raise such a clueless child?"

"With Granny's help."

"Thank God for her."

We're quiet for a moment. I bite at the broken cuticle around my thumb. I wonder if he misses the snorty laugh she'd let out while watching reruns of her favorite old sitcom, *Living Single*. The scent of her lilac perfume on Sunday mornings before church. I haven't stepped foot in her bedroom since she died. Dad asked her to move in with us when I was born.

*I hated the idea of her living alone,* he told me. *Plus, she couldn't get enough of you!*

G'Pa passed away right after Dad graduated college.

"Grits?" Dad offers, scooting his chair back from the table.

"Only if you make them the way I like." Also known as Granny-style: lots of butter and sugar.

He rolls his eyes. "Heathen. Don't ever change, TJ."

"I don't plan to!"

Mounted on the wall opposite me is a big dry-erase board. Scribbled in Dad's chaotic handwriting is The Plan. A step-by-step checklist of the things we must accomplish to secure my optimum future.

Yes. *We.*

There's a column for me and one for Dad. Mine is the basic playbook: GPA expectations, ideal SAT scores, track goals. He's already begun mapping out my senior year, including a job at Crumbtious, a local doughnut shop whose owner is another Brook-Oak alumnus.

Dad's side is mostly numbers. The weekly hours he needs to work plus overtime. Scholarship and grants deadlines. Things he can cut out of his budget to save more money. A "Top Ten Colleges for TJ" list.

Number one, written in blue marker: *DUKE!!!*

Duke's been Dad's first choice since I joined the track team. A top-twenty-ranked D1 school in the sport. Nationally respected undergrad programs. Strong community. Only an eight-hour drive from Louisville, a safe, still-reachable distance for Dad but enough space where he won't feel as though I'm reliving his story.

Everyone assumed Dad would end up at Howard, maybe

somewhere up north or the West Coast after graduating Brook-Oak.

Instead, he attended Kentucky State University in Frankfort.

*I wanted to stay close to my folks,* he tells everyone. *And you can't go wrong attending an HBCU!*

Truth is money was tight around the Wright household. My grandparents couldn't afford tuition *and* the out-of-state living costs that Dad's nominal scholarships didn't cover. Postgraduation, he landed a job back home. Bought this house. He never married. Then I came around. Every Wright Dad's ever known has lived, worked, and died here.

I'm destined to "break the cycle," according to him.

"Real food." Dad sets a plate of eggs and bacon plus a steaming bowl of grits—melting butter oozing in the center—down in front of me before flopping back into his chair. "Eat up."

When did he make all of this? I must've spaced out, staring at The Plan. I mumble a "thanks," already halfway into my eggs.

"Any plans today?" he asks.

I peek at my phone. The lie comes effortlessly. "We're having a big game night at Jay's later. Maybe sleep over?"

Dad frowns, chin on his knuckles. "I thought we'd watch *The Last Knight.*"

Any given Saturday night, you can find us slouching on the couch, marathoning the Transformers movies. They're the kind of awful CGI disaster you just laugh through the entire time. It's replaced the way we used to spend Saturday evenings: watching films with Mario and Aleah.

I swallow down a spoonful of grits.

*Should I give Dad a heads-up about Mario?*

No. Then he might ask about Aleah. I'm not ready to face that conversation.

"Well . . ." My eyes drift from Dad to The Plan. "It's our only chance to hang out before spring break. After this weekend, I won't have any time."

Dad and I made a deal: spring break isn't a vacation from Brook-Oak. I'm doing a free response for Mr. London's class. An extra take-home quiz for Algebra 2. Catching up on readings. Anything to increase my 3.6 GPA. Better my chances of getting into Duke, or at least our second and third choices.

Dad folds his arms, studying me.

I wonder if he sees right through my lie.

It's not as if he'll be mad that I'm going to a party. Dad went to his fair share of kickbacks in high school. But my grandparents enforced a strict curfew—*home before midnight*, a tradition Dad's continued with me. I can't have a Cinderella-esque restriction killing my vibes with Christian. What am I supposed to say if he wants to hang out after the party?

*Sorry, I gotta bounce! These Jordans are about to turn into a pair of Crocs.*

"TJ," Dad starts to say.

"Just tonight," I plead. "I'll be at the Scotts'. No foolishness. Promise."

He rubs his chin. I know that face. It's the same one I get every Christmas Eve when I beg to open gifts early before he finally gives in.

"Phone charged and on at all times. Be polite. No spontaneous trips around the city because y'all got bored," Dad warns. "Sleep in the living room, not Jay's bedroom. No sleeping nude—"

"Dad!"

Since I came out, he's implemented a few revisions to The Talk:

*I know what it's like to be a teen*, he'd said. *Hormones are real. Things happen. Sexuality is fluid. Who we think we are today might not be who we are tomorrow. I want you and your partner safe. Everything should be consensual.*

Darren and Jay might be like brothers, but Dad insists that could change one day.

He's not done with his speech yet. "I'm serious, TJ. If you feel like something's about to happen, check for consent. Verbally give your own consent too. If you're not ready to do anything, you don't have to. Condoms. *Plural.* Do we need to rewatch the video on how to . . . ?"

He pauses to reach for his phone.

"Dad! No! They're my best friends."

"You think nothing happened between me and my 'friends'?"

"I don't actually want to know, thanks."

God, if he ever says he and Jay's mom hooked up, I'll perish right then and there.

Dad cackles, kicking me under the table. I grin. Finally, he drops the subject as I demolish the rest of my grits.

"Come to think of it—going to the Scotts would be good for you," he notes. "The perfect opportunity to talk to, uh. Justin." Dad's cringey expression after saying Jay's father's name tells the whole story. Most of it, anyway.

To say neither of us are Mr. Scott's biggest fan is a gross understatement. He's not a horrible person. Simply . . . *businesslike* with a lukewarm sense of humor. He reminds me of an undercooked Hot Pocket—generally inviting on the outside but cold in the center.

Quite the opposite of Jay's mom's endless friendliness.

Anyway, my little meeting with Dr. Bernard last week? It was about acquiring a recommendation letter from a Duke alumnus.

*It can't hurt your chances!* she'd said with a this-might-be-your-only-shot smile. Between my grades, extracurriculars, and praise from other teachers, I'm still not a guarantee.

Enter Mr. Scott, proud Duke graduate.

I can count on a single hand how many one-on-one conversations we've had in the past twelve years. The number of times he's been around TNT and only acknowledged Jay. Let's not tally the "We voted for Obama" reminders he drops Dad's way with a grin. As if he's done our very Black family a favor by being slightly less racist than his neighbors.

*I do it for Jess*, Dad told me when I asked why he never says anything back. *She's been there for me over the years. More than you know, TJ. You make sacrifices for friends. You make difficult choices.*

So here I am. Depending on one of those "difficult choices" to change my future.

I shrug. "Yeah, I'll mention it to him."

Dad scrubs a hand over the top of my head. "That's my baby boy." He restarts his crime drama. "We're moving closer to The Plan."

"Yup," I say with as much brightness as I can stomach.

I feel guilty for lying about my true intentions for tonight. And I'll talk to Mr. Scott about the recommendation letter. Eventually.

But right now, the Theo Wright Plan is going exactly the way I want.

Nothing's going to mess that up.

# 5

# DID SOMEONE SAY PREGAME?

**Darren was right.** When it comes to social gatherings, punctuality is a nonexistent concept for me.

Even with roughly eight hours' notice, I'm still not ready. That two-hour nap I had after my shower—the need to rinse off the grime from my morning run, plus the stress from my talk with Dad—didn't help. Neither did the post-nap erection I had to take care of.

Overall, it's the outfit selection that does me in. What can I say? I take pride in my appearance. Choosing which socks to wear is a thirty-minute process alone. My drip must be flawless when I ask Christian to prom.

That's what I type in the group chat at 4:45 p.m.

**Darren**
Disappointed but not surprised.
4:46 P.M.

**Jay**

Broooooo quit being a girl and put something on!

Its all about what u SAY not what u WEAR

Flirt game on _100_

Wait . . . u suck at flirtin nvrmnd 😖

4:48 P.M.

The urge to reply with a paragraph-long clapback about Jay's misogynistic comment and that Jayla *chose him secondhand* because Marcus Whitman was already in a relationship at the time delays me an extra minute. I toss my phone on the bed to focus on selecting a shirt to pair with my light denim jeans. The key to tonight's fit is adding little details so Christian sees an upgraded version of the Brook-Oak Theo.

I choose a black *Star Wars: The Last Jedi* T-shirt, the signature title font in blood red. Dad and Granny introduced me to the franchise when I was younger. I was indifferent about the original trilogy—we don't discuss the prequels—but the second I saw Finn on-screen in the newer films, a Black character who was as important as the others, I was hooked. Mad love to Lando Calrissian, but Finn made me feel like I could single-handedly destroy an empire.

I wish Granny had been around to see him on-screen.

The shirt goes perfectly with my Air Jordan 12 Retros. Tiny diamond studs in my ears. But the real gems are my neon green socks with strawberries on them.

I can't remember the origin of my love for patterned socks. A stocking stuffer from Granny possibly? Anyway, I own over thirty pairs now. Argyle to Nike swooshes to *Bob's Burgers* ones.

At 5:10 p.m., Dad yells, "TJ! There's a suspicious blue SUV outside our house with two boys inside!" from downstairs.

"On the way!" I shout back, continuing to curl-sponge my twists in the bathroom mirror.

"Darren has that 'I've been kidnapped' face on."

"Okay, okay!" I rush through a final rotation on my hair before gargling a capful of mouthwash. I check my reflection. Brook-Oak parties are a funny thing. At least the few I've been to. We pretend it's all about the dancing and drinking games and casual hookups. Being ourselves without adults judging our every move.

In reality, it's a fashion competition.

No one wants to stick out for any reason, let alone your wardrobe. The key is to blend in with your name-brand-wearing, summer-vacations-at-the-beach peers. I don't intentionally try to be like those kids. I simply don't want to fall into that other category.

"TJ!"

I sprint back into my room for my phone and overnight backpack.

"Wait!" Dad stops me as I yank open the front door. He tugs out his wallet. "Take some money. I know Jess will happily order in for you guys, but I don't want her paying for you. She doesn't need to . . ."

He trails off as he stuffs two twenty-dollar bills in my hand.

I wait for him to say he doesn't want anyone feeling obligated to take care of Miles Wright's son. He doesn't want Mr. Scott's pity money, even though Jay would never let it come off that way.

Sometimes, I think the reason Dad found this house in the South End rather than one in the West End where he grew up was to show everyone from Brook-Oak he's good. He's made it.

Is that the point, though? Proving your success to everyone else rather than doing it for yourself?

"Thanks," I mumble as he pecks a kiss to my temple.

"Be good. No trouble," he cautions as I jog out the door. "I love you, TJ!"

"Love you too, Dad!"

The interior of Jay's BMW X3 is more or less what you'd expect from the seventeen-year-old son of a health-care consultant and a lawyer: all-black leather, climate-control system with pollen filter, touch screen navigation, and an overpriced sound system currently vibrating Drake through my bones. I adjust the volume on "Passionfruit," catching Jay's side-eye in my periphery. He worships Drake like a god.

"So you made us wait for . . . *that*," Darren comments from the back seat.

Our eyes meet in the rearview.

"What?"

Darren pops his head between the driver's and passenger seat. "You look . . . respectable. Not at all basic."

"Oh, screw you," I say with a chuckle. "Tell me, D, are they still offering generous employee discounts at the J.Crew you work at?"

Darren's wardrobe has two dimensions: activewear or fitted,

collared shirts with black skinny jeans. There's no happy middle ground. Either option is always completed with a clean pair of high-tops.

His muscles are almost bursting out of today's red, white, and navy polo shirt.

He gasps, fake scandalized. "Shut up!"

"Ignore him." Jay smirks, eyes on the road. "You look . . . swell."

"More like swol," I mumble into my hand.

For his part, Jay's playing the casually wealthy role—white boat shoes, rolled-up khakis, and a loose-fit T-shirt with a very distinct green Lacoste crocodile on his chest.

"I'm a ten," Darren says, slouching back in his seat.

"An eleven," Jay affirms. "Theo's just jealous."

"Of what?" I scoff.

"That D's going to smash with Mack tonight," Jay declares, merging onto Interstate 65. Chloe lives on the north side of Jefferson County, in Prospect. It's a cool thirty-minute drive from Brook-Oak on a good day.

"Makayla?" I peek at Darren in the mirror. He's red-faced, looking down at his hands.

"The one and only Swipe Right Mack," Jay answers for him.

"*Makayla*," Darren firmly corrects. Then he's back between our seats, phone in hand. "And we're not going to, you know . . . But she followed me back!" He scrolls through his notifications to confirm @theonetruemakayla is now following @funko_dj.

Makayla's profile photo is one of those semiprofessional masterpieces: a sunset beach in the background. Golden light kissing her shiny cheeks. Wind-wrecked ponytail sweeping honey-blond strands across her smile. Just enough It-White-Girl vibes to explain her nearly four thousand followers.

"Congrats," I say, passing back Darren's phone. "Are you gonna *talk* to her this time?"

"Doubt it," mumbles Darren, wiggling into his seat.

"Oh, ye of little game." Jay guffaws. "It doesn't take much with her."

I roll my eyes. While Darren might be the king of unearthing gossip in our group, Jay feasts on the rumors and garbage takes like a raccoon. He treats Sharpie-written messages on bathroom walls as facts.

"Whatever," says Darren. He grins conspiratorially. "Theo's the one destined for action tonight. Right?"

I slouch low, knees pressed to the dashboard.

"No comment."

"We should be worried about someone walking in on Theo making out with Christian tonight, bro," Darren continues, shaking Jay's seat.

In the corner of my eye, I see Jay bite his lip. He's quiet for a minute. Fingers tightening on the wheel. Finally, he cracks a smile. "Now, that'd be a sight. Make sure to strap up, Theo."

He cranks the volume on another Drake song, bobbing his head along.

Discussion ended.

An anxious feeling crawls beneath my skin. It's not that I *want* Jay's analysis of my romantic—or sex—life. But I get weird when he acts like this. As if there's a comfort level he hasn't reached yet.

With my sexuality.

With . . . me.

Just then Drake is interrupted by a phone ringing through Jay's Bluetooth. It's his mom. He answers on speaker, the sharpness of Mrs. Scott's voice echoing through the SUV as she says, "Hello! Jay, sweetie!"

"Yes?"

"You're answering hands-free, right? You better not be holding the—"

"Mom, no." His jaw flexes. "You're on speaker. The boys are here."

"Hi, Darren!" she says. Then, an octave higher, "Hey, Theo, sweetheart. Miss you!"

I laugh. "Miss you too."

Jay rolls his shoulders like he's annoyed. "Did you need something, Mom?"

"You bet I do! I need you to be here tomorrow morning," she says, her voice losing some of that sugariness from a second ago. "Jules is visiting. We're all doing brunch."

Jay exhales loudly through his nose.

"I can hear you," admonishes Mrs. Scott. "It's already work getting your father on board. Your support is crucial."

"Yes, Mom."

"It's bad enough your sister's only giving us a small window to be a family," she continues to rant. "Seriously, she can't see her friends another time? Of course not! Why would my only daughter come into town and act like any other college student—study, spend time with family, *act* like an adult . . ."

I scratch my ear, cheating my eyes in Jay's direction.

His posture is stiff. He's white-knuckled, laser-focused on the road. This is him anytime his parents bring up Jules.

Jay's older sister is a rising junior at the University of Kentucky. Last time we spoke, she was still undeclared. It's safe to say whatever she gets a degree in won't garner any praise from her parents. They weren't fans of her decision to not apply to any Ivy Leagues. Or her partying lifestyle. Her overspending on non-school-related things freshman year. The list goes on.

"Thank goodness you're not turning out like her," Mrs. Scott says.

"Yeah." Jay sighs.

"Yale won't know what to do with how great you're going to be."

"Nope. Can't wait."

Half of Jay's bedroom is Yale paraphernalia. All provided by Mrs. Scott. Sometimes I wonder if Jay even wants to go there. Then again, that's hypocritical, right? Dad name-drops Duke at least once a week and I mostly go along with it.

I can hear Mrs. Scott beaming through the speakers when she says, "Such a great role model for Jasper."

Jay and I have talked about this before. The pressure from our parents. I'm an only child, so I don't always get what it's like for him. But in the quiet moments in his bedroom when we're surrounded by books and unfinished papers and uncapped highlighters, we whisper about constantly having to think about what's next. The steps we have to take. The people we have to impress. Jay does it with a half smile though, as if he kind of enjoys the challenge.

I wish I could tell him I don't.

"I'm sure that's all thanks to Darren and my golden boy, Theo!" Mrs. Scott adds.

On cue, Darren and I shout, "You're welcome!"

Jay's eyes flit from the road to me. I can't read his expression, but it's not the same one that was teasing Darren minutes ago.

"Yeah," he huffs. "D and Golden Boy have my back."

"Always," Darren insists.

I nod.

*TNT forever.*

After Mrs. Scott lists off her expectations for tomorrow, she ends the call. A buffered silence hangs in the air. Drake resumes his half singing, half rapping about love. The GPS occasionally interrupts to give directions.

"Fuck," Jay finally hisses. He thumps the steering wheel twice as we come to a stop at a red light.

"Jay," I say, low and calm. I know how he gets after a bad call with his mom. "You good?"

He exhales a few tight breaths through his teeth, then absent-mindedly digs into the center console. "Thank you, Alicia, for coming through with some pregame paraphernalia." He produces a baggie with two rolled joints and several mini alcohol bottles.

Darren hoots from the back.

Jay's mouth eventually relaxes into a smile.

"We need snacks first," I say. "I'm not dealing with two trashed besties on an empty stomach."

"Don't forget—I need Sonic!" Darren mentions. He's created this infallible hangover-prevention method. Greasy burgers are a main component.

"Deal!" Jay agrees after checking the time on the dash.

Chloe's party doesn't formally start until nine p.m. That's eight p.m. for Chloe's inner circle. Ten p.m. for the fashionably late, but polite-enough-to-not-show-up-empty-handed crew. Anything after that is for the already-drunk crowd looking for more booze and provisions before their next party stop.

We're aiming for around nine thirty.

After a lane change, Jay's elbow nudges mine. He whispers, "Thanks" without looking my way. I nod and leave it at that.

He never wants to talk about these things in front of Darren.

One Drake song later, we're pulling into a SpeedEx gas station parking lot. Pregaming before a party is another mandatory ritual for us.

Today, we all need it.

Familiar faces from Brook-Oak roam around SpeedEx's convenience store. Darren's chatting up two girls I think he knows from Yearbook at the checkout area. A group of seniors argue over the best doughnut-and-beer combos near the mini-bakery. P. J. Wahid from my Algebra 2 class is doing the Shiggy dance to, you guessed it, Jay's bro-crush Drake by the self-service coffee bar. We've entered the unofficial pre-party waiting zone.

I'm not interacting with anyone.

Thing is, I'm in my own head. I've been standing in the middle of the candy and chips aisle for five minutes. Something about the scent of hot dogs roasting under a heat lamp and the BOGO cranberry Sprite sale advertised on the soda fridges derails my brain. Now all I'm thinking about is Christian. More to the point: needing actual *words* to ask him to prom.

I can't go all *Love, Actually*. Show up to Chloe's party with a series of oversize cue cards that basically add up to: *Will You Go to Prom with Me?*

I'm all for sentimental gestures, but not that clichéd.

Netflix makes it look so easy. He's gay. I'm gay. We're both out. I'm supposed to say something clumsy but cute. He'll laugh. The world will freeze around us. The perfect obscure pop song will come on as I ask him to prom.

We kiss. Everyone claps. Roll the credits.

Except, outside of TV and movies, I've only ever seen that happen for straight kids.

What are the chances it goes so smoothly for me?

"Jay!"

I spy Jay being tugged into a bro-hug from Cole Nelson, former BOHS wrestling captain. He graduated last year. We never really socialized. Jay's people-person skills far exceed Darren's and mine. He might know more people around here than Dad does.

"Tell me you're headed to Chloe's tonight," begs Cole.

"Where else would I be?" Jay replies easily.

"Sweet." Cole fist-bumps him. "Flying solo?"

"No. My boys Darren and Theo are coming."

"Hmm." Cole's eyes flit around as he grips a Mountain Dew bottle. I slink behind a candy station. Cole leans toward Jay. "Theo's a chill guy. At least I've heard. Gay, right?"

One of Jay's eyebrows lifts. "Uh, yeah."

"Cool for him," says Cole. "I've got no problem with it."

Here's the thing: the moment anyone says they don't have a problem with something, it means they do.

Case in point: "I always felt like he was slick checking out my junk in the showers," Cole adds. "Appraising the merchandise, you know?"

"What?"

Cole shrugs, pushing back his messy brown hair. "I don't think he's a creep. You two been friends for a long time?"

"Since we were, like, five," replies Jay, face flushed.

"We all do it. Size each other up and shit. It's a guy thing," Cole continues, bobbing his head like this is nothing but casual talk between buddies. "It just felt like he wanted . . . *something*."

There's a buzz catching like fire in my nerves, waiting for Jay to correct Cole. Shut him down. But all Jay does is blink, lips opening and closing.

"N-no, it's not like that," he finally stammers. "Theo's chill."

"You sure?"

"I swear."

"Good." Cole taps a friendly fist to Jay's shoulder. "Like I said, I don't have any problems with dudes like *that*. I didn't want any awkwardness if we see each other later."

Jay chews on his bottom lip, rocking on his heels.

"There won't be."

He doesn't add anything else. Cole disappears into the checkout line. Jay holds on to a smile that doesn't reach very high. Eventually, he starts up an animated conversation with Mya Anthony by the frozen yogurts. Like the last five minutes never happened.

Except they did.

I want to ask Jay why he even entertained the conversation for longer than ten seconds. Is it something he always does when I'm not around? Let some B-movie asshole spit homophobic lies about his best friend?

But I'm frozen in place, trying to cool the anger building in my throat.

*Never in public*, Dad's reminded me multiple times. *Don't be that angry Black boy everyone loves to hate.*

"Theo?"

My head whips to the left. It's Luca, an eyebrow arched curiously.

"Um, yeah?" I croak.

He waves a hand in the vicinity of where I'm resting against a candy rack. "Do you mind? I've got a theme going here."

That's when I notice the collection of goods cradled in his arm: tropical-flavored Red Bull; a pack of Reese's Peanut Butter Lovers cups; a can of stackable salt and vinegar chips; and a bottled water, hopefully to balance all the salty-sweet flavors.

I snort. "What's the theme? Chaos?"

"Ha. Ha." A seamless smile unrolls across his mouth. "Don't hate."

Hands up, palms out, I say, "Wouldn't dream of it." I back away from the candy shelf, eyeing him. "Let me guess. The missing ingredient is . . . Sour Patch Kids? No, Lemonheads. Stabilizes the harshness of the chips, right?"

He chews his lip like he's holding back a laugh. His chin juts toward an assortments of Starburst candies.

"Hmmm." I tap my chin, grinning. "You look like . . ."

I access his outfit: White Air Force 1s. Tan, black, and red plaid pants. It's the black T-shirt with FOOD VIBES ONLY in yellow lettering across his chest that seals the deal.

I swipe up a blue-green pack. "Tropical, obviously."

"Wrong." He plucks the yellow pack from the shelf. "Original. I'm a pink-Starburst-only guy."

It's so ridiculous. Not his love for the strawberry-flavored Starburst. They're the only redeemable ones, lemon being a close second. It's the way he says it, with this sheepish grin and a strange confidence in his brown eyes. I want to laugh.

Luca must detect my trembling smile. "Are you done food-shaming me?" He sounds more amused than exasperated.

"Whoa! No judgment here!" I motion toward the chips in the crook of his elbow. "Those are my favorite."

"Thanks." He readjusts his snacks before the can falls. "Your approval is all I was waiting for."

*Okay, asshole.* I can't help beaming.

From anyone else, that'd feel like a jab to the throat. An outright *your opinion wasn't asked for, so mind your business* that'd send me reeling, ashamed for daring to speak. But Luca attaches this crooked smirk to the end of his sentence like a postscript on an email.

"That's an exceptional haul for a Saturday afternoon," I note. "Going to a movie?"

"Party." He eyes a bag of spicy, white cheddar cheese puffs.

"Chloe's?"

"Strong possibility."

"Me too." I'm not quite sure why my voice rises to an octave that would make Sam Smith proud.

"Cool." He hovers over a rack of M&M's. "Warning—don't plan an epic promposal by the pool with fireworks and the cheer squad dancing behind you. It might end tragically."

My eyes widen. Does he know about the dare? Has Darren been running his mouth again?

"Hell no." I shake my head, chuckling. "I'd never do something that pathe—"

The word almost slips out. Doesn't matter. Luca's expression shifts dramatically. His nostrils flare. The skin around his eyes tightens. I'm a half second too slow with an apology.

"That's not what I—"

"No. I get it." He sniffs, then reaches down. Clumsily, he grabs a pack of honey roasted peanuts. Tosses them at my feet. "Here. You need these since you clearly didn't have the nuts to tell me I was making a mistake yesterday."

"Wait, I meant . . ."

Again, my words aren't fast enough.

Luca's gone, ducking into the line. Never looking my way when I say, "I wish I was half as brave as you were."

# 6

# THE SAME POST MALONE SONGS ON REPEAT

**"Let phase four** begin!"

In the back seat, Darren crumples a Sonic wrapper, mouth half-full of bacon cheeseburger. He brandishes two pink, chewable antacid tablets.

"You're a masochist, D," Jay says from the passenger seat. He dumps twin mini bottles of vodka into two thirty-two-ounce SpeedEx cups three-quarters filled with lemon-lime soda.

We've been aimlessly driving around Prospect to kill time. I'm behind the wheel. There's an unsaid code between TNT—I'm always the designated driver.

I haven't touched any alcohol since the Night of Too Many Jell-O Shots.

Everyone has their "and that's why I'm never doing *that* again" war story. Mine involves Darren's parents' sixteenth-wedding-anniversary celebration. Technically, we weren't *invited* to the party. Jay and I were there to keep Darren occupied while his parents danced the night away with their adult friends. It didn't stop us from swiping a tray of Jell-O shots from the kitchen.

Honestly, what's more fun than puking your guts up while playing *Halo*? Try adding rainbow chunks to it.

My impulse control is a solid eight now.

"It's called preparation, Jay," Darren says while happily accepting the cup passed to him.

His No Hangover Super Soldier Serum consists of a teaspoon of olive oil, at least two greasy burgers from a fast-food restaurant, an adult dose of the pink stomach stuff, and, finally, lots of water before and after. He's the only proven statistic. Though, I can vouch he hasn't crashed miserably after a night of drinking so far.

"You too can live hangover-free if you'd follow my methods, Theo," Darren says, slurping through his straw.

"Then who'd drive?"

He rubs his chin, considering. "Good point."

We cruise through serene, antiquated neighborhoods. Long driveways lead up to brick homes and pristine green lawns. The sinking sun bounces orange light off the windows. It's weird how every house appears untouchable and cozy at the same time. Nothing like the South End where everything looks well loved.

Passenger window down, Jay takes hits from his blunt. I don't mind the scent. It's his car, so whatever. But between the woodsy aroma and Sonic, we're going to show up at Chloe's smelling like a bad, early-aughts teen rom-com.

"Wait, wait, wait! Chill, chill, chill!" Jay almost tips over his cup excitedly. "Check the memories post that just popped up on IG."

I pull to a complete stop at the end of the road to look at his phone.

It's a photo of TNT. Our first day of track practice. New cleats and shorts and still-dry white T-shirts. Official members of the squad.

"Badasses," says Darren after another sip.

"Speak for yourself." Jay guffaws. "Theo, what was up with your hair?"

"Probably the same thing that was up with your face." I thump his shoulder. "Puberty's a scam, right?"

"True."

Darren laments, "Palo Alto will never be able to upgrade you two."

"Neither will the Ivies," Jay agrees.

We don't talk about this often. Life after high school. Darren's applying to Stanford and Cal Tech. The Scotts won't settle for anything short of Yale for Jay. *Maybe* Princeton, Cornell, or Brown. All to spite Jules. Apparently, it's Duke for me.

The fact that The Nameless Trio won't be on the same campus in less than two years blows my mind. In Darren's case, not even in the same time zone.

I keep wondering what happens to us after we toss our graduation caps in the air. How many more miles does our friendship have? Are before-college friendships like bookmarks on your web browser? You occasionally revisit them or completely forget they're there. Are they like those tabs you keep open for no apparent reason?

Is that how it was for Dad and his high school friends?

One day, they woke up. Moved on. From shared lunches and study guides and secrets to perfunctory hellos in the Starbucks line.

I can't imagine Jay missing my birthday.

Every November 8 at 12:01 a.m. he posts a vintage photo of us as Batman and Joker on Halloween. It'll include one long, sappy-as-hell caption that's guaranteed to leave me choked up, not that I ever tell him or Darren.

He never forgets.

Just like he remembers to bring an extra T-shirt and shorts in case I forget practice clothes for track. His trunk remains stocked with bottled water. In the center console are five different kinds of phone plugs so everyone can stay charged.

It's who he is.

Friendly. Thoughtful.

That's why it's so hard to swallow what happened back at SpeedEx. The way he didn't call Cole out for his homophobia. His *lies*.

"God, we were such rookies back then," Jay reflects.

I pull back onto the main road. "That's your fault," I tease.

We're all quiet for a second. Stuck in that time loop. Then Jay says, "It's actually *your* fault. Both of you."

"What d'you mean?" Darren asks, chewing on his straw.

Jay pulls his knees to his chest, folding into a small ball in the passenger seat.

"When Theo dared me to run around the quad shirtless that day," he starts, "Coach Devers saw me. I was in deep shit for semi-nudity, of course. But . . . she encouraged me to try out for the team. Said I was one of the fastest freshmen she'd ever seen. Well, one who wasn't late for class."

We all laugh.

"My parents really wanted me to find an extracurricular," he admits. "Something for my college résumé. Can you believe it? I was fourteen!"

I can believe it. Dad was the same way.

"Hey." Darren smacks the side of Jay's seat. "You never told us that."

"I know, I know."

At the next red light, I glance at Jay. He's wincing, watching kids biking down the street. "It's why I love our dares. They make us invincible. Do things we'd never do."

"True," Darren mumbles.

As I follow the GPS's directions, I turn down the music. Just to listen to this side of Jay. The one that's so different from the SpeedEx version.

"Even tonight. Look at Theo. Going after his crush."

I roll my eyes. If *ready to shit my pants* translates to *going after my crush*, then sure. That's what I'm doing.

Jay taps his phone screen. "This is what started it all. Us against our fears."

Okay, Darren has forfeited the Most Dramatic Friend spot.

I ask, "Wasn't that back when we were all on the relay team?"

"Ye-yeah." Jay clears his throat.

In the beginning, the three of us were determined to compete in the same event. We had the best synergy on the team. If one of us won, we all won. Coach eventually saw Darren's potential in the hurdles. She liked Jay and me on the relay team, but there was only one spot available.

We raced for it.

I beat him by half a second.

She moved Jay over to solo events, which was better for him anyway. He loves a spotlight.

"We've come a long way." Jay turns to the window to finish his blunt.

A scummy guilt swishes around my stomach. I know why I'm holding back on questioning Jay about what happened. I need him. Well, I need *his dad* for the recommendation letter.

I don't want our friendship to become transactional. Right now, it feels that way.

Jay exhales a cloud of smoke, smiling. "Tonight's a night for big things."

"Oh yeah?" I ask.

"I have this feeling."

Darren thumps his chest, burping loudly. He points accusingly at Jay. "This asshat is going to treat you to the best prom experience ever after you lock down this dare."

My eyes bounce back and forth between them. My boys. The two people I can always count on to get me out of a funk.

"Okay. Let's get this night started."

The Campbells live in a castle. "Six bedrooms and seven bathrooms," Jay whispered when we pulled up. It's a riverfront property. Over four acres of brick and glass and immaculately kept landscape.

From the outside, the two-story looks as though my house and the properties on either side combined to create a Transformer.

Already, the driveway is near max capacity. I park on the street. A nervous feeling sinks into my bones. I wonder if Chloe's neighbors know her family is out of town for spring break. We drove by at least two other palaces housing a car lot worth of vehicles in their expansive driveways. There are clearly multiple parties happening in Innisbrook. Hopefully, it keeps the cops from shutting this one down.

At least until *after* I ask Christian to prom.

I shoot Dad a quick "check-in" text. We dodge a troupe of theater kids recording numerous live videos on the way to the front door. Their exuberant squealing is considerably more tolerable than the overplayed Post Malone music that assaults us as the door swings open.

"QR code," demands Octavia Ballard, blocking the entryway. She's flanked on either side by Regina and Christy, two other Ballers benchwarmers. Octavia's six three, all muscle, no give. I bet she bench-presses guys like me before her first sip of iced coffee in the morning.

"QR code!"

Darren startles. "Whoa, what the—"

I glare at Jay. He never mentioned needing a special digital code to get in. What are we walking into? The Red Keep?

Jay, smooth as ever, flashes his phone screen for Octavia.

Christy uses an app on her phone to scan and verify Jay's code, then perkily announces, "They're with Jayla."

"Are y'all keeping tabs?" I ask.

Regina replies dryly, "If anyone starts shit, we need account-ability. A 'don't fuck around and you won't have to find out' system, if you will."

Inside is the kind of chaotic energy I expected. Neon-orange plastic cups stacked on any surface available. Decent music. Bad dancing, or, in Arvin's case, dry humping a wall. Varied levels of socializing happening everywhere.

Having visited Chloe's previously, Jay takes us on a tour. The foyer opens to a living room, then an overcrowded kitchen, fol-lowed by a decked-out family room. Vaulted ceilings, arched windows, hardwood *plus* marble floors. Jay mentions a finished basement we don't visit along with an "off-limits" second floor. French doors lead to a partially covered patio, pool and outdoor firepit included.

The hot tub is already packed, the pool less so. Someone's portable Bluetooth speaker competes with the noisy soundtrack coming from inside.

So far, no Christian.

"Do you see him anywhere?" I whisper-shout once we're back in the living room.

In the middle of all the bodies, Chloe sits cross-legged on a sofa. Seniors and previous graduates bracket her. Her chestnut hair is purposefully messy. When she notices us, Chloe waves politely. I do the same, but she's already absorbed in a nearby conversation.

"Uh, D?"

Next to me, Darren vigorously shuffles in place like Elmo cele-brating his birthday. It's his favorite go-to dance. A *pay no attention to my clumsiness* Jedi mind trick.

"You're supposed to be *helping*," I remind him.

"I am!"

"Really?" I wave a hand at his . . . spasming. "This isn't helping."

He hiccups, then cackles. Any other day, I'd fully appreciate tipsy Darren. Hell, I'd *encourage* it. But not when Jay, my other wingman, is suddenly distracted by the happily squealed "Bae!" from the entryway.

Jayla stands in a semicircle of cheerleaders. Her box braids are scooped up in a ponytail to show off a pair of chunky gold hoop earrings. The cerulean BOHS Cheer Squad T-shirt she's wearing looks—unsurprisingly—great against her pale-brown skin.

"Jay?" I elbow him. "A little assistance?"

He gives me a half-assed apologetic face.

"Sorry. We're looking for . . . ?"

"*Christian*," I say, not that it matters. His eyes keep drifting toward Jayla. I clear my throat aggressively until his head snaps back around.

"My bad." He laughs, cheeks reddening. "I'm here for you. Do you want to search downstairs?"

Beyond his shoulder, I clock the severe stink eye Jayla is throwing us. Throwing *me*, to be precise. As much as I want Jay around, it's not worth her wrath.

"No. Go." I sigh. "Do your . . . hetero things."

He looks mostly relieved when I wave him off.

"I won't be far," he promises. "When you find Christian, just . . . uh, make sure I'm around. You know, dare rules and all."

How could I forget? At least one of us must be present when the other is doing a dare.

"He's probably not even here yet," Jay adds while backing away. "You know the gays like to make an entrance."

I blink three times. That scummy feeling surfaces in my stomach again. Before I gather a retort, Jay has Jayla lifted in his arms. Phones are out to capture the moment in all its sickening adorableness.

#TheStraightsAreAtItAgain.

I exhale loudly, turning toward Darren, ready to rant.

"Darren! O-M-G!"

The two girls from SpeedEx sidle up to Darren, bouncing on their toes.

"They're playing Kings downstairs!" one cheers.

"You're coming, right?" the other asks, barely hiding her eagerness.

Darren's eyes don't know where to look. I cough into my fist. He presents me with an abashed smile. The one he always uses when convincing me to share the mochi ice cream.

"Jesus, just go," I relent.

Before he gets too far, I say, "Turn your location on. Stop at three *mixed* drinks. No shots," going full-on Miles Wright.

I shudder.

"Promise to do reconnaissance while I'm gone," he yells, tripping over his own feet to chase the girls.

Whatever. This is fine. As much as I love Jay and Darren, their lack of game will slow me down. I only need them around to witness my big moment. Project: Win a Prom Date with Christian Harris has always been a one-man job anyway.

• • •

Except trying to find Christian is like a big, drunk game of *Where's Waldo?* at this party.

Somewhere between nonchalantly mingling with the wallflowers and lasting one round of Beirut: Name That Tune! Edition with the Rolling Tones, I scale back on my search. It's been forty-five minutes. I'm exhausted. Catching up with classmates about our worst essays or the latest viral video is more my speed.

Eventually, I end up in the family room—AKA Club Brook-Oak.

The "dancing" is as awful as you'd expect. All the furniture has been pushed against the walls to maximize floor space. The overwhelming odor of sweat, alcohol, and countless body sprays saturate the room.

At the heart of the swaying bodies is something that catches me off guard.

It's Luca and Makayla . . . *grinding.*

This is, dare I say, scandalous? Modern-age *Dirty Dancing* hip action is happening between them. My entire face is on fire from watching.

Strands of Luca's hair stick to his temples. Makayla's arms are linked around his neck. His hands can't find traction on her swiveling waist. Her exaggerated smile seems almost performative. Like this is all for the audience they've amassed.

A sharp, rippling sensation moves through my chest.

Somewhere in my brain, I know if that was *me* instead of Makayla flirting and tugging on Luca's collar, everyone wouldn't be whistling and catcalling. If that were me and Christian, they'd turn the other way. Pretend we didn't exist.

I can't tell if that's how I truly feel or if Cole's words have gotten to me.

The music changes: an old Nicki Minaj song.

Someone shrieks, "Theo!" Kendra from chemistry grabs my hands. "Middle school! Remember?"

I definitely do.

It's a truth universally known that while I'm never the center of attention at these gatherings—a slot permanently filled by one Jayson Scott—I rarely turn down an opportunity to show off my sweet feet and hips. Studying choreography from YouTube videos, on top of the library of nineties Black comedies Dad's introduced me to, shouldn't go to waste. It's my birthright. Besides, watching all these amateurs struggling to twerk hurts my soul.

"Let's go!" calls Kendra.

The music's suddenly louder. Eyes track me, waiting. It takes midway through the first verse to ignore their stares and find my groove. But after that? It's over.

This is my jam.

I don't go for the instant kill. Instead, I start with moves I've learned from K-pop videos. A shoot dance here, part of the Renegade there. All for laughs. I feed off their energy.

Once the second chorus kicks in, I'm fully committed. Winding my hips to the drumbeat. Feet shuffling as I glide across the hardwood. I even snag Kendra to mimic the choreography from the music video.

"O-M-fucking-G, marry me, Theo!" a girl shrieks over the song's thudding bass.

Our audience multiplies. Bodies squeeze into the circle. My

eyes catch Luca's. He surveys me with a blank expression. A weird rush of nerves vibrates up my spine until Kendra spins me.

I lose him in all the faces.

When the song fades, I turn to Kendra for a quick high five before a senior politely asks her to dance. She winks at me before obliging.

I stumble away to get some fresh air.

The endorphins buzz in my system. I'm not even mad about the sweat rolling down my cheek. It's like I'm walking on the clouds.

Every first day of summer break, Jay, Darren, and I go to Sonic Drive-In for slushes. My favorite is blue raspberry. That first sip, sitting with my friends under a giant sun with nothing to stop us, is just like this feeling.

*Phenomenal.*

It takes a lot of negotiating to squeeze through the crowd. More and more people are flooding the opposite direction, anxious to flee the house for the cool promise of water and night air. I'm fighting the tide. But honestly? It's so worth it.

When I reach the front of the house, I hear a recognizable laugh.

Christian Harris's laugh.

Things unfold like every movie has promised: Christian slowly descends the stairs. Light from the upstairs hallway haloes over him. Some chill pop song plays *ironically* as our eyes meet.

He stops on the last step, beaming at me.

"Hey, Theo."

"Hi. Uh, hello. Christian." My ears burn. "Hey."

He ignores my sputtering to hold his phone screen in my

direction. A video of me dancing two minutes ago plays. "Sorry I missed the show." He tilts his head in a genuinely amused way.

I suck in my cheeks to level out my smile. "That's me. Future Lil Nas X backup dancer."

"Not a bad gig."

He steps down onto the landing. I've got a good three inches on him. I wonder how far I'd have to lean to kiss him. That's a thing I should plan for, maybe? Hopefully better than I planned for this moment where I'm too busy staring into his crinkled eyes to ask what I'm supposed to.

My eyes search our surroundings. If I'm going to do this, I need one of my boys around. Relief washes over me when I find Jay seated among a group of athletes trading shot glasses and orange cups in the living room.

He's keenly watching us.

"I never see you at these things," comments Christian.

I turn back to him, rubbing the back of my neck. "I, uh, wasn't sure you'd be here either."

"I don't make it a habit." He snorts. "But tonight felt appropriate? Like we all needed it."

"Facts."

"Were you, um . . . looking for me?"

*Yes!* I want to scream. *And I just need you to move about twenty paces to your left.*

My gaze drifts back to Jay, who's shaking a finger at me like, *I can't hear you all the way over there.*

Shit. Okay, I don't have the right words. No fancy poem to recite. No cheerleaders or a cappella group or even a good song playing—seriously, whoever's DJing is killing all my vibes with *another* Post Malone tune—but I have Wright genes in my blood.

"Hey, do you want to go over—"

"Holy fuck, what's *she* doing here?"

I'm startled by a voice that's not Christian's. He's looking past me. I follow his stare. And there she is. My ex-friend standing in the foyer wearing an expression matching the acronym spelled out in gold letters on her black shirt:

IDGAF.

# 7

# OPEN-DOOR POLICY

**Aleah Bird is** at Chloe's party. Less than ten feet from me.

Thing is, since we started at Brook-Oak, Aleah and I have never shared a class. I'm in the HSU program. She's in YPT, for singing, I've heard. I've never asked anyone. I didn't even know she was attending BOHS until the second week of freshman year.

We've barely crossed paths in the hallways. Even then, I was probably too busy joking with Darren and Jay to acknowledge it. She was most likely with the Ballers. Between two campuses—a separate one for all the YPT studios and performance spaces— there are over a thousand students attending our school. It's easy to become just a face in the crowd.

But part of me has always had a Spidey-sense about Aleah. I've trained myself not to look her way. Keep a distance only noticeable by me.

Until tonight, I guess.

Static clings to the air. Has someone lowered the music? Or maybe the whispers are louder. A handful of phones are not-so-discreetly pointed toward Aleah. I step closer to Christian like he's a shield I can hide behind.

It's unnecessary.

The awkwardness of Aleah's arrival dies quickly when a tipsy freshman yells, "Mario Party downstairs!" He proceeds to crash into a tray of plastic shot glasses filled with various colored liquor. Soon, he's just another victim of #BOHSFail as people encircle him with their phones recording.

The music returns to its previous ear-aching thud. Voices carry from all over the house. Everyone has moved on.

Except me.

I watch Aleah stand in the foyer for a second. She doesn't make eye contact with anyone. Her teeth tug on her bottom lip. Long fingers toy with the thin chain of her silver necklace, an anxious move I remember from when we were kids.

But maybe she's changed? Maybe she's not nervous.

I don't know . . . *this* Aleah.

A line of shirtless guys marches past Christian and me. They repeatedly grunt, "Pool time!"

We edge back onto the stairs.

When my vision clears, Aleah's disappeared. Lost in the constant ebb and flow of bodies shifting around the party. I don't know why I waste another ten seconds searching for her. What am I going to do? Walk up to her? Ask if she's okay? Can we sit down and hash out five years of absence and absolute douchery on my part?

*Yeah, right.*

"Hey." It's Christian's voice—of course—that pulls me back.

I whip in his direction, cheeks warm, smiling goofily.

He's gripping an orange cup now, grinning back. Eyes twinkling. Yes, I've reached peak Thirsty Theo once more.

"Were you saying something?" he asks.

"Huh?"

"Before the whole . . ." He trails off, waving a hand toward the door.

"Ah. Yes. I think so?"

A laugh bursts from his lips. He's wearing a lemon-yellow shirt. The maybe-a-dimple in his left cheek flexes, setting off an alarm inside me—I can't simply improvise asking him to prom with sweaty armpits from dancing. Possible burger breath from earlier. I don't even know what condition my hair is in.

"Theo?"

I glance over my shoulder. Jay's still observing us while Jayla rants in his ear. Twisting back to Christian, I say, "I was gonna ask if you know where the bathroom is?"

Wow, not at all what I wanted to ask.

"One that doesn't have a long line?" I try to add convincingly.

Christian blinks twice. "Um, sure." He leans closer. I can smell his cologne. Something sweet, like oranges. He whispers, "Don't tell anyone, but . . . upstairs. Third bedroom on the right. All the other doors are locked."

I swallow as he inches back. It's like my body already misses his heat.

"Thanks," I say hurriedly. "Would you mind hanging out here for, like, five minutes? I need to . . ."

He blinks again, frowning.

"Not that, I mean," I wheeze out. "Shit. No, not like. Seriously. I don't have to, you know. Fucking shit."

Christian laughs. *Hard.* Literally wiping tears from his eyelashes before he says, "Whatever you need, Theo. Do you."

"It's not like that," I repeat.

"Noted."

I shake my head, biting the inside of my cheek.

"Take care of business." He nudges me with a teasing grin. "I'll be around."

Then he wiggles into a small group of band nerds shouting near the kitchen.

I take a beat to memorize his exact position. The kind of jeans he's wearing. Shoes too. My brain downloads every indicator that'll bring me right back to this boy once I pull myself together. Then I check my surroundings. No one's watching. Jay's lost in an aggressively loud game of Heads Up! with our track teammates.

Once it's safe, I take the stairs two at a time, leaving the noise behind.

All the framed photos on one wall imply the unlocked bedroom belongs to Chloe's little sister.

I shut the door behind me. No one needs to know I'm here. I don't bother with the overhead light switch. Thanks to strings of fairy lights tacked above a queen-size bed, I'm not in complete darkness. Everything's bathed in soft, artificial yellows and pinks. A collage of Disney princes is painted on the opposite wall. A pastel green bean bag sits in a corner next to the tween-size desk with a MacBook decorated in mermaid stickers.

"Okay, *Maddie*," I whisper after clocking her name engraved on a trophy. "Bedroom challenge accepted."

My own room has a chaos-meets-*GQ* vibe. Framed graffiti art I've found online. All-black furniture and bed frame. Chrome-painted standing lamps. My white desk has scribbled art from highlighters and Sharpies.

Dad helped set it up. More than once, he's offered to bring in vintage pieces from Granny's old room, but I always decline.

I think he's relieved every time I do.

After two minutes assessing myself in the attached bathroom's mirror—I don't stink, my clothes aren't a mess, and I gargled a precautionary capful of mouthwash—I hop onto Maddie's bed. When I pull out my phone, several notifications await me.

Dad sent a photo as a response to my earlier check-in text. His sock-covered feet kicked up on our coffee table next to a takeout box of wings and fries, plus a two-liter bottle of cherry Coke, his favorite. On the television, slightly out of focus, is the original live-action Transformers movie. The only one we genuinely like.

There's a message underneath.

**Dad:**
👍
BIG party plans over here!
9:32 P.M.

I grin. My fingers blur over the keyboard—**lol dont party too hard!** Then I think a simple text isn't enough. Pics or it didn't happen, right? I scroll through my camera roll. There's a randomly saved photo of a half-eaten pizza pie—pepperoni, pineapple, and jalapeño, a truly lethal combo—from a few months back when TNT crashed at Darren's after bowling and laser tag. I send it along with another message—**this pizza is sus but im killin it on this new mario!!!**

His reply is instantaneous.

**Dad:**
NEEDS MORE PEPPERS! Looks tasty! Have fun!
10:34 P.M.

For the record: Miles Davis Wright is an emphatic fan of the exclamation point in text. But it's the ensuing message that makes my stomach jump, then knot. It has me seeing double, thankful I turned off my read notifications.

**Dad:**
While youre kicking butt be sure to talk to Mr Scott before it gets too late! remember to smile and say THANK YOU!
10:35 P.M.

Quickly, I exit out of my messages. No reply. No thumbs-up or prayer-hands emojis. Nothing except tight shoulders and the sour taste of guilt at the back of my throat. It's not the lying to Dad about where I am, what I'm doing that's overwhelming. It's that, once Dad's found a new way to improve The Plan, it becomes his entire focus. The sooner he can X something off the list, the better.

I'll get a recommendation letter. But why does it have to be tonight? And why *him*? There are over 150,000 Duke alumni. I searched it. I'm not even done with junior year. Haven't taken the SATs yet. Every portion of the college application process is so *urgent* only to become another name in the pile of applicants they won't decide on until a couple months before you graduate. A continuous cycle of anxiety over what you can do to help tip the scales in your favor when, really, no one knows the exact formula.

Yet Dad keeps trying to crack the code. I'm going to be the exception. Duke-bound, come hell or high water.

I don't feel like thinking that far into my future tonight. I only want to concentrate on winning this dare. Going to prom with Christian.

I flop backward on the bed. Log in to YouTube. It's time for research. Ignoring all the *Craig of the Creek* clips recommended to me—I'll watch them later—I type in the search bar:

*Best promposal ideas.*

Over a hundred results pop up. I don't have time to watch them all. Who knows where Christian might be by now? Instead, I set a timer on my phone for seven minutes, then click on the first video.

It's a tutorial by a white guy. He's asking a girl to prom using cardboard, lights, and his friend's pickup truck. Sweet as it is, it's out of my current capabilities being that I'm lying in a kid's bedroom watched over by an army of stuffed mermaids.

The next one involves cheerleaders. Immediate skip. I'm saving my one BFF favor for the recommendation letter, not to have Jay ask his Theo-hating girlfriend for aid with a promposal.

I settle on a compilation video with a high viewer count. It hits all the cliché check marks—over-the-top cuteness, poorly constructed signs, super-cheesy music—but I can't stop the way my heart races. Ninety percent of the clips are of straight couples, and yet . . . I can picture myself in every scenario. Putting myself out there. Waiting for Christian to shout, "Yes!"

I'm so distracted I don't notice the next video automatically cueing up is from the Brook-Oak YT channel.

It's another compilation. Titled *WORST PROMPOSAL IDEA*. A user named NotThatZain posted it. The tiny channel icon reveals it *is* that Zain, though. The one from the Rolling Tones.

Despite being uploaded six hours ago, it hasn't been taken down yet. Maybe no one's reported it? The video has already amassed two thousand views.

It's a four-minute-and-thirty-seven-second car wreck set to Lorde's "Supercut." A meticulously spliced-together anthology of Luca and Devya's relationship through photos from their Instagram accounts along with excerpts from *that* promposal.

"Oh, fuck."

I want to look away, but I can't.

This is art. The magic indie films are made of. From chaste kisses to sofa cuddling to sharing iced coffees at Starbucks, all interrupted by scenes of Devya's cringe face during the promposal. For every *aww*, red-heart-emoji moment, you're hit with another angle of Luca flat on his ass as another boy swoops in to steal his spotlight. To my utter shock and humiliation, there's even a few zoomed-in cuts of me—eyes bulging, brow raised, jaw unhinged— sprinkled in.

Perfect reaction GIF or meme material.

My timer goes off as the video ends on a slow-motion close-up of Luca's distraught face.

The comments section is outrageous. Skull emojis, copious amounts of LOLs, *thoughts and prayers*, and *what's his @?* I barely scroll halfway before catching way too much secondhand embarrassment to continue.

I stare at Luca's paused face. He looks nothing like the boy I saw dancing with Makayla. Maybe he's already over Devya? That's all high school relationships are, right? A good time, a bad breakup, a quick transition to the next.

At least, for Luca's sake, I hope so.

I jolt when, out of nowhere, the bedroom's doorknob jiggles. Once, twice. Then a wave of hallway light singes my retinas as the door flings open. Slowly, my vision adjusts. I squint at someone standing in the entryway.

"Luca?"

I take in a pair of dark brown eyes, confused pout, FOOD VIBES ONLY T-shirt, and silver rings on his fingers before Luca replies, "I need the bathroom."

"Um . . . TMI."

"Not like that," he says, his voice strained. "I need to—"

"Dude, it's your business," I say, hands raised, "not mine." I grin broadly. A hint of déjà vu hits me. It reminds me of the last conversation Christian and I had, except I'm not the one looking like he needs to poop.

The hallway light still irritates my eyes, so I say, "Could you maybe close the door?"

He obliges with a sigh.

"This house is a maze. The bathrooms on the main floor are clogged. There's a line in the basement. Every door up here's locked. And—" He pauses to take a breath, cheeks flushed. "This wouldn't be a problem if Aja hadn't spilled an entire cup of beer on my *pants*!"

Sure enough, one quick glance reveals the darkened stain around his . . . er, crotch.

I quickly bring my eyes back up.

"I smell like Coors Light!" His face scrunches. It's kind of adorable. "My nuts are cold. And all of this happened right in front of Devya."

I bite down on my knuckles to silence my amusement. Oh, the irony. But he clearly doesn't get the humor.

"Luca, you literally—and figuratively—handed me my nuts back at SpeedEx." I shake my head. "This is karma. The universe has spoken. 'Thou shall not disrespect Theodore Wright's balls.' It's hilarious!"

"I just need the bathroom." Luca exhales.

I jerk my head behind me. "Have at it."

The door slams shut behind him.

I drop my face into my hands, holding in a scream. What was I thinking? Making testicle jokes like I'm a six-year-old? How does this keep happening? Every time Luca's around, suddenly, I'm this unfiltered asshole. On the wrong end of his bad moment.

"Get it together, Theo," I whisper into my palms.

I stare at the bathroom door. I can hear the faucet, Luca's mumblings. Should I leave him to deal with this embarrassment alone? Get back downstairs and finish my dare? What if he needs someone to talk to? Maybe the Devya situation isn't as cut-and-dried as I thought.

The door swings open, startling me. I lurch back. Something hard and rectangular digs into my right butt cheek.

My phone.

Lorde's "Supercut" floods the room. Simultaneously, our eyes widen. I can't move fast enough. Wiggling around, I unearth my phone. My clumsy hands bobble until it lands faceup on the carpet.

On-screen, a mini-Luca blinks furiously, mouth agape like a goldfish.

*Shitshitshit.*

My heart beats brutally against my ribs as I scoop up my phone. I exit YouTube like I've been caught watching porn.

When I raise my eyes, I'm fully anticipating rage-dilated pupils. A long string of (deserved) profanity followed by a possible punch to the jaw. I don't know Luca's history with violence, but it's what I'd consider doing.

Instead . . . I'm met by a smile?

Luca looks entertained, arms folded across his chest, eyes bright.

"Not my best idea, I'll admit." He chuckles. "Check the BOHS Fail tag. George, my lab partner, uploaded a much better video to that Ariana song. 'Thank U, Next'?"

"I'm sorry," I say, choking. "Your lab partner meme'd you?"

He shrugs. "I told him to use Vampire Weekend."

"You *helped* him?" My lips inch upward. "Vampire Weekend? For someone who proposed to One Direction, I didn't expect for you to have such A-plus taste."

"First off, that was for *Devya*. She was obsessed with them when we started dating. I mean, who doesn't have a thing for Zayn?"

"Facts."

I'm probably looking too deep into this, but did Luca just confess to having a crush on a former boy band member? Man crushes are a real thing, though that phrase is often used to affirm some fuckboy's heterosexuality. Thinking someone of the same gender is objectively hot doesn't equate to queerness.

He could've been joking too.

But I must be making a weird face because Luca deadpans, "I'm bi, Theo. Sorry I didn't CC you on the eblast."

"Oh. That's cool." I run a hand over my hair. "I'm gay, since we're doing the whole coming out thing."

Luca motions toward the spot next to me on the bed, eyebrows raised like he's asking for permission. I scoot over. He sits with one foot under him, phone propped on his knee as he recites an oral history of the Devya and Luca Romance. First meet-cute in the bleachers during a soccer game to dinner with his family last December. He twists a scratched-up silver ring on his left thumb while speaking.

The whole thing is decidedly dreamy. Not in that sarcastic way I look at Jay and Jayla. Devya and Luca were good for each other. Well, up until she admitted to being "bored" with him and ended things after winter break.

"Ouch. That's harsh."

"But honest." He keeps rotating his ring. "Don't get me wrong. At first, things were great. Social media helped. All the likes and 'hashtag goals' in the comments."

He swipes down his Instagram grid. Sixty percent of it is them. "Thing is, after coming out to my fam, they became obsessed with Dev. Commenting on every post. Making it a big deal."

I tilt my head, confused.

"Because she's a girl," he sighs. "My papá and mamá have never said anything *bad* about me liking boys too. In fact, they've never acknowledged it at all. They kind of . . . avoid it." His lips turn down defeatedly.

I want to say sorry, but I know that won't help.

Dad's always been up-front about his experiences being bi. The dismissive behavior from family at cookouts. Unfollows on social media when he added it to his bios. Casual "Oh, is Alex a girl or a . . . ?" during conversations.

*And my favorite*, he'd said with a stiff smile, *are you gay yet? Or was this just an experiment?*

I nudge my knee against Luca's until he looks up.

"They'll come around," I whisper. His lips pucker, so I add, "If they don't, all you can be is yourself. Horrible music choices and all."

His laugh leaves a warm sensation in my belly.

"What about Makayla, though?" I ask as he closes out Instagram.

He raises both eyebrows.

"You two were all over each other downstairs. I wasn't sure if I was watching dancing or porn."

"It wasn't that bad!"

I lean in. He smells like a weird mix of cardamom, beer, and cranberry. I whisper, "It really was." I grin when his cheeks go a full shade darker.

"We're friends." He throws his hands over his face, mumbling more words into his palms.

"I'm sorry, what?"

"She's my fake girlfriend!" he shouts, dropping his hands. I crack up again as he explains, "I asked her to pretend like we're dating. She took it to another level on her own. What do you expect from a drama student?"

That's unsurprising. Makayla's had her fair share of starring roles in the plays and musicals at Brook-Oak over the years. She slayed as Sophie in *Mamma Mia!*

"Luca, tell me you're not out here fanfic'ing your own life!"

He rubs his phone screen across his shirt, cleaning it. "Is that bad?"

"Nah." My eyes scan the modest space between our knees. "But why fake a relationship with Makayla?"

He stares blankly at me for five seconds until . . .

*Oh.*

"You wanted to make Devya jealous," I say.

He nods. "Dramatic, right?"

"A little," I confirm, smiling. "What's high school if we're not a teeny bit extra about everything?" That earns me a wide, appreciative grin. I'll take it. With tonight going the way it has, any win feels deserved.

"So, what're you—" he starts, but an unexpected, squeaky noise interrupts him. A sneeze that doesn't come from either of us.

I leap off the bed. "What the fu—"

Another *achoo*. From under the bed. Luca joins me in the middle of the room, a hand clapped over his mouth. We wait for the monster underneath to reveal themselves.

"Whoever the hell is down there, you better come out right now or . . ."

*Or I'll scream*, I think, because I'm in a tween's bedroom with the closest "blunt" object being a stuffed Flounder from *The Little Mermaid* movie.

"Okay! Okay!" comes a voice. Then someone wiggles from beneath the bed, standing.

It only takes two seconds before I recognize that shaggy, copper haircut.

I groan, shoulders falling.

"Seriously? This is my life right now?"

# 8

# HI, MY NAME IS . . .

**I can't believe** this.

Shaggy haircut. Crooked, full-rimmed glasses. Five color-ful, woven bracelets running up a thin forearm. It's the student I collided with in the quad yesterday. The reason I failed to ask Christian to prom and was at the top of the #BOHSFail pile for hours after lunch.

After my heartbeat slows to a reasonable level, I say, "Why were you hiding under the bed? And who are y—"

"Sick shirt!" Luca proclaims.

I pause to inspect it.

At first glance, it's only an oversize, black graphic tee. But I guess it's the artwork that has Luca bouncing on his toes. Katsuki Bakugo, one of the more popular characters from the anime *Buko no Hero Academia*. I'm behind on the last two seasons, but Bakugo's literally explosive personality always makes me laugh.

He's drawn with his trademark scowl, wearing the classic blazer-and-tie UA uniform rather than his hero costume.

Above his spiky blond hair is one of those adhesive name badges. I quirk an eyebrow at the Sharpie scribbled on it.

**HELLO**
MY NAME IS

RIVER (THEY/THEM/THEIRS)

"River?" I ask, studying them as they push their glasses up a thin nose. Oval face, warm ivory skin. Their lengthy bangs cut right into their eyes. "Nice name tag."

Up close, I realize I recognize River from somewhere else. I've seen them shuffling down the halls of Brook-Oak with a Black boy. *Devaughn.* Well, I *used* to see them together.

He died last year.

River smiles nervously. "Oh! Hold on," they say with this smoky voice. "Be right back!"

And just like that, they're scurrying back under the bed like an anxious mouse.

Who *is* this person?

When River reemerges, they're clutching a drawstring cinch bags. It's red like the borders of their name badge with anime stickers all over. They fish around in it, tongue peeking out the corner of their mouth, before yanking out a stack of blank adhesive name badges. Every shade of the rainbow is represented.

"Here!" River holds up two Sharpies. "Um, if you want to . . . ?"

I hesitate.

"Hell yes!" Luca whoops, plucking a green badge from the stack. "Thank you!"

He scribbles his name and pronouns in a funky cursive script, smacking the sticker over one of the *O*s in FOOD on his chest.

After taking my own blank name badge and Sharpie, I ask, "Is Bakugo your fav?"

River shakes their head. "Todoroki. But I got a stain on that shirt before coming here."

"Join the club," sighs Luca, fanning a hand at his still-darkened pants.

"Do you have a favorite?" River asks, trading glances between Luca and me.

Without hesitation, Luca lists his top five characters. Then his favorite episodes, which turns into a rant about why the manga's emotional journey is superior to the anime. I like watching this side of him. Nothing like the defeated boy knocked on his ass in the middle of a hallway. Or the boy trying too hard on the dance floor. He's natural, relaxed. I wouldn't mind listening to him more.

The entire time, River flails like one of those trailer-reaction-video analysts geeked up on too many energy drinks.

"This is all very . . . nerdy," I finally say, grinning.

Luca sizes me up. "Let me guess: Your favorite is Midoriya, right?"

I duck my head, not answering.

"I thought so!" He laughs. "Reserved but not shy. Overachiever without being annoying. Slightly dramatic. Tendency to overanalyze. Underdog who's A1 when it comes to friendships."

"Whoa, whoa! I'm *not* reserved," I practically screech, clearly owning the Wright extra-ness in my DNA. Fine, I might've read that Scorpios *can be* reserved. Cautious, actually.

"Also, I'm not an underdog," I point out.

I'm not, right? Do Jay and Darren think the same thing? Wow, way to *not* overanalyze.

"If you say so." Luca smiles amusedly. On my other side, River's thrown a hand over their mouth, but it's barely hiding the grin I know is there.

"This is an attack!"

"Ooh, thoughts on *Attack on Titan*?" River asks Luca.

It takes them two seconds to fall down another rabbit hole about a series I could never get into. Way too dark.

"There's nothing wrong with liking the main character. It doesn't mean anything," I note with a hint of defensiveness. Ignoring their eye rolls, I say to Luca, "Er, I didn't know you were so into anime."

He frowns. "Anime club, freshman year? Remember? We were both there."

I try not to think too much about my first year at Brook-Oak. The weirdness of being new again. Adjusting to how much more competitive high school was at every level, not just academics. All the awkwardness of feeling like I still didn't belong. Even with Jay and Darren by my side. Even being the son of Miles Wright.

Anime club was a blip in a series of attempts to figure myself out.

Two years later, I still haven't solved that equation.

Anyway, I attended the initial meeting. We sat around in a circle. Mr. Onyebuchi, the club's faculty advisor, who you'll only ever catch in T-shirts around the halls, brought these delicious red velvet cupcakes. There weren't a ton of us, but enough that I can't recall faces.

Mr. Onyebuchi suggested we start with a typical icebreaker: "What's your name and favorite anime?"

I wasn't prepared for the five- to ten-minute dialogues about the art and history and character arcs most of the others gave. Yes, I love anime, but in that moment, I felt like everyone else loved it *more*. Like I had no right to call this my thing because I didn't have the vocabulary to discuss it in the way they did.

Luckily, time ran out before I had to answer.

I never went back.

"I mean . . ." I shrug. "I vaguely remember?"

We're all sitting now. River, pretzel-legged on the floor. Luca and me on the bed. Something flickers across his face. Either disappointment or indifference. He's twisting a different ring now—the crying-heart-inscribed one on his ring finger.

River clears their throat. "I was hiding under the bed because . . ." Their voice drifts off when Luca and I look their way.

"Because?"

"Don't laugh. This is kind of weird." It takes them a second to continue. "Not everyone at school knows I'm nonbinary. I thought it'd be cool if this party were kind of my 'Hey, this is my name! This is who I am!' thing."

We're all quiet for a beat. Then Luca asks, "How is that weird?"

River tugs on their bracelets. "Isn't it?"

"Nah," I quickly say. "Not at all."

A hopeful smile pulls at their lips. "My older sister Katie suggested using the name badges. As an opener. Everyone could wear one. Know what pronouns to use when talking to or about each other."

I rest my chin on my knuckles, beaming.

Luca gives River an awkward fist bump. "I like that. Normalize being respectful and inclusive to everyone. Assumptions are for assholes."

"I was so confident when Katie dropped me off. Then I walked in and . . ." River trails off, picking at the edges of their name badge. "I got some strange looks. Real invasive questions whenever I tried to make conversation, so." They nod toward the bed. "Been under there for almost two hours."

"I'm sorry people are dicks," I say.

I don't include that I hope my friends weren't among them. That I hope Jay didn't say the wrong thing like he tends to after getting buzzed.

River sweeps hair out of their eyes. "Is it bad that I wanted to stay in here until my sister came back to pick me up?"

"Not at all," Luca replies.

I paste on my best maybe-a-little grin, but frankly? It's not the worst thing. In here, the music's softened. A continuous tremor of unrecognizable hip-hop songs, one after another, beneath our feet. It's warm, but not stuffy like downstairs. The fairy lights sketch a waterfall of stars across our faces.

I bet Maddie never has a reason to leave.

"Maybe . . . we could all hang out?" River suggests.

I blink at them.

"Uh, unless," they stammer, trading nervous glances between Luca and me. "You have other places to be?"

I bite on my thumbnail, considering. It's way past the five minutes I told Christian I'd be. More like twenty-five. Though, for whatever reason, I don't feel as pressed to get back.

"Nah," I reply. "No rush. These things go on for hours."

Luca's knee brushes mine as he nods.

"Good." River throws us a funny look. "Or I can leave, if I'm interrupting something . . . ?"

*Interrupting what?*

My eyes shade in Luca's direction. He's rotating his thumb ring, not staring at anything in particular. Talking with him *was* the easiest part of my night. It was as if we speak all the time during classes instead of in passing. Nothing like my conversation with Christian, who I *have* shared a class with. Who's been my project partner before. But our conversation earlier was more about my nerves.

Talking to the boy you like should be tricky, I think.

*But maybe . . .*

I shake my head before my brain can go there. Out of the question. Christian's the endgame. I just need ample time to prepare. And I guess I'm doing that by hanging out with these two.

Luca says, "You're not interrupting" convincingly. Great. So, he agrees. Nothing's happening here.

"Besides," I say to River, ignoring the new knot in my stomach, "you were here first. We're trespassing. Our fate is in your hands."

"Hmm." River taps an index finger along their jaw. "I suppose there are worse people I could hang with."

"Much worse," I confirm.

River waits a beat, fully drawing this out, before declaring, "Fine, you may stay . . . but only if we do one thing."

"What's that?"

"One sec." River scampers under the bed again. They seem to have an affection for dark, cramped spaces.

While River's waist-deep in their Narnia world, I chance a look at Luca. His eyes slowly skim over my face. Like he wants to say something. Ask something. He doesn't. However, the left corner of his mouth ticks up a little. Mine does too.

I wonder if he's thinking about what River suggested. The two of us sitting on a bed in a semi-dark room . . . alone.

I wonder why *I'm* thinking about it.

When they return, River's clutching a board game box—a special edition Disney Monopoly.

(The obsession is real for Maddie.)

"Whenever Katie's friends come around," River begins to explain, "I get a little anxious. They're so cool and I'm . . . not?"

I pucker my lips disapprovingly.

"Not yet!" corrects River with only a hint of uncertainty. "Anyway, to calm me down, she cooks, then we have game night."

"So, like an icebreaker?" I ask.

*Dear God, don't let this turn into anime club all over again.*

River shrugs, like they're afraid it's a bad idea. "It's . . . fun." For emphasis, they shake the Monopoly box. The pieces rattle around inside.

Luca barely holds in a snort.

I tilt my chin up, putting on my best thoughtful face. The opportunity to torture River in a teasing way like they did us minutes ago is too tempting. But I don't drag it out.

"Fine." I smirk. "But only if I'm the banker."

Before I know it, the game board is in the center of the floor. Tokens are selected: I seize Pinocchio while Luca grabs Peter Pan and River goes for Lady and the Tramp. Luca wastes no time buying everything he lands on. River is ruthless about collecting on their castle-front properties. I end up in jail on my third roll.

We laugh so hard tears cling to the corners of my eyes.

River was right—I love this.

I open the music app on my phone. We listen to my Thunderstorm Vibes playlist, a collection of chill synthpop songs. River's "borrowed" a pink-and-purple feather boa from the end of Maddie's bed. Luca's wearing a pair of yellow heart-shaped sunglasses. A plastic, bejeweled crown sits lopsidedly on my head.

Between dice rolls, River paints Luca's nails licorice black from a bottle swiped off the dresser.

"Not to be dramatic," he starts, "but if my papá or tíos saw me now, it wouldn't be a pretty sitch."

"Why?" I ask.

He rants in Spanish for a minute before realizing River and I aren't following along. "This isn't *masculine*." He wiggles his painted fingers. Then, in a rough, forced voice, he says, "It's too feminine. Not for men. Boys should be strong and unbreakable, not 'delicate' or 'soft.' "

I guess he's mimicking his dad.

"He always comments on what I'm wearing," Luca continues, the lines around his mouth deepening. " 'Are those flowers on your shirt? No bueno.' And 'Why are your pants so tight?' 'Did you accidentally shop in the chicas section, mijo? Change. Don't be a bad example to your hermanos!' Like what I wear has anything to do with being a role model for my brothers."

"Like they're not capable of making up their own minds about who they want to be," adds River.

"Exactly!"

"Just another subscriber to the social constructs of gender norms," grumbles River.

"It's such bullshit."

I don't comment. My eyes lower to my shrinking pile of fake money.

Thing is, I know what that's like. The expectation for Black or brown boys to constantly be *strong*. Stand, dress, and talk a certain way. Carry a particular type of swagger. Repress tendencies that don't fit in our communities.

Dad hasn't impressed this on me. Everyone else has.

We're supposed to live up to that toxic definition of *masculinity*, no matter what.

Case in point: our nails should be polish-free. Dirty nailbeds might even get you bonus points if it gives people the illusion you've been working hard with your hands.

*Real man stuff.*

Everywhere I look, it's acceptable for white, cis guys to paint their nails. Wear a dress or skirt for a photoshoot. To step outside the boundaries. It's "trendy," then. But if a Black or brown boy does it, we're being a word I refuse to use, but have heard enough times to hate and fear it all the same.

Suddenly, we're "corrupting" instead of existing.

I adjust the crown on my head, then ask, "What does your mom say?"

Luca's frown softens. "Things like, 'Papá is old school, mijo. He'll get better. Be strong.'"

"Words from the patriarchy," grunts River.

Luca stares at his nails. "It's not that I think he doesn't love me. It's that it feels conditional, sometimes."

Every hint of synthetic starlight in the room catches on the sheen in his eyes. Reflections of pink and gold and sadness. I keep waiting for those stars to spill down his cheeks. But Luca doesn't let them. He flashes a weak smile and that's it.

This is him being their definition of *strong*.

I nod at his nails. "They look fire."

It's true—the black polish with his skin tone and silver rings is a vibe. But I feel a bit hypocritical. Deep down, I know I wouldn't be brave enough to do the same.

If Jay or Darren saw my nails painted . . .

They wouldn't unfriend me. Delete my number. Darren definitely wouldn't. I'm mostly confident about Jay too. But my teammates—well, there might be several looks in the locker room. Whispered comments. Inappropriate jokes I'd take with a smirk. Because it's what we do. We pick out each other's flaws, roast one another, then bro-hug it out.

Except . . . I know I'd go home and immediately scrub the polish off to avoid it ever happening again.

While Luca's being strong, I'm a fucking coward.

"Should I stop?" River indicates Luca's unfinished hand. "I don't want—"

"No." He beams. "I didn't come here tonight to be *that* guy."

River resumes painting.

My index finger lazily swipes over my playlist before selecting a new tune. It's a good one. Last-dance-at-prom-worthy. I think of Christian. Whether it would matter to him if my nails were painted.

Would he be okay with it the way Luca seems to be?

Out of nowhere, a cool shiver tickles up my forearms.

*Somebody walking over your grave*, Granny used to call it.

The bedroom door flies open, smacking against the wall. It's not the noise that startles me. It's the girl standing in the entryway, tearstains on her cheeks.

When she sees me, she says, "God, why now," her voice choked.

My frown and pinched brow feel oddly familiar.

So does the sudden urge to run.

# 9

# THE PAST NEVER FORGETS YOU

**People who win** staring contests have the fortitude of a god. The kind of strength it requires to maintain eye contact with anyone, unblinking, for long stretches of time is something I never mastered. Especially when doing it with someone who hates me.

Ironically, as kids, I used to lose all the time to Aleah.

She was so ruthlessly focused. Blank face, lips puckered, breathing easy like her eyes weren't watering. I couldn't compete.

Now here we are, just like then, staring at each other with wide eyes. I swear she hasn't blinked once. Not at all.

She hasn't moved from the doorway either.

I'm standing by the bed, pretending that noise in my chest isn't as loud as the music coming from downstairs.

"Aleah," says Luca as I finally blink. How does she *do* that?

When her head whips in Luca's direction, he asks, "You okay?"

She sniffs hard, dragging knuckles across her cheeks. "'m fine," she says to the floor. "Just need the bathroom."

"Are you su—"

"Could you not?" she snaps, cutting Luca off. "I'm not really in the mood for Twenty Questions."

Luca throws up both hands like a shield. Wise move to surrender. It shifts her mood slightly. An inch of anger gives way to . . . sad frustration, I think. Like she's fighting too many wars at once. I know that feeling, but even approaching the idea of speaking to Aleah Bird intimidates me on a good day. To do so while she's crying, ready to unleash her dragons on anyone who looks at her funny? It's a death sentence.

She sighs, then hiccups. "I just need a minute."

No one speaks as she crosses the room. The bathroom door clicks softly shut. A long, exaggerated exhale finally leaves my lungs. This is my cue to exit. I need to go. Tonight's been weird enough.

When I pocket my phone, my playlist is replaced by whimpers behind the bathroom door. The occasional broken sob muffled by either a hand or a towel. A chorus of pain I can't get out of my head.

River speaks first. "Should we check on her?"

"I don't think she wants us to," says Luca, twisting his thumb ring. "She had some real 'bother me and I'll end you' vibes."

*Exactly*, I want to say. As a unit, we should back out of the room very slowly. But my feet are stuck. The soundtrack in my head is Aleah's stifled, broken voice.

That's the last noise I heard the day I told her I'd moved on from our friendship.

It was two weeks after Dad's breakup with Mario. After he moved to Texas. Without him around to bring her over, we hadn't seen each other since then.

Dad and I were at the supermarket. In the frozen foods aisle is where we saw her. All I remember was Dad's wounded, lost expression while staring at Aleah. The way he shook at the sound of her laughter. It's not just that Aleah and Mario share physical traits. They're both loud and unafraid and love ferociously.

Except, maybe Mario didn't love Dad enough.

Not enough to stay.

I don't know the details behind their breakup. Dad never explained. I've always been too scared to ask, fearing another meltdown from Dad about it.

But I had sufficient courage to ditch Aleah the next day.

"Didn't something happen . . ."

I freeze like I've been caught. Like River knows.

They say, ". . . with the basketball team?" in this low, concerned whisper. It's nothing like the excited murmurs you hear around school when someone wants details on the latest gossip.

Luca gives River the abridged version of what happened. I don't bother comparing his version with Darren's to figure out the truth.

It's none of my business.

As hard as I fight it, my brain starts to thumb through the history of Theo and Aleah—TJ and Birdie, to be exact—like a reader searching for their favorite part of a book.

It lands on this:

Psalms of Hope, Granny's church. The place Mario and Dad met one Christmas morning. I was ten years old, wearing a clip-on bow tie, anxious to get home to open gifts. Granny wanted Dad to meet every member of the choir. Mario was last. He sat in the back pews with his arm tucked around Aleah's shoulders as she played Pokémon on his phone.

Back then, I think I knew Dad's overeager smile at Mario's gentle, deep "Hey" meant something. I'd seen it before. But this one lasted longer. *Much longer.* So did my pouting in the pews next to Aleah while they talked for nearly an hour.

"Wanna play?" she offered, vibrant smile attacking me.

I lost myself in the game. In her ramblings about which Pokémon were her favorite. Suddenly, I didn't care about gifts anymore.

Just that she talked like she'd known me forever.

Like a friend.

Another memory bleeds into that one:

A sweaty Saturday afternoon at the church. Aleah and me tucked into the pews again. Mario rehearsing with the choir. Dad pretending to be invested in behind-the-scenes stuff to spend more time around him.

Aleah had her own phone by then. Her dad drives trucks overnight. He wanted a way to always be in contact.

We were sharing earbuds, listening to music. The *Sister Act 2* soundtrack was our favorite. Dad and Mario had already converted us to nineties-comedies enthusiasts. While the choir belted their way through foot-stomping medleys, we sung along to "His Eye Is on the Sparrow" like we were re-creating a scene from the movie. Her pitch-perfect alto to my off-key tenor.

"I'm gonna be a singer one day," she declared with her brightest smile. "You'll be my backup singer. Way, way, way back!"

"Hey!" I pouted. "I'm no one's backup."

"True. You'll find your own thing," she told me.

"You think so, Birdie?"

She scrubbed a hand over my 'fro and whispered, "Duh, TJ. We're gonna be happy like your pops and my uncle. Nobody's gonna stop us."

There was so much conviction in her voice. It's hard to imagine a version of Aleah that's anything but that—confident.

Maybe she's not that Birdie anymore. And I'm not her TJ.

I'm so far in my own head, I don't hear the toilet flush. The faucet run, then stop. Only the squeaky bathroom door as it's yanked open.

Aleah reemerges, posture stiff, face dry and passive. Her expression says it all—*the last three minutes never happened.*

If only I could say the same about the last five years.

Aleah plays with her necklace again. Her long black hair is braided into twin French braids. Edges perfectly gelled like when she was younger, and Mario styled her hair. She glances around, taking everything in. Her slow assessment starts with River, then Luca, and finally me. Her eyes quickly move on. As if she's deemed I'm not important anymore.

I don't know why it stings so badly.

How many times in the past have I done the same thing to avoid acknowledging what I did to her?

"Thanks for . . . you know," she says to Luca. He's barely

nodded before she's making the hasty exit I should've made five minutes ago.

"Wait!" River calls out. "Aleah!"

Aleah whirls around, face contorted in one of those *Do I know you?* ways.

"You don't have to go back there if you don't want to." River pastes on an enthusiastic smile.

"Why wouldn't I *want* to?"

There's an edge to Aleah's voice, but it's not mean.

River shrugs, withholding all the information Luca disclosed. "If you want, you can chill with us."

I almost shout, *I'm sorry, what?*

Listen, River seems cool. I respect that they were in Maddie's bedroom first, so it's their decision, but I like our current setup. Three's a great number. Enough to distill any awkwardness between conversations. Never too overwhelming. Perfect like TNT. We don't need a fourth.

I don't need Aleah's evil glares every two seconds.

Aleah snorts, crossing her arms. "With you three?"

Her eyes land on each of us again. "Since when have any of you ever hung out?" She squints right at me.

It's another hard and fast uppercut to the jaw.

"Tonight!" River announces as I mumble, "Surprise, never."

Aleah's lips pucker as my joke lands flat.

"Things is," says River, "we're trying a social experiment: avoid the boring, narcissistic, uncultured people downstairs who have hostile breath from consuming way too many Doritos and alcohol."

Aleah blinks like she can't believe what she's just heard.

I can't either.

*Who the hell is River?*

But it works. Aleah laughs. Beside me, Luca snorts into his hand. I smile at River, who's tipped up their chin, shoulders proudly drawn back.

Aleah exhales as if she's buying time to find her next words. "I don't think this is the place for me. The house. The party. This . . ." Her long pause is accompanied by a momentary glance my way. ". . . room."

"Yes, it is," River insists, and I really, really want them to just let Aleah go. For both of our sakes. Unfortunately, River doesn't receive my telepathic plea. "All of us have reasons for not going back downstairs yet."

I bite my cheek. Luca and River have perfectly acceptable motives for kicking back in Maddie's room. Do I? There's an obvious reason why I *should* go back to the party. But I haven't left yet.

"Things have been pretty chill up here," confirms Luca, rubbing the back of his neck.

Aleah says to River, "Sorry, I thought all the narcissists were downstairs." She jerks a thumb at Luca. "What's he doing here?"

He clutches his chest. *"Ouch."*

"Oh, whatevs." Aleah flicks a braid behind her shoulder. "You'd rather be at home doing problem sets anyway."

"Jesus, you monster! I'm not *that much* of a math nerd."

"Ramírez, you love that shit," counters Aleah. "I bet you get a boner anytime someone mentions the Pythagorean theorem."

"Brutal and incorrect," he says, then cackles.

"Do you two . . ." I wiggle my index finger between Aleah and Luca. ". . . know each other?"

Instantly, Aleah's smile is ingested by a scowl and harshly narrowed eyes. "It's kind of hard to miss people you share classes and hallways and an entire *school* with," she says coolly. "Among other things."

"I didn't mean . . ." I pause. Now would be the time to shut up. No need to defend myself. Let it go. But I say, "It's not always intentional."

*Just with you,* I don't say.

"Really? People exist in the same place as you? You notice them? Don't ig—" Aleah cuts herself off.

We both know what she wanted to say.

Yeah, I deserve it. But does it have to be right now? In front of River? In front of . . . Luca?

Why am I so embarrassed thinking about how *he* perceives this interaction?

It doesn't appear to bother him, though. "I tutored Aleah last year," Luca explains casually, like it's common knowledge.

How has this become a Six Degrees of Theodore Wright thing? Like, *by the way, the cute, superior-taste-in-snacks guy standing next to you knows the girl you used to spend almost 24-7 with (and who currently looks like she wants to throw up at the sight of your face) because her uncle dated your dad, who is, well,* your dad, *and . . .*

Wait, do I think Luca's cute?

"I hate math," groans River. It's what finally snaps me out of wherever my brain was going with that tangent.

"Ugh. Me too," Aleah says. She flops onto the carpet next to River. The bluish glow of her phone's screen shines off her face. "Fuck. It's barely eleven. I can't call my unc—"

She stops abruptly, flinching.

I chew hard on my lower lip, waiting.

"My *ride* will think I'm a total loser if I call him this early," she recovers, her expression settling back into the detached one she wears so well.

"Great!"

Luca bounces onto the bed. I stare at him, then River, contemplating my options. But I already know what choice I'm going to make.

I'm not the kind of guy who's going to abandon them. Not when they clearly don't want to go back downstairs. Plus, seeing Aleah with those tearstained cheeks, hearing her broken sob behind a door . . . it tugs at a piece of me I know I haven't left in the past.

A second later, I join Luca on the bed.

It's decided—we're all staying.

"I'm River Zhao," say River, officially extending their hand to Aleah.

Aleah returns the gesture, shaking. "I've seen you around school. Loving this look, B-T-dub," she comments. "Glasses, feathers, name tags, and cartoon character shirts."

River's still wearing the boa. Luca has Maddie's sunglasses pushed up into his hair. The plastic crown sits between us. With Aleah here, I feel like less than a king.

"Anime," River and Luca quickly say, pointing at River's shirt.

Aleah shrugs, seemingly unfazed by the correction. "I never

knew your name. Or your pronouns? They/them. That's dope."

Pink blooms across River's cheeks.

"I'm Aleah. She/her pronouns."

"I have more, if you want?" River offers.

As they trade Sharpies and name badges, River relays a brief—albeit enthusiastic—history of *Boku no Hero Academia*. Aleah diligently nods along. I turn to Luca.

"Hey." I grin. "I didn't know you tutored?"

He's in the same STEM program as Jay, but I never put it together. I would've hit him up last semester when I was drowning in Mr. Montgomery's obsession with radicals and square roots. If I could afford his rates, that is.

Another bonus of the Wright-Scott family connection: Jay's assistance is *free*.

A shy smile curls Luca's lips. "Pays for new fits and shoes." He gestures to his wardrobe. "You'd be surprised how much desperate-to-appease-their-demanding-but-stacked-parents kids will pay to pass an Algebra 1 class with a high C."

"Whatever." Aleah feigns annoyance at his comment before suggestively wiggling her eyebrows. "Is 'polynomial' your safe word?"

"Shut up!" Luca guffaws.

He pulls up his website on his phone, then passes it to me. Through the cracked screen, I see he has a contact form, prices, a frequently-asked-questions section. He's even got a testimonial page. "Damn," I whisper, handing back his phone.

I don't mention the way his thumb lingers against my knuckles during the exchange.

Instead, my mind goes on autopilot.

How can Aleah afford his fees? She's not one of the flashy rich kids we matriculate with. The ones you never see in the same outfit twice, have their own cars, and have zero problems telling you their zip code. Aleah lives in the West End. As long as I can remember, her mom's been in and out of rehab or prison. Never in the picture. Her dad's truck driving is their sole income. Mario was there to help, both financially and as a positive influence on Aleah.

We're a lot alike—only children with fathers who work above and beyond to secure our futures. We make up that 10 percent of Brook-Oak's population that walks through those pristine glass doors knowing every day isn't just another day.

It's our one shot at improving our lives if we play the game right.

*Be sure to talk to Mr. Scott* rattles around my head in Dad's voice.

"No offense . . ." I overhear Aleah say to River. "But how old are you?"

"Sixteen."

"No shit. You look younger." When River lets out an affronted squeak, Aleah adds, "It's a compliment! No acne. Baby cheeks. Drop that skin-care routine, babe!"

I imagine River's blushing. I'm too busy fiddling with my phone to look.

"Whoa, nice!"

Luca points toward my latest wallpaper. I saved this Finn artwork from Pinterest months ago. He's holding a blue lightsaber while dressed in a hoodie and joggers, giant headphones around his neck. Just a normal Black boy doing Jedi things. It's so dope.

The artist—a fourteen-year-old Nigerian girl from Surrey—has a serious art portfolio. Something about her being that young simultaneously intimidates and motivates me. The same way Jay being faster than me when we started track did. The gap feels concurrently huge and minuscule.

"Thanks," I finally say to Luca.

"I've been meaning to change mine."

It's no surprise his wallpaper is of him and Devya.

She's smiling, hair windswept across her face. He's kissing her temple. A fiery pink sky in the background. The kind of stuff you'll find all over his Insta.

"You don't have to . . ." I hesitate. *Am I really going to say this?* "If that's what you want, keep it. It's okay to still feel a certain way about someone."

It's true. Moving on isn't a one-step process.

"Can we skip the weepy montages?" Aleah interjects. "All these *deep* feels like we're in a damn Pixar movie. I'm not here for that." She fakes dry heaving into her hands.

"Why not?" I ask.

"I'm just not," she replies, emphasizing every word.

Again, shutting up is so simple. I can ignore her offended tone. Turn back to Luca. Reset. But this is the thing about Aleah—when she doesn't like something or is bored with a topic, she dismisses it as if you should *know* better. Like it's not even worth the time. Why bother?

I've always hated that. Which is why I ask, "Sore subject?" with just a pinch of pettiness.

Her eyes widen. Luca kicks my ankle. I ignore what he's trying to tell me to watch Aleah for another reaction.

"Fine." She swivels to face Luca. "Here's the deal—if your first instinct isn't to remove your ex's face from your phone screen after months of not dating, her getting another boyfriend . . ." Aleah lists every offense on her fingers. "A very public dismissal during a promposal—yes, we've all seen the video, let's not pretend—then clearly your pathetic attachment isn't to that person, but the *idea* of having someone to be in love with and them loving you back."

"Jesus!" Luca squirms anxiously. "You didn't have to drag me like that."

"I'm keeping it real. Move on from your past."

"What if it's not that easy?" I counter. "What if it's deeper than just filling an empty space?"

Aleah flicks an eyebrow up.

I sigh. "Walking away from things isn't always that simple."

"Oh yeah?" she challenges. "Hello, kettle, welcome to the chat!"

Luca clears his throat. "Is this still about me and Devya?"

"I don't think so," River whisper-shouts.

I'm still talking about Luca, aren't I? Or relationships, in general. I've never had a boyfriend, so I'm working with limited data, but—this isn't about me . . . is it?

"It's nothing, right, Theo?" Aleah asks through clenched teeth.

It's a bullet—the way she says my name. Not TJ. *Theo*. The sharp reminder of where we stand in each other's lives. A puncture to my ribs, digging in, refusing to come out clean.

I snatch up my phone and stand.

"Theo," Luca starts, but I'm already stomping toward the door.

Fuck this. I'm going back to the party. Staying here with Aleah and all our unresolved bullshit is a choice I'm opting out of.

It's too bad I'm so in my head, so intent on running from my issues—again—that I don't see the bedroom door fling open before it nearly clocks me in the face. My reflexes kick in just in time to send me falling to the floor.

"Holy shit!" I gasp, breathing hard as another familiar face looms over me.

# 10

# LET'S GO TO THE BACK OF YOUR CAR

**"Theo, why are** you on the floor?"

Makayla stands over me, eyebrows lifted curiously.

I want to tell her it's because she almost ended my life—a mild concussion at the very minimum—by carelessly tossing open the door without checking to see if maybe someone else was on the other side. Instead, I reply, "Stargazing?"

She steps over me like everyone did in the quad yesterday.

"And where the hell have you been?" Makayla asks, arms crossed, annoyed glare directed at Luca. "What kind of date are you? MIA for God knows how long."

"No worries, I'm okay down here," I grumble after no one volunteers to help me up. I roll onto my stomach, then easily push up to a seated position. Thanks, Coach Devers, for your gauntlet plank workout during the off-season.

"We had an agreement," Makayla says to Luca, continuing to ignore me.

"My bad." Luca guiltily rubs the back of his head.

Makayla's hazel eyes are narrowed, but something cracks in the hardness of her expression. She leans toward him. "I agreed to be your—*you know*." Her voice is slightly louder than a whisper. "And you'd stay by my side, all night. We'd look out for each other."

Luca remorsefully lowers his chin.

"Ditching me wasn't cool, Luca."

"Aja spilled a whole cup of beer on me and . . ." He hesitantly waves a hand at his pants. The damp patch seems to have shrunk. Not that I look long enough to gauge.

Makayla throws a hand over her mouth. "It kinda looks like you . . . jizzed your pants?"

"I know, I know." Luca's face scrunches. Someone snorts. Without looking, I know it's Aleah. Luca turns pleading eyes on Makayla. "It won't happen again."

"Whatever." She fluffs her wavy blond hair. Her loose-fit cotton hoodie hangs off one shoulder. It's unzipped, exposing a black crop top. Makayla really is one of those girls who looks drop-dead gorgeous in ill-fitting sweats and old-school Chucks. It's almost like she put zero effort into her attire and yet.

I get the appeal for Darren.

She smirks. "Reliable sources tell me Devya has been asking about you."

"Wait, seriously?"

The excited pitch of Luca's voice unnerves me. Ten minutes ago, he admitted he wasn't over her. Well, his wallpaper made that confession. Something pangs in my stomach. It tightens as Luca asks a million and one questions about Devya.

What did she say? Where was she at? How did she look? Who else heard? Everything but why the fuck should he care?

(Okay, that was a whole new level of petty, even for me.)

I hug my knees to my chest.

After Makayla fields most of Luca's inquiries with vague answers, she surveys the room. It's amusing watching her expression change as she takes us in. Curiosity and confusion for River. Familiarity and a subtle meh-ness for me—a look courtesy of her friendship with Jayla, no doubt. Then offense and disappointment for Aleah.

Aleah seems delighted to mirror the same expression back.

Like most of the sports teams, the Ballers and cheer squad are a tight group. The fallout of whatever happened with Aleah, Lexi, and Derek must've changed things. It's clear whose side Makayla has chosen.

"Is this a drama club meeting?" she asks.

"That's a hell and a no," I answer.

"Obvi. I'm co-prez of this year's senior drama troupe. Thanks, Theo," Makayla says dryly.

I'm quite aware. A video of her clutching an acceptance letter from Florida State University, all while fake sobbing—YPT truly is a great program—with her family celebrating in the background is still talked about daily.

"Luca, this isn't your . . . usual crowd," Makayla insists, hands on her hips.

"Are there applications for what crowds we can hang out with now?" Aleah asks, interrupting Luca's already feeble-sounding response. "Please, Lawrence, lay down the rules. What're the qualifications to be on Luca's team, because I'm only signing up if there's free 'Traitors' merch given out with every admission."

"Traitor?" Makayla scoffs.

"Would you like a definition? Google is free."

"So is not being bitchy to people who don't deserve it," Makayla snaps.

I hug my knees tighter. If I'm being honest, it's nice having Aleah's wrath aimed somewhere else. Whatever's happened seems deeper than just a breakup between one of our school's sweetheart couples. It's certainly disrupted the flow of the party. In fact, Aleah rarely attends these functions. I figured it was lack of transportation from the West End to whichever wealthy kid's northside residence was hosting. The city bus line doesn't run as late as most parties last.

The questions keep piling up. I'm not going to ask any of them.

Not now, at least.

Aleah barks a laugh. "That's the thing about being popular—everyone who doesn't fit in your clique is bitchy." She shakes her head, *pfft*ing. "Problem is, the real assholes are the ones you call *friend*."

Makayla bares her teeth, ready to go right back at her. But she doesn't.

The bedroom door creaks open.

"Hey-yo!"

A white boy with golden-copper hair leans in the doorway. He looks a little older than us. College freshman, maybe. He lazily holds an orange cup, smiling goofily with bright blue eyes and a constellation of freckles across his nose and cheeks.

"Unlocked bedroom equals bathroom," he announces. "Score one for me and my need for a long piss."

I blink at him for a minute. Is he for real?

"Uh, who the fuck are you?" Aleah asks, brow furrowed.

"Jack," he replies with a bigger grin. "Oh, wait. No. *This* is Jack." He lifts his cup. "Jack and ginger . . . like me!"

River sputters out a laugh. Luca hides his eyes behind a hand while Makayla's jaw drops open, clearly amazed by the levels of intoxicated this boy has reached. I rub deep circles into my left temple. It takes a moment for my brain cells to recalibrate.

"I'm Bry," Drunk Boy says. "Short for Bryan. Actually, short for Bryant. I have no earthly clue what my parents were smoking when they—"

"Save it for the Wiki entry, *Bry*," interrupts Aleah.

"Yasssss!" He snaps his fingers in a circle. I swear Aleah's about to go full velociraptor on him, clawing out his spleen.

Bryant turns to Makayla with a sleazy look that makes my skin itch.

"Are you guys having an orgy?" he asks her.

"Excuse me?"

"Y'know . . ." He clumsily swirls his cup around the room like it's supposed to explain something. "Bedroom. Multiple—uh, respectably hot people." His nose wrinkles before he quickly adds, "No homo, dudes."

Correction: I'm going to gnaw out Bryant's jugular. And enjoy it.

"Then there's you." Bryant licks his lips while eyeing Makayla.

"Swipe Right Mack, yeah? Kind of obvious what's gonna happen if you're here."

Makayla swallows slowly. Her chest rises and falls rapidly.

The name—Swipe Right Mack—is the worst. No one dares say it to Makayla's face. It's whispered in locker rooms, bathrooms, hallways. On private text chains I've seen secondhand. From asshats who think they're funny. Groups where sex is a victory and currency. I don't know the origin of the nickname. Only that it's followed her since late freshman year. A play off a dating app function: *Mack Lawrence swipes right on every boy who wants to hook up at a party. She never turns anyone down.*

It's not just the boys at Brook-Oak who whisper about Makayla.

It's the girls at corner lunch tables. In the bleachers at games. Ruthless mid-tier social climbers doing whatever it takes to scratch their way to the top.

Makayla's their favorite target.

"So, mind if I join?"

Even with the cup to his lips, it's obvious Bryant's grinning, waiting on Makayla's reply. A dog anticipating his treat. She gives him nothing.

River steps forward. "Leave."

The height difference between them and Bryant is staggering. That doesn't matter. River stands as tall as possible, shoulders drawn back.

"Excuse you?" Bryant peers down, offended.

"There's no orgy. No vacancy for you here." They push up their glasses. "Go away."

"I didn't ask you—"

"You heard them," Aleah says from behind River. "Peace out, Bry."

To Aleah's right, Luca's fists clench at his sides.

Bryant wobbles while trying to walk backward. I'm not sure if it's the alcohol or sheer terror at Aleah's unwavering glare. He huffs, "Cool. Time for a refill anyway," tossing his empty cup on the ground before stumbling down the hall.

I shoulder the door closed and lock it.

I'm done with uninvited guests.

When I turn around, everyone but Aleah is huddled around Makayla. Aleah's on the floor, legs crisscrossed, phone in hand. Luca guides Makayla to sit on the bed. In the same spot he and I were before. I'm an asshole for this, I know, but . . . for five whole seconds, I'm annoyed.

I shouldn't be.

I was almost out the door. Back downstairs. Looking for my friends and Christian. No more insults from Aleah. No River leaving me bankrupt during Monopoly. Luca was going to be just another boy at school again.

Now I'm watching him comfort Makayla.

"Are you okay?" Aleah finally asks.

Makayla's eyes flutter. "Do you care?"

Aleah exhales like she wants to scream. I feel the same, but for different reasons. "Why are you like this?" she says.

"Me?" Makayla's pitch rises as if she's surprised.

"Yes. You." Aleah rolls her eyes. "The same you who stopped talking to *everyone* at Kenzie's Halloween Bash when you found out Ashton lied about the veggie burgers?"

"I have a food allergy to sesame!"

"You locked yourself in a bathroom and cried," Aleah says flatly.

"I could've died!"

I watch as Aleah's body trembles with laughter she can't contain. Makayla tries to fight her own, but it doesn't work. She snorts so hard, her hair flies over her face.

Aleah kicks her foot. "And who showed up with an antihistamine and a bottle of water, waiting for you to calm the hell down?"

Eyes closed, Makayla replies, "The same girl who wouldn't let me hold her hair when she got sick after the Ballers made it to the semis for the first time in . . ."

"Ten years," Aleah finishes with a smile I haven't seen in forever. Soft and wide, almost crooked on the left side.

Just as quickly as it appears, Aleah shakes it off. "One, don't touch my hair." She holds up her index finger. Then her middle one. "Two, the tequila came in a plastic bottle. That's vile. Three, everyone in here didn't need to know that!"

"I kind of did," Luca whispers.

Aleah gives him a swift side-eye. To Makayla, she says, "I'm just checking to see if you're okay" with a low, gentle tone.

"Yes." Makayla shrugs. "It's all gossip, anyway. I'm used to it."

"Doesn't make it right," says River.

A tiny smile stirs across Makayla's lips. Like no one's ever said that before. She tucks hair behind her ear before continuing her play-by-play with Aleah of their past hangouts.

I lean against the wall. Outside the door, a Megan Thee Stallion song plays. My head bobs along. It's a failed diversion tactic as

Makayla's and Aleah's laughter echoes louder than the music.

The back of my neck prickles. Am I really salty about their friendship? About the way they can brush off whatever's happened lately? Do I have any right to be upset when I'm the one who fucked up things with Aleah? I mean, technically, Mario and Dad did. At least, that's what I've told myself for years.

No. I'm being ridiculous. Good for Makayla and Aleah. They can stay BFFs. After all, I have the same connection with TNT. Finishing each other's sentences. Inside jokes. Embarrassing party stories. Deep, personal secrets.

*Theo's a chill guy. At least I've heard. Gay, right?*

*I don't think he's a creep.*

*I don't have any problems with dudes like* that.

Cole's words rotate around in my skull. They're accompanied by Jay's silence. By the things he could've—*should've*—said but didn't.

I tug out my phone. It's been an hour since I first crept upstairs. Too long.

I'm supposed to be with Christian, not with semi-strangers and an ex–best friend.

Unlocking the screen, I pull up my web browser. Time to solidify my plans for accomplishing this dare. But when my tabs load, I'm met with the last one I had open.

My hand trembles, ears burning.

No, it's not porn. It's Duke's website. Dad and I were exploring the *THINGS TO DO* option. He wants us to visit the campus in the fall. Another reminder I need to come out on the other side of tonight with a W.

I open a new tab, not bothering to close out Duke's page. I'm that guy who has dozens of tabs open at once, always telling myself I need each of them. Like closing out just one means I'll never get it back.

My search is pretty basic:

*How to ask a boy to prom.*

Thirty-two million results. Otherwise known as too many options for a boy chilling in a tween's bedroom on a Saturday night.

*Seventeen. Teen Vogue.* Pinterest. All the usual suspects fly across the screen as I scroll. Each one *very* heteronormative.

My eyes flick up to Luca. He's sitting cross-legged on the bed, full attention on the group. Warm brown cheeks flushed. His hair is pushed off his face by a thin, yellow headband. Another stolen article from the Museum of Maddie Campbell. In his lap is my forgotten toy crown. It looks a little like a prom court crown, in all its plastic glory.

I wonder if he used any of these resources for Devya's promposal. A brief flash of his face when Makayla mentioned her name glazes my vision. Between that and his phone's wallpaper, it's clear where his head is at.

Deleting my previous search, I key in a new one.

*How to ask a boy to prom if you're queer.*

*Specificity matters*, I remind myself.

Twenty million less results, but worthy, respectable sources. BuzzFeed and Reddit and . . . Okay, I'm not diving down a Quora rabbit hole to ask Christian out. Some lines aren't worth crossing.

I skim the articles. Click through photos. Bypass the ad-filled videos because I'm without my earbuds and don't want the others to know what I'm doing.

"We need drinks!" announces Makayla.

Confused, I ask, "For what?"

"If we're staying here"—Makayla pauses to fluff her hair until it has more volume than when she arrived—"I need alcohol and mixers to go along with this prime stash."

I look down. There's a magical snack spread across the Monopoly board: trail mix, various candies, small bags of chips, pop-top plastic cups of mini-cookies, granola bars. River keeps adding more items to the pile. The depths of their bag are limitless.

As if sensing my weird gaze, they explain, "You don't have an emergency snack kit?"

"Forgot mine at home," I tease.

"What goes good with . . . beef jerky?" Aleah's face scrunches. "Vodka?"

"Beer, probably," offers Luca.

"We need booze ASAP," Makayla confirms. She hip-bumps Luca. "Coming with?"

He hesitates, biting his bottom lip.

"Come on," begs Makayla. "We made a deal."

*What is with them and this deal?* I want to ask.

"I know. It's just . . ." His words trail off.

Across the room, our eyes meet. His are wide. Mine are squinted to match my crinkled brow. A strange quiet sits between us. Neither of us knows what the other is saying with their stare. Of course not. This isn't me and Darren. Why would I expect Luca to understand what I'm trying to ask?

"Isn't this your chance to talk to Devya? Find out why she was looking for you?"

I don't mean for my words to come out so accusatory.

He blinks.

"That's why you . . ." I wave a hand around, hoping it says everything I can't. Correction: everything I *shouldn't* say. He and Devya are none of my concern. Whether he gets over her or sits like a hopeful puppy, waiting for her to finally acknowledge his existence, has nothing to do with me.

Yet, once again, my brain and mouth are operating on separate servers.

"It's why you're doing the fake—" I stop when Makayla startles before she glares at Luca. I smile nervously, stammering, "You're doing the 'best thing you never had' thing, right? Maybe it worked. Queen Bey doesn't miss."

My weak chuckle isn't as loud as the alarms ringing in my head.

Luca's not amused. His jaw tenses. The sharpness nearly punctures his skin.

I count the seconds until he finally says, "Is that the only reason you think I stayed up here?"

"N-no."

Part of me hopes he stuck around because we were having fun. Because he likes River. Because of . . . me.

"You think I'm only up here biding my time? Playing Monopoly and hoping Dev will magically dump Peter for me?" His words are pointed. "Have I really sounded like a pathetic, whiny dude praying his ex will see his potential?"

"That's not what I said."

"What you *said* and what you *meant* are two different things," he notes stiffly.

"Luca, enough," says Makayla, stepping between us, blocking my view of him. "I need your help grabbing drinks."

They bicker for a minute. I look away. Exhaling out the frustration is easy. Trying to get my heartbeat to slow down—not so much.

What's wrong with me? I wasn't supposed to end up in a bedroom with any of them, let alone Aleah tonight. I wasn't supposed to feel so raw about her friendship with Makayla. Or Luca's situation with his ex.

I need fresh air. I need my boys.

As if on cue, my phone *bzzt*s in my palm.

A new message from Jay. It's a direct one; not from our WhatsApp chat. My shoulders tense. One-on-one texts are rare. Anything we say to one of us, we should be able to say to the group.

A photo uploads in his gray bubble. It's partially grainy from the pool's artificial lighting and dark skies outside, but I instantly know who it is: *Christian*. He has an orange Solo cup in his left hand. Even slightly out of focus, he's beautiful. Perfection in a five-foot-eight body. The fuzzy faces in the background resemble band geeks.

My heart catches. He's still at the party.

The next text reads:

WYA?? looks like he wants some company. How are u 💅 BLOCKING urself?! lmao

I ignore the burning urge to reply with a string of middle finger emojis to scroll back to Christian's face.

He's caught mid-laugh. White teeth and crinkled nose. Mildly wrinkled yellow shirt still looking great on him. He's the sun and all I want is to be close to him. To absorb that energy.

All I want is this same Christian at prom as we dance to songs we've heard exhaustively all year. His laugh when I whisper bad jokes in his ear during photos. Our first kiss that I'll inevitably fuck up. I always do. But it's what first kisses are for—to mess up and try again.

Again and *again*.

I close out Jay's message. My eyes catch on the text underneath. The unanswered one from Dad. My thumb hovers over it. He'll be passed out on the sofa now. I imagine him snoring away in a Duke T-shirt. Because he's so certain of where I'm going to land after graduation.

He knows The Plan is bulletproof.

*Sorry, Dad, I agreed to a foolish—but necessary—dare with the potential to screw with our entire endgame. Just a teeny bit.*

I ignore the tightness in my chest. Failure isn't on tonight's agenda. Jay's photo means he's nearby. Greedy as it is, I'm determined to have the boy and prom *and* convince my marginally intoxicated best friend to persuade his dickish father to write me a recommendation letter.

"I'll go," I volunteer. Makayla and Luca share a glance as I say, "I'll help you, Makayla."

"I thought you were leaving," says Aleah, looking thoroughly unimpressed when I reply, "Plans changed."

More like they've reverted to the original ones.

"Fine," Makayla huffs after her silent communication with Luca fails to work. His gaze roams from the crown to me. But he doesn't say a thing.

"Cool." I shrug nonchalantly.

I disregard every impulse to glance back at Luca while following Makayla to the door. I have one boy in my head. One goal. It's time to stop running from it.

No one else is getting in the way of me asking Christian to prom.

# 11

# DANCING ON MY OWN

**Except *everyone* is** in the way.

The moment Makayla and I walk down the stairs, I'm hit by the thud of a song that has people shouting the lyrics at the top of their lungs. The heat from too many bodies crammed in one space quickly leeches onto my skin. Rum and sweat and coconut water fill my nose. Somehow, the crowd has gotten thicker inside the house.

I trail Makayla at a respectable distance.

Before we can reach the bottom step, a group stands in the way, recording a live video. Sophomores, I gather from the way they don't appear completely out of place, but also have that wide-eyed wonder as Makayla seamlessly hops onto screen with them. She doesn't need to ask for permission. They worship her like Aphrodite descending from the heavens to frolic with mortals.

Makayla's a pro. All air kisses and impeccable selfie angles before she reaches back to pull on my wrist. "Send me those!" she yells, smiling but never exchanging numbers with any of her new fans.

If Christian is a prom prince in the making, Makayla's a certified nominee for prom queen at Brook-Oak.

"Was that necessary?" I shout over the music.

"As if you have to ask."

I ignore her sarcasm. My eyes are busy searching every poorly lit corner. Tracking faces. My neck cranes to investigate rooms. I listen for *that laugh*. Any indication of Christian.

He's here. I just need to locate him.

Makayla doesn't make it easy, though. She all but drags me through the house. It's annoying, but something inside me wants to keep my Christian plan to myself, so I don't complain.

"Theo? Theo!"

I blink hard. Makayla glares at me. When did we get to the kitchen? People are shotgunning beers around the marble-topped island. A couple makes out against the fridge.

Makayla lifts a bottle in each hand. "Whiskey or vodka?"

Her face falls when I reply, "Neither? I don't drink."

As the tipsy pack finishes their shotguns, their faces become clearer. No Christian, unfortunately.

"I'm the DD," I explain after Makayla shakes another bottle in my face. "I drive while TNT—" I cut myself off at the confused tilt of her head. "My boys, Jay and Darren?"

People around school don't really acknowledge our nickname. It's not as if we have custom-printed T-shirts or anything.

We're more known for our dares. Our track accomplishments. Or as individuals in our respective programs.

Darren, the goofy TMZ nerd. Jay, the popular STEM guy. Me, the . . .

Actually, I don't know how everyone perceives me.

The athlete? Dancer? Mariah Carey dude? Son of the great Miles Wright?

Or do they see me like my magnet program—general? Basic? *Nothing special or extraordinary required.*

Makayla gives me an indiscernible look. "Right. Your friend *Jay.*" Something hangs on the way she says his name.

"And Darren," I repeat, maybe a little too hopeful. Here I am, playing wingman for a friend I haven't seen or heard from since I let him run off with those Yearbook girls. My birthday gift better be epic come November. "You know, Darren Jacobs?"

"Yeah," she says unconvincingly.

Was that mutual follow back earlier an error?

"Anyway, drinking's their thing. I'm good without it."

"Sounds responsible," she notes, turning to pick through a cabinet stocked with several half-empty bottles of alcohol.

I grin.

"And *so* boring," she adds, my shoulders deflating at her smile. "Mixers for you, then."

Before I can protest, she loads my arms with supplies: a stack of Solo cups, orange juice, and sodas. I fumble to arrange everything as she moves through the Campbells' kitchen like it's her own.

"Vodka, rum, *and* good old Jim Beam," Makayla says. She

balances the bottles in her hands like it's nothing. "No discriminating in this house."

She takes stock of everything I'm holding, then nods. "Let's go."

It's even more difficult navigating the party with supplies. The struggle is obnoxiously real. We're detoured thanks to the boys' basketball team clogging the main kitchen entrance to loudly discuss their failed season. Makayla twirls to avoid sloppy drunks. Mingles easily as we pass familiar faces. Every few seconds, she checks to make sure I'm not too far, even stopping when I get caught behind a line of kids—poorly—doing the Wobble.

I'm two steps behind when I hear it.

His laugh.

I don't care how many people complain as they maneuver around me. How thirsty I look when the path clears, and I clock Christian standing outside by the pool. Whatever Makayla shouts as I clumsily drop our supplies on a nearby couch goes unheard.

Christian's right there.

Makayla cuts in front of me. "Where are you going?" she asks frantically. "Theo? We have—"

"I'm going to take care of something," I interrupt, staring past her at a dimpled left cheek, lemon-yellow shirt. Carelessly, I add, "I'm about to have the best prom ever."

Makayla's eyes track my line of vision. Her mouth falls open at the sight of Christian. I can relate. "Wait, Theo," she rushes out, but I'm uninterested in her babbling.

The only person I'm fascinated by is taking a sip from an orange Solo cup, looking like he needs a new reason to smile.

"Hey."

Christian jerks when I pop up in front of him. Okay, I could've made a subtler entrance. But his eyes brighten when he realizes it's me. My heartbeat finally settles.

"There you are."

"Here I am," I confirm, grinning uncontrollably.

"Thought you ghosted me." He laughs softly.

"I would never."

His eyebrows raise, as if to say, *Boy, please*. That's fair. I wasted too much time upstairs trying to psych myself up for this. I was distracted by the wrong things. Well, not *wrong*. Things that weren't a priority. It still doesn't sound right in my head.

Whatever.

I'm in front of Christian now. The hint of a teasing smile is visible as he sips his drink. The pool's artificial light gives him a charming alien glow. Random kids splash around in the water. The air's warm and fresh. We gradually rock back on our heels to a song I don't know but feels perfect.

When Christian lowers his cup, he stares my way like he's waiting for me to speak first.

I scan the area. If I'm going to do this, I need . . .

*There he is.*

Jay is near the hot tub, within earshot of me and Christian. He's drinking and chatting with a Black boy I can't identify. Their conversation seems chill. Quiet enough that, if I project, he'll hear me.

"Hey, uh," I stammer. Great. All my hype evaporates in an exhale. "Sorry about being gone so long."

"You got lost?" Christian asks.

"Something like that."

"Let me guess," he starts, swirling the contents of his cup. "The toilet clogged. You flooded the whole upstairs. You tried to clean it all up but there were no towels. Only toilet paper. And then—"

"Wow," I interrupt. I don't fight the smirk pulling at my lips. "Were you there watching instead of helping? That's rude."

His own lips twitch into a grin.

"Anyway." I half laugh, feeling everything inside my belly go warm and soft. A star-filled sky gazes down on us. Christian's full attention is on me. "Speaking of time going by pretty fast—prom's coming up, you know."

"I do. It's gonna be fun."

"Yup." My lips tick higher. "Even more fun with a pretty cool, sweet, funny date."

*Way to go, Theo. Really using those SAT Word of the Day apps to their full potential.*

Christian's forehead wrinkles. "I hope so."

I'm dizzy with adrenaline. The music's turned to a low hum. The slosh of pool water like an undercurrent to our voices. I can sense Jay's eyes on us. It feels like everyone's staring.

"Theo . . . ?"

Christian's free hand carefully grabs my elbow. His wide eyes anchor me. Our surroundings stop spinning.

I clear my throat, raise my voice.

"I was thinking maybe you'd like to go to—"

"Hold on," begs Christian. "Oh, shit. *Stop.*"

I freeze. My unsaid words lodge into my throat like a giant jaw-breaker I forgot to let fully dissolve before swallowing.

The dead air between us makes my palms sweat.

"Er . . . did I read this wrong?" I say quietly.

Christian's fingers drop away from my elbow. "Theo," he begins, but then someone else joins us. The boy Jay was talking to wedges himself next to Christian's side.

"Hey, sorry to interrupt," he says, his voice a tad deep but jubilant. He extends a hand. "I heard you two talking. I'm Kenneth-David. You can call me KD."

"Okay," I say, dragging out the word.

Up close, he's cute. Fawn-brown skin. We're around the same height. He has short curls and wears those square hipster glasses everyone loves. His smile is lopsided, endearing.

"Nice to, uh, meet you . . . KD," I say, taming the wariness in my voice. "I was kind of asking Christian something import—"

"You can also call me Chris's boyfriend," KD interrupts.

Numbness shoots through my chest.

*Did I hear him correctly?*

KD's smile tightens. "Because that's who I am," he continues, easing an arm around Christian's tight shoulders. "His boyfriend."

Something thick and awful bobs in my stomach.

I blink at Christian. "He's your . . ."

Christian rests his head on KD's chest, nodding. He looks on the verge of a frown. Can't say I blame him. Pathetic, clueless, bizarre Theo, thirsting over another guy's boyfriend. Asking him to prom in front of said boyfriend.

Maybe those are all the things my classmates think of me.

My eyes dart around. The people scattered outside gawk at

us. Some whisper to each other. I think someone's documenting everything on their phone. At least one boy openly chuckles into his cup.

And then there's Jay—leaning against a brick pillar, grimacing. He cuts a hand across his throat. He's telling me to abandon ship.

I can't move.

"KD's a senior at Mountainview," explains Christian, grinding my already shattered heart into dust for the wind to blow away. "We met at—"

"That's really cool," I sputter before he finishes, stumbling backward. There's a Class F fire spreading across the back of my neck. "Love that for you two."

"Theo, I—"

"No worries!" I hold up both hands. "Forget I asked."

Even though I didn't. The full question never made it out my mouth.

KD's brow lowers. His mouth flexes like he might say something. And as much as I want to defend myself, I can't tear my eyes from the apologetic expression softening Christian's face.

"Seriously . . ." My voice cuts out, eyes burning. "I'm happy for you."

"Thanks," he whispers.

We nod in unison. A silent agreement. This conversation never needs to be repeated. No need for KD's cold stare. Christian can explain the confusion later. And my trembling lower lip won't be commented on.

All the dares I've completed. The gaping and snickers from

other students. King of #BOHSFail at least four times a year since I was a freshman.

Nothing feels like this.

I don't think anything ever will.

A breathless Makayla materializes out of nowhere, surprising me. "Theo, finally!" she gasps out. "I was searching everywhere for you!"

Really? Because it's barely been ten minutes since I was her personal grocery cart.

"Sorry," Makayla says to Christian, then KD. I pointedly look *anywhere* but his face. "I need this guy and these . . ." She firmly squeezes my biceps. ". . . for a small, but necessary home improvement project."

In my ear, Makayla whispers, "Unclench your ass cheeks and follow me."

I try not to wince at the way her nails dig into my skin.

"Catch up with you soon?" She offers Christian the most earnest, believable smile ever. Her Hulk-like grip tugs on me. My numb body willingly obeys. Anything to get far, far from whatever just happened.

On the way, I catch a glimpse of Jay. His curious blue eyes. The lit-up phone in his hand. His uncomfortable posture, pale expression. His lips part like he might say something, then he shakes his head.

What the hell was that?

It's not until we're back in the house, Makayla reloading my arms with the contraband, that I hear what she's shouting over the music.

"Who does that? Goes after a boy who's clearly in a relation-ship?" Makayla shakes her head. "I mean, I know you're friends with trash, but . . . Theo Wright, a skank? Never figured you for—"

"Trash?" I interrupt her, eyes wide. *Is she talking about Darren or Jay?* "I didn't know he had a boyfriend."

"You didn't know?"

"No."

Her scandalized expression tells me she doesn't believe me. "How?" She continues to pile things into my cradled arms. "Anyone who's ever been to a Brook-Oak sport that ends in 'ball' has seen Christian low-key flirting with KD, despite him going to the *wrong* school."

I recycle through the last ten minutes. Christian's surprised face, followed by the horrified one, then sympathy. Like he'd just figured out how oblivious I am.

"You really didn't know Christian Harris had a boyfriend?"

*I didn't.*

Those two words fill up my throat, but never make it out.

How could I have known?

It's not all over Christian's *public* social media accounts. That's curated to show off his music stuff. Band performances. His solos. I'm not anti-athletics outside my own, but I don't have time to attend any of our school's sporting events. I'm too busy studying. Working on bonus-credit assignments. Then there's helping at home while Dad picks up overtime shifts. Chilling with Darren and Jay—when the latter isn't hugged up with Jayla—on the weekends.

Not to mention avoiding every single Brook-Oak Ballers game because of Aleah.

The only time Christian and I interact is during school. I wouldn't have signed up for this idiotic dare if I had the smallest notion he was taken.

I frown at the ground.

"If it's any consolation," she starts, obvious pity in her tone, "it's still newish? Christian and KD. Only a few months old. HoCo at the earliest."

It's not the slightest bit comforting, actually.

Makayla smiles sadly, leaving it at that.

"The others are waiting on us," she says.

I don't know why *that* sounds soothing. My desire to run out the front door, drop out of Brook-Oak, and scrub the internet clean of my existence vanishes. Being in the same space as Aleah— and, to a degree, Luca—shouldn't be so appealing, but I don't turn down the invitation.

"Could we maybe not mention . . . y'know." Since my arms are stuffed, I waggle my eyebrows to fill in the blanks.

Makayla's face says exactly what I need: *No judgment here.*

I appreciate Makayla Lawrence beyond words. That is, until she abruptly stops ten feet from the stairs.

"Hi, Lexi!" she says, her voice instantly falling into that over-enthusiastic peppiness her social circle's known for. "When did you get here?"

"Ugh, Mack. Thank God. Someone I *like*." Lexi says it with all the affection of a bored socialite *finally* talking to someone other than the staff at a gala. "Do any of these people even know Chloe?"

Lexi Johnson is beloved at Brook-Oak. From her talent to wardrobe to beauty, the idolization is endless. She did more for Derek's popularity than he ever could for hers.

Makayla giggles loudly. "I don't know half these people."

"It's the worst," says Lexi.

I stand back, trying to maintain a solid hold on our contraband. It's not as if my existence is acknowledged.

Watching Makayla mingle is intriguing. She's great at peopling. Laughs on cue. Maintains eye contact. Tosses her hair in that fun way. Nothing against any of the cheer squad—I don't know 60 percent of them beyond their ponytails and the occasional group project—but Makayla comes off as the most genuine in public situations.

Lexi says, "Can you believe *she's* here?"

Makayla blinks twice. "Who?"

For a future Hollywood ingenue, her confused act needs work.

My back tightens in anticipation of Lexi's next words. She sighs melodramatically. "Aleah, that sneaky bitch."

I hate that last word. Whatever anger I've been storing deep in my belly bubbles up. My fingers squeeze around the last cup in the stack in my arms, crunching until it cracks. Sharp plastic edges dig into my palm. I'm unfazed. My glare intensifies when Lexi jumps, surprised.

I keep waiting for Makayla to correct Lexi, but her silence says enough.

It's as loud as Jay's was back at SpeedEx.

I'm so tired of popular kids protecting their own rep at the expense of someone else's by staying quiet. Never denying the blatant lies. Letting shit happen.

"Oh, hi, Theo," says Lexi, cool and casual, like I'm in their little squad.

"Don't call her that," I say, ignoring Lexi's aghast expression. "She's not a . . ."

I *refuse* to say it. Ever. Especially when referring to another person.

Lexi folds her arms. She's wearing a body-hugging LeBron James jersey that stops mid-thigh. The barest trim of black shorts peeks from underneath. Her ponytail swings wildly as she assesses me. "And you know this, because . . . what? You were there?"

I bite out a "No."

"Derek told you?"

"Nope."

"Are you and . . . *Aleah*"—Lexi struggles not to say the other word—"besties?"

I shake my head. We're nothing close to friends, which really makes me reconsider this hill I've suddenly decided to die on. But I'm having a shitty night. And Aleah isn't here to defend herself. I can't let it go.

I can't be another Jay.

"Last I checked, she was *my* best friend," Lexi snaps. "Before she fucked up. You have no right—"

"To stand up for someone who's not around when her 'bestie' shits on her reputation?"

Lexi sucks air through her teeth.

"Look, I don't know what happened," I clarify lowly when I realize a trio of seniors has taken a serious interest in our conversation, "but she deserves better than to be disrespected behind her back."

*Better than me*, I don't say.

Discreetly, Makayla pinches my hip. She grins tightly at Lexi. Pretty sure it's her way of telling me to shut up.

She's doing a fantastic job of being quiet for both of us.

Lexi hasn't budged. Her usually bronze face is crimson. Whatever. Guess I'll have a list of people who hate me by the end of tonight. She can fall in line behind KD and Aleah.

"Gee, Mack." Lexi rotates to face Makayla. "I heard you were cuddled up with Luca Ramírez earlier? Damn, girl. You move quick."

Makayla shifts uncomfortably.

Lexi drags her eyes up me. "Never suspected fuckboys were your taste."

I don't have a response. It seems Makayla doesn't either.

"I'm not hating," says Lexi, smirking in a way that confirms she most certainly is. "When you're done swiping right on bigmouth track boy, find me, 'kay?"

"Lexi," Makayla says gently.

They whisper to each other. The current rotation of dance-pop drowns out their words. From their body language, I gather there's a lot of pleading and apologies on Makayla's part while Lexi blinks disinterestedly. It ends with a short, compulsory hug before Makayla drags me away.

I glance over my shoulder as Lexi disappears into a congregation of cheerleaders and basketball players. At the heart of the chatter is Jay. He's never had a problem fitting in with them. The Jayla factor. She's currently under his arm. He's a dedicated boyfriend, jumping through hoops to attend every event the cheer squad performs at despite track commitments.

*Anyone who's ever been to a Brook-Oak sport that ends in "ball" has seen Christian low-key flirting with KD . . .*

Makayla's words rebound around my head, taunting me.

I stop at the top of the stairs. My stomach churns. I fight against the need to vomit. Everything is hitting me too quickly. The dare. Jay's insistence it happen at Chloe's party. Texting me that photo of Christian to show they were in the same place, at the same time.

"Theo?" Makayla calls.

I gasp out, "Holy shit."

# 12

# LIKE A NINETIES THROWBACK

**He knew.**

HE KNEW.

Hefuckingknew.

Jay, my best friend, has been to multiple Brook-Oak games to support Jayla. Games where Christian's performed with the band. Where he's no doubt been seen with KD.

He's known they were a Thing.

It's all I can focus on. Not being rejected in front of an audience. Nor the ways I'm certain his *boyfriend* is planning to hide my corpse if we ever cross paths again.

Why would Jay set me up with a dare I could never win?

It makes zero sense.

Maddie's bathroom is relatively spacious. At least for a kid who has a step stool to reach the sink. The width of her counterspace is nearly the size of my entire bathroom. I'm sitting on it now. The back of my head is pressed against the mirror. A calm, consistent drip from the faucet echoes in my ears. I try to match it with my breaths.

Autopilot took over the second Makayla and I walked back into the bedroom. I made a beeline for the bathroom once I unloaded all our supplies. No greetings. No snappy retorts for all the questions tossed our way. No eye contact.

Everything in my brain was suffocating enough.

I needed a break.

Jay's key fob digs into my thigh. It might've been more practical to leave the party. Drive around the city alone. Clear my head. Then again, someone could've said I "stole" Jay's SUV. The last thing I need is an alert going out about an underage Black boy cruising through one of the wealthiest communities in Kentucky at night.

*Ding.*

An Instagram notification lights up my phone. I've been tagged in a new post.

I sigh before hesitantly checking the tag only to be hit by a low-quality video of Christian turning me down by the pool. The two-second glimpse of KD's exasperated face is enough for me to hit pause. I block @BOHSFails12345—unquestionably a burner account—then click on Jay's grid.

He hasn't been active in hours.

The bathroom's lighting is selfie-worthy. Sky-blue walls. Heavy scents of vanilla and bubblegum shampoo. What it lacks are the kind of acoustics that prevent anyone on the other side of the door from hearing you whimpering like a toddler in need of a nap.

I sniffle quietly. My feet swing back and forth while I swipe through old photos. Sporadic tears wet my cheeks. I scrub them away as quick as they fall.

There are now three versions of Jay living rent-free in my head:

The frowny one near the pool.

The quiet one who didn't defend me at SpeedEx, but who I want to believe would've in any other situation.

The Jay from the Throwback Thursday post I'm staring at.

It's from the day we found out we'd made the track team. Jay was a no-brainer since he's always been fast. Darren made a strong case for himself during tryouts. I'd just made the cut. Funny thing is, I remember Jay's reaction after my name was called. He caught me in one of those smothering bear hugs, lifting me off my feet. I screamed and he hollered and Darren pounced on us, laughing.

All I could hear was Jay's elated, "Holy shit, we're doing this together!" like he wanted to cry.

A light knock startles me. "Theo?"

The door gently eases open as I wipe another tear from my cheek.

"Hey?" Luca bites his lip. "Okay?"

I clear my throat, nodding. "Incredible."

"Anyone ever tell you that your lying is abysmal? Like, one-star, will-not-be-recommending-to-my-friends bad?"

A smile tickles my lips. "Anyone ever tell you to wait for an invitation before entering a room?"

He leans against the now closed bathroom door. Genuine concern encircles his eyes. Considering the way we left things, it's startling.

After a beat, I say, "I thought you were pissed at me?"

"Theo, I have two younger brothers and a six-year-old sister." He smiles. "We fight constantly. Literally, just this morning. We had a blowout about bathroom time."

I wonder if he takes extra-long showers like me. With that many siblings, maybe mornings are the only time he can properly "clean" himself? I bite my lip to hold in a laugh, but something in the way my shoulders shake must give me away.

He flips me off, chuckling softly. "Don't go there. Grudges aren't my thing. I'm a Libra."

"I have no idea what that means."

He gasps theatrically. I can't stop the laugh as it flies from my mouth. He waits until I'm quiet again before motioning to the gap between us.

I like how Luca asks for permission to step closer.

I slide over so he can join me on the countertop. We drift into silence. It's far from awkward. More like a thing we share. I like that too.

"Sorry I've been shitty tonight," I whisper, turning my phone over and over in my hands.

"I'm not complaining." He winks.

"In my feelings, I guess."

"You're allowed."

Our thighs are pressed together. We're shoulder to shoulder too. The warmth extends all the way into my face. Having a friend like Darren, personal space is something I abandoned long ago. But it's different with Luca.

I don't know how, but it is.

"I unloaded a lot of things about my family earlier," he says, tipping his head back against the mirror. Without the headband or sunglasses, his hair flops onto his brow. "But I really do love them. How could I not? My sibs drag me out of bed every single Saturday to play Xbox or build Lego structures."

He swipes through a few photos on his cracked phone screen. The entire Ramírez brood assembling a re-creation of the Death Star.

I glance down at my *Last Jedi* shirt. He does too, mouth twitching.

"My tías taught me to cook *and* throw a punch!" He snorts into his palm.

"And these—" He holds up both hands, wiggling the fingers with rings on them. "Family gifts."

Luca explains each one to me: the plain silver band with scratches from old age on his left thumb belonged to his grandfather. A crying-heart signet on his ring finger is from his favorite cousin. Interconnecting silver hearts on his left index finger from his mom.

As I tentatively brush my thumb over the metal, he says, "It's a reminder: 'All things are possible with someone you love.' That's what my mamá told me."

My eyes flicker to his face as I continue to trace the last ring.

"I'm not giving them a pass for what they say about my queerness." He frowns. "Family, friends, relationships—all of it's complicated. They do foolish shit. We do too. No one's above fucking up."

I think about Jay.

Is that all the dare was? Something silly between friends? I can be furious, but I'll have to forgive him, won't I? We have too much history.

Warm, damp skin touches mine. Luca's turned his hand over in mine. My fingers skim his sweaty palm. He doesn't pull away. Silently, we've established new boundaries.

"Would you—" I stop when my throat constricts. Considering Luca's been spilling his guts on the regular, I don't know why the question I want to ask feels so personal. It takes a second to speak again. "Would you ever forgive Devya? For what happened yesterday? Or what she said when you broke up?"

He stares at me, brow knit. "What makes you think I haven't?" He bumps my shoulder. I lean into him as he says, "I don't hate her. I didn't completely believe she'd say yes, anyway. It was a gamble."

*A big one*, I think, my index finger drawing circles across the belly of his palm.

"My feelings are . . . complicated."

That word again. It's the same for me and Jay. Darren too. He hasn't responded to the texts I've sent since I first started sulking in here. I'm not even on read, which presents two possibilities: his battery is dead or he's drunkenly hooking up with someone.

Most likely the former.

"Why'd you ask that?" Luca says.

My shrug is automatic. I almost lay out the whole Jay and Christian dilemma to him. But despite us virtually holding hands, I'm not on that level with Luca yet.

"Research purposes," I reply, smirking.

His laugh comes out sharply, like he wasn't expecting it.

Staring into those dark brown eyes, it's impossible not to want what I thought I had out by the pool. The Christian thing is still tragic, a little less painful now, but I want the dream that sits like mist above my head. My Big Gay Night at Prom.

"Whatever you're 'researching,'" he says, adding exaggerated air quotes to his last word, "I hope you know it doesn't have to be anything like my situation. Don't get me wrong, if I ever promposé to anyone again and it ends like that, I'll be sure to burn it all down."

My laugh echoes loudly.

"Just do you," he insists, smiling. "Good or bad, it's your life."

*It's my life.* Too bad it hasn't felt that way, at all.

"For what it's worth," I start to say, letting our shoulders brush, "your promposal was really sweet."

Luca doesn't instantly respond. He blinks slowly. Did I say the wrong thing again? Then he reaches out and twists my left nipple through my shirt.

"Ow!"

"How are you so bad at lying?" he huffs.

"It's true!"

Luca flinches as if he's about to go in for the right nipple. I throw my hands up in defense. We crack up.

"Come on." He hops off the counter. "Time to get out of our own heads."

Something about the look in Luca's eyes, the way his fingers brush against mine as we both move for the door, feels like he's the one person left who won't let me down tonight.

• • •

Back in the bedroom, Makayla and River are organizing a small picnic over the Monopoly board. We should probably feel a tad guilty for claiming Maddie's bedroom—and all the things in it—as our own personal party space. It's mad disrespectful. I almost lean into that vibe . . . until I spot the latest MacBook and AirPods on her desk, a pair of designer sneakers under her bed. Yeah, she'll get over us borrowing her fleece throw blanket to set our snacks on.

"So . . . about that video on Insta," I start.

"What video?" River asks while making snack piles.

I blink. Aleah hums while cleaning up game pieces. Makayla sets up cups around the board. In the bathroom, Luca never mentioned the low-quality vid of my Christian debacle from that burner account. No one's been on their phones. It's as if they've blocked out the rest of the world. They're living in this moment.

I clear my throat. "Uh, never mind."

Makayla shoots me a curious look as I sit down. The group hasn't commented on *why* Luca and I were in the bathroom. In my head, that sounds a lot sleazier than it is. It doesn't help that Makayla whispers in Luca's ear until his cheeks turn two shades darker.

I can't fight the apprehension I have toward her now. Don't get me wrong, I'm grateful she bailed me out at the pool. But it's her voluntary silence when Lexi was attacking Aleah that's left me uneasy. All the pleading she did to win Lexi back.

Luca bites open a pack of sour candies. "I was thinking—"

"That's never a good idea," Aleah interjects. She pours vodka and orange juice into a cup. After taste-testing, she adds more OJ.

"Like I was saying," Luca continues, side-eyeing her. "We need to have some fun."

"Are we going to learn quadratic equations?" asks River, pushing up their glasses. "I'm only sixteen. I'm not ready."

"Roasted!" Aleah high-fives a beaming River.

I tip over on my side laughing. The socked foot digging into my stomach most definitely belongs to Luca, but I can't stop. Once I'm upright again, I wipe tears from my lashes.

"Two words." Luca holds up his index and middle finger. "Dance. Contest."

"What're we, ten?" Makayla asks.

Luca drops his index finger.

"Oh God," says Makayla while mixing her own drink. "You're serious, aren't you?"

Luca's expression is adorably determined. Pouty bottom lip. A tight knot between his dark eyebrows. Cheeks puffed out from holding his breath. When his eyes lock on me like a puppy hoping you'll drop some scraps while eating, I flush.

"What're you looking at?" I say, head tilted.

"I saw you earlier."

I shoot him an expression that says, *That's a rather ominous, almost threatening statement.*

"I saw you *dancing* earlier," he amends. "You were really good."

"Thanks."

"Not as good as me, though," he adds, *nearly* pulling off a smug grin. I respect the effort.

"What you and Makayla were doing wasn't dancing."

"Excuse me," gasps Makayla, elbowing me hard before sipping her drink.

After a quick search on my phone, I read, "Dancing is *to move rhythmically to music*" from the screen. "That wasn't you two."

Aleah splutters into her cup. The level of fire in my cheeks rises. Never in a million years did I imagine being able to make Aleah Bird laugh again, but here we are.

"Bullshit," Makayla disputes after another gulp. "We were just as good as you."

"Is that a challenge?"

"Hell yes," Luca replies. He chews aggressively on a sour gummy worm. I'd be lying if I didn't say this defiant, cocky version of him is mildly . . . hot?

Pulling my knees to my chest to hide a slow-rising erection, I say, "What're we talking here? One-on-one? Me against you two or—"

"Team competition!" River fist-pumps the air. "Makayla and Luca versus Theo and Aleah!"

My face falls.

Aleah protests before I can. "Hard pass!" She shakes her head. "I don't have anything to prove to anyone, especially not with—"

Makayla reaches across our circle to grasp Aleah's hands, smiling tenderly. "*Please.* It'll be way better than going back downstairs."

It's clear: no one wants to return to the party. Especially not me. Which means I have two choices—lock myself in the bathroom again or accept my fate, being partnered with the one person in this room who looks like she wants to murder me.

Aleah asks River, "Why aren't you participating?"

"Impartial judge," they reply.

"Why can't I be the judge?" Aleah asks, insulted.

"I also have an unfair advantage over all of you," explains River. "Multiple years of tap, jazz, hip-hop, and contemporary dance classes."

Aleah looks impressed.

River brushes back their bangs. Pink blush freckles their cheeks. "My sister had a lot of . . . ambitions growing up. She's also a noncommittal monster. She'd drag me to all her latest phases until she got tired and moved on." They pointedly eye the ground. "My parents always gave Katie the freedom to discover herself. But with me, it's—"

They stop abruptly.

We all wait. Our silence is only interrupted by the crash of something falling over downstairs. No one asks River to finish. We have a mutual understanding: *Now's not the time.*

Though we're all here voluntarily, we're still primarily—in the most basic definition—strangers.

"Let's get this over with," Aleah finally says, and sighs. She glares at an overeager Luca. "Don't make me regret this."

Without acknowledging each other, Aleah and I end up on the same side of the room. Makayla and Luca are opposite us. River settles into the middle of the blanket, scrolling through their phone.

As the challengers, River insists Team KayLu—ugh, gross—goes first. They whisper fervently before calling out what song to play.

Makayla and Luca scurry into position, backs to us. Is this a dance competition or an audition for YPT? A K-pop song I vaguely recognize thanks to students humming it between classes comes on. Luca and Makayla break into synchronized steps. They smoothly meld an amalgam of TikTok dances.

It's not bad.

"Get it, girl!" Aleah shouts over the synth-heavy chorus.

To my surprise, Makayla's more than hair flips and jerky hips. She has rhythm. There's a fluidness to her arm movements. She's easily better than Jay, who's one offbeat clap away from white-frat-bro purgatory, and Darren, whose moves are borrowed from the Dad's Guide to Dancing playbook.

But it's Luca who has me absentmindedly biting my thumbnail jagged.

He floats between dances. His feet are light and smooth. No stiffness in his shoulders. No hesitation when his motions speed up. And his hips . . .

At one point, he rotates them while lifting the hem of his shirt and, *sweet baby Jesus.*

My eyes discreetly peek down. Wow. SpongeBob boxer briefs never looked so appealing.

None of this is helping the situation in my jeans.

When the song ends, River cheers. Luca lifts Makayla into a hug, twirling in a wild circle. "Don't drop me!" she says, giggling.

"Withholding scores until the end," announces River. "Team Wright Bird, you're next."

For a breath, all I hear is my banging heart trying to match its beats to Aleah's uneven, heavy exhales. She plays idly with her necklace. I run a hand over my twists.

Why is this so hard? It's a silly dance-off. We're not recommitting to a lifelong friendship.

"Er . . ." I glance at River as they wait for our music selection. "There's this nineties song by Montell Jordan . . ."

Behind me, Aleah groans, annoyed.

River grins like they know which song I'm talking about.

As I walk toward Aleah, the recognizable timbre of Montell's voice declaring *This is how we do it* rings out in the bedroom. It's an anthem heard at almost every sporting event, old-school house party, or Black family reunion.

Aleah and I know it from another place, another time.

Back on Saturday nights when nineties Black comedies kept us up past bedtime. When Dad pushed the furniture in our living room around, then Mario would cue up a playlist of the songs he and Dad loved as teens. They'd teach us all the dances from the movies.

Unfortunately, Miles Wright's best move is the Carlton from *The Fresh Prince of Bel-Air.* So embarrassing. It never stopped Mario from laughing and pecking kisses to Dad's cheek when they thought we weren't looking.

Aleah and I giddily learned every step. We'd stay up even later, practicing on our own.

The song suddenly stops. The first chorus came and neither of us budged.

Makayla sips her drink, bored expression ruling her face.

"Any day now, you two."

"Aleah?" I try to force the apprehension from my voice.

The music begins again. She taps her foot to the melody. Reluctantly, she whispers, "On three . . ."

The smile curling my lips barely has time to reach full height before she's counting down.

"One . . . two . . . three!"

We start with something remedial: the Reebok, which is basically shuffling in place while our shoulders bounce. Then it's the Roger Rabbit. Soon, we're cycling through every dance we learned. I'm sweating, trying to match her. The hesitation is gone. We're in a groove. It's like we never missed five years' worth of steps.

I initiate our next dance: the Kid 'N Play. We can't leave it out. Aleah syncs with me, kick for kick. She adds her stank-face, which indicates she's really into it.

I'm caught off guard when she switches to another dance, one we've never performed outside my bedroom.

Almost every viral video I've seen paying tribute to *House Party* focuses on Kid 'N Play's dance sequence. It's iconic for a reason. As problematic as the movie is, I still go back to watch that scene, but not for them. Seconds before their big moment, Sydney and Sharane, the two love interests, outclass the guys. Only Aleah knows how obsessed I am with it. She'd cue up the movie on her phone. We perfected the whole routine in a single weekend.

A weird shame always prevented me from letting others watch me perform this routine. As if they'd think I'm wrong for liking the girls' routine over the boys'.

Now my eyes jump to Luca. He's bouncing in place on the carpet, grinning. He brushes hair off his forehead. Gold and pink light glitters off his black nails. I reject the humiliating sensation trying to creep into my muscles. All the lies people taught us about being a boy.

Why should anyone decide our limits of masculinity? Or femininity? Why can't we have both? Or neither? Why do I have to hate myself for liking things that don't fit into someone else's parameters?

Fuck those rules.

I sidle up to Aleah's side. Tonight's been *awful*. I don't have a date—or a way—to prom. There's undiscussed tension between me and Jay now. The least I can do is finally enjoy myself.

By the time the song ends, everyone is on their feet, cheering. Aleah's breathless and smirking. I'm buzzing.

"Nailed it!" Makayla shouts.

Luca whistles sharply.

An overwhelming wave of joy crashes on me when River lifts both our arms in the air like boxers after a heavyweight battle. "Winners!" they declare.

I can't help myself. I rush over to Aleah, wrapping her in my arms. "Hell yeah!" I say, caught in a laughter that feels never-ending.

But it does end.

"Get off me!" Aleah roars, jerking away. Our disengagement is clumsy, but her reflexes are quick. She stands stiffly by the door. "What the hell's wrong with you?"

I stutter, "I—uh."

"You what? Think we're cool again? Friends?"

A dry itchiness grabs my throat.

"That's over," Aleah says with the finality she never used when we were younger. Because I was the one saying it when I turned my back on her.

Why did I think I could suddenly undo the past?

"I'm *done*, do you hear me?" she seethes, her voice cracking at the edges. "No one else is gonna burn me. Never again."

# 13

# WHY ARE YOU HERE?

**"So . . ." Luca says** at the peak of my brutal stare-down with Aleah, "you two know-*know* each other."

Silence.

Frankly, I don't know *how* to reply.

"You were friends?" Makayla asks, gazing more at Aleah than me. When Aleah doesn't speak, she continues: "I've never seen you two interact before tonight. Which I guess isn't strange. Brook-Oak is huge. I don't recognize half the people I say hi to. But that performance you two just put on . . . you can't be total strangers."

The more Makayla talks, the more Aleah's hands tremble as she rubs her arms. She's a volcanic geyser waiting to erupt. And I have no escape route because Aleah's blocking the door.

"You're clearly not friends with his friends," Makayla says, snorting.

My head swivels in her direction. What does that mean? *His friends.* It's the second time she's taken a shot at TNT. What, are we talked about over hand-washing time at bathroom sinks? Are our names written in Sharpie across stalls?

"That also explains why Theo—"

Makayla stops when I shake my head so hard, I see stars.

Aleah doesn't need to know what happened with Lexi. She doesn't need to know I stood up for her. Or that Makayla didn't.

"God, let it go," hisses Aleah.

"Sorry, sorry." Makayla raises both hands in surrender. "Another sensitive topic for you."

"I don't know why I came here tonight!" Aleah groans. "Why are any of you hiding out in some kid's bedroom? What're you running from?"

Luca waves a hand around. "Hello, I'm the guy with the semi-viral video of his ex turning him down during a promposal." He pops a few gummies in his mouth, chewing angrily. "Said ex is downstairs, noticeably unfazed by my attempt to make her jealous with my new, *fake* girlfriend."

"Wow," says River, blinking back their awe. "That's a mouthful."

"That's what—"

Makayla smacks Luca's arm, hard. "Don't you dare finish that joke."

"Now we're getting somewhere," Aleah says, rubbing her hands together. "Who else?"

No one volunteers. I brush invisible lint off my T-shirt. I can feel everyone's eyes on me.

I already know Luca's story. River's too. To some degree, we all know Aleah's reasons. No offense, but I'm pretty confident

Makayla's here because of Luca. But none of them know why *I'm* here. Not the excuse that originally landed me in this bedroom—my *real* motive.

Carrying around the weight of your failures and mistakes is exhausting. The Christian thing. Prom. The uncertainty of where my friendship with Jay truly lies. I'm convinced I'll mess up The Plan next.

I'm going to fail Dad.

My bottom lip is raw by the time I lift my eyes. Expectant faces add another layer of tension to my muscles. I'm just so fucking tired.

"It was a dare," I exhale out. "I'm not *hiding*. I'm here because of a dare."

River's head tilts sideways. "A dare?"

Makayla says, "You mean those absurd stunts you and your friends pull on Fridays?"

I clutch my chest, fully affronted. Silly stunts? Absolutely. Reckless? Maybe. But absurd is a level of harshness TNT has yet to reach. Then again, I'm the one avoiding a crowded party of people who've most likely seen some version of Christian rejecting me online, so maybe Makayla's not that far off.

"They're not *all* silly," counters Luca, smiling up at me. "There's the one where you sang Mariah Carey."

"You saw that?"

"Who didn't?" He guffaws. "I was at the table next to yours. Front-row seat."

Mortification burns against my neck. Once again, I overlooked him in a group situation. How many times has he been in my periphery? Sitting so close to the margins, he's been blurred. Never fully in focus.

"I didn't see you," I whisper, unable to come up with anything better.

He shrugs nonchalantly, like it's a common thing.

But the more I think about it, how could anyone not notice a boy as genuine as Luca Ramírez?

"What was the dare?" River asks. The hesitance in their tone tells me it's more sincere curiosity than nosiness.

I sigh. "It was—"

"Oh, shit!" Makayla slumps back against the bed, eyes wide. "That's why you were asking Christian to prom, isn't it?"

She might as well have shoved a butcher knife into my gut with the way I nearly double over in pain.

"Christian?" Luca's eyes dart around. "As in Drumline Christian?"

"The one and only," Makayla says as I defeatedly flop onto the floor. *Sweet.* Now they all know. Theo Wright, king of asinine life choices.

"You wanted to ask . . . Christian?" Luca shoots me an indecipherable look.

"He has a boyfriend," comments Aleah, as if I needed that extra layer of embarrassment.

I pull my knees to my chest. "I didn't know," I whisper to my feet.

*Jay didn't tell me* sits on the tip of my tongue.

A new round of anger and confusion fuses to my marrow. Jay's like a bother. He couldn't—no, *wouldn't*—do that to me. What would be his motivation? Fine, he can be a dick about losing at video games or placing anything but first at a track meet. He's never gotten off on cruel public humiliation before. At least, not when it comes to Darren and me.

"So you're squatting in a bedroom because of a dare?" Aleah asks skeptically.

"I wanted to go to prom. Badly." I shrug awkwardly, still hugging my shins. My eyes close. I don't want to tell them the rest. But the pressure of everything else forces me to speak.

"The other reason is . . . I don't know where I stand with my friends right now."

In one long breath, I break down The Nameless Trio's history at Brook-Oak. The dares and what they did for us. How much we mean to each other. And how, more and more, I'm starting to see the ways we differ. I can't shake this obligation to keep things status quo, even though I know words like "obligation" shouldn't be associated with friendships.

I even mention the party being Jay's idea, which elicits a huff from Makayla and a pursed lips and eye roll combo from Aleah.

"It's been a shit-tastic Saturday."

I pinch a few of my twists between my thumb and forefinger, turning them clockwise, waiting for someone to call me out for being too melodramatic. When their silence is undercut by the party's music, I glance up.

No one's glaring at me. No signs of pity or disappointment. Only a few slow nods.

"I'm kind of hiding too," Makayla says. "I know what that

pressure's like. Maintaining the same relationships I've had since forever. Pretending like I don't have any shitty friendships when . . ." Her voice drifts.

I chew my lip, waiting.

Loose wavy hair falls in front of her face but doesn't cover the sad line of her mouth. The deep wrinkles around her eyes.

"It'd be great if just one of them said something when an asshole like Bryant calls me Swipe Right Mack," she says, a mild tremble in her voice. "If they didn't laugh it off. Like it's no big deal. I'll get over it, right?"

Makayla tugs on her hoodie like it's choking her.

"*Friends* are supposed to have each other's backs," she continues. "To be honest, I can't wait to graduate. Go to college. Get the hell away from them. Start over."

Behind her, Aleah teeters from foot to foot. Her eyes are wide, glassy, umber pools.

Makayla laughs weakly. "Which is ridiculous, since no one knows the real me anyway."

Everyone's quiet for a beat. Luca twists his rings. Aleah refuses to look at anyone. I crack my knuckles as Makayla's words settle in my chest. *Does anyone at Brook-Oak know the real me?*

"I do," River says eventually.

"What?"

"@ReadingByLaw, right?" River flashes an Instagram account on their phone. The grid is all aesthetically beautiful photos of book spines and colorful stacks and covers hiding a blond girl reading.

There are a few scattered images of the account's owner—Makayla.

"How'd you find that?" she asks, blinking hard.

"We've met. Kind of," replies River, smiling. "A year ago, at Epilogues. Nic Stone's new-book release party. You probably don't remember." They shrug in that self-conscious way I do when no one else in the room knows what I'm rambling about.

Makayla's eyes light up. "You had longer hair?"

River's face wrinkles, smile intact. "Ugh. Yeah."

"You took our photo? Nic and me?"

River nods, then brings up the image. Makayla standing with a brown-skinned woman wearing a popping shade of blue lipstick.

"Wait—you're a book blogger?" Aleah asks, head cocked sideways.

"Bookstagrammer," Makayla confirms sheepishly.

"You've never mentioned that."

"When do any of us ever talk about our lives outside of Brook-Oak? It's only relationships or the occasional hookups." There's something accusing in her voice. Like she knows what parts of Aleah are only shown for the Brook-Oak crowd and what she's keeping close to her chest.

I wonder if Aleah's ever told Lexi—anyone—about life at home. Her dad or Uncle Mario. Her mom.

"Everyone's different at school. Who's interested in a girl secretly sitting at home on Friday nights reading teen rom-coms?" huffs Makayla.

"That's low-key judgmental, don't you think?" I say.

"It's the truth."

"Bullshit." I shake my head. "You don't know if anyone would like you any less if they knew you were into that. Also, is life that hard for you? Being at the top?"

"I thought you liked the attention," Luca confesses, shrugging one shoulder.

"You mean *this*?" Makayla thrusts her phone screen in our faces. "Getting this shit every day? That's not attention. It's fucking . . ."

Again, her voice dies, but in a broken whimper. A choked death that doesn't require a follow-up. The words on the screen are enough.

Comments on her main Instagram page. DM after DM. Screenshots of text messages. A compilation of the foulest, grossest, most unrestrained sexual commentary I've ever seen. Most of it from a host of fuckboys—some recognizable from their bite-size profile pictures, others merely anonymous, probably fake accounts.

I try to swallow down the bile racing up my throat as I read.

It's one thing to see these things play out on TV. I've never known anyone in real life dealing with it.

Watching Makayla's breaths come fast and frustrated, her eyes on the brink of tears, shakes me.

"Why don't you go private?" I ask around the nausea.

Aleah *pffts* loudly. "Why should she have to?"

"For protection?" I offer, unsure if that's the right word.

It's clearly not. Aleah's face darkens.

"Oh, that's right! Girls should hide in order to be safe. Keep their lives private or suffer the consequences for being themselves.

We should 'protect' ourselves." Even her air quotes are threatening. "While boys get to, what? Exist unchecked? Free balling, no worries, mansplaining on level ten because the patriarchy is real, y'all! Fucking deal with it."

"That's not what I'm saying."

"It *is*," Makayla argues.

"We have to hide for safety . . ." Aleah drags a finger between me and Luca. "Instead of boys like you speaking up when this shit happens. Stop co-signing your vile-as-fuck brethren with your silence."

Luca and I don't have the words to defend ourselves. But is that what I'm doing? Defending instead of listening?

I suck in my lower lip, nodding.

"It only took one boy to start all of this," says Makayla. "Sam Bailey."

I barely recognize the name. A faceless, trophy-winning, former jock at BOHS pops up in my head.

"Well, two boys," Makayla amends. "Sam and Cole Nelson."

It takes everything inside me not to react.

Cole. Jay's SpeedEx buddy, Cole.

Makayla gives us the abridged version of where her—degrading, undeserved—nickname originated. Her sophomore year, at a similar party. She and Sam Bailey hooked up. Completely casual. Then Sam bragged to his best friend, Cole, who *liked* Makayla. She knew but wasn't interested. Naturally, that means Makayla broke some form of "bro code" by having sex with Sam. Cole and Sam started telling people Makayla had sex with both of them. She was "that girl at a party who liked to have fun."

"Because being sexual or enjoying intimacy is wrong for anyone who's not a cis man," she says, sighing. "But for them, it's cool. Acceptable. No slut-shaming involved."

It's true. The countless times my teammates have bragged about their sex lives to applause, jokes, or stunned awe runs through my mind. No dragging. No derogatory name-calling. Not a peep about how if it was coming from someone who didn't identify as a man, the responses would be different.

Much different.

It's hard to stomach more of Makayla's story. The way two boys become four. Then ten. Twenty-five. Guys she's never spoken to outside of a quick, meaningless hello are suddenly people she's messed around with.

"The part that gets me every fucking time," she says, laughing sadly, "is the girls who call me Swipe Right Mack. Girls I don't even know."

Her eyes peek toward Aleah. Guilt mixes with the frustration in her expression.

"The ones I'm friends with."

Aleah and I simultaneously swallow. I can't imagine the Aleah I knew using such a gross nickname.

"I'd never call you that," River says.

"Thank you," Makayla whispers, tucking strands of hair behind her ear.

"Is that why you got pissed when I left you downstairs?" Luca inquires.

"Random dudes approach me all the time. Ask me to blow them or, worse, touch me without permission," Makayla replies.

Luca looks as remorseful as Aleah did a second ago.

Makayla's eyes are glistening, but she never lets a single tear fall.

Is that what we're all doing tonight? Being strong? Refusing to let the world crush us completely?

"I never called you that either," I swear. "I never meant to let others hurt you."

I don't know what's worse: that this is Makayla's reality or that I never did anything to change it.

How many times has Jay called her Swipe Right Mack? Too many.

How many times did I confront him about it? Not enough.

"They never do." Makayla mimics me—knees pulled to her chest, arms cradling her shins. She sniffles while looking at all of us. "Maybe reconsider the friends you keep."

I think about what Makayla said earlier. Feeling more committed to your history with someone than the actual relationship. My friendship with Jay is complicated. But is that enough to walk away?

*Can* I walk away? Our families celebrate holidays together. Then there's the track team. Summers at Sonic. The dares. So many things connecting us. Places where I'd see him.

How long have I pretended to only see the Jay I want versus the one that's right in front of me?

I'm grateful for the Jay who brings me energy bars. Posts sentimental shit on my birthday. But how can I ignore the Jay who casually slut-shames Makayla? The same Jay who couldn't warn me about Christian having a boyfriend before I made a total ass out of myself?

I bite hard on my lip. Tears sting my eyes. I hold them in.

What about the Duke recommendation letter from Mr. Scott? What about Dad? If The Plan wasn't such a big factor in my future, would this be easier? Is one silly letter really what's holding me back? Or is it something else?

Aleah pivots toward River. "What about you? I know coming out's a big deal, but . . ." Her index finger taps the name tag stuck to her chest. "Seems like tonight's bigger than just *this*."

River rocks in place. Tiny, multicolored feathers from the boa are stuck to the ends of their hair.

"Hey," Luca says, breaking the silence twisting over our heads like a vicious ghost. He squints at Aleah. "You never answered your own question."

I smile, wondering if he knew what I was thinking: *River hates this kind of attention.*

"Why are *you* here?"

Aleah crosses her arms. She's managing to maintain an invisible force field, keeping us all out, but the edges are cracking. Her resolve's fading.

Her next words are drowned out by a wave of music, the bedroom flooded with hallway light as the door opens.

"Finally! We've been looking everywhere for you!"

# 14

# SINCERELY YOURS, THE EDIBLES CLUB

**I stare blankly** at the two people huddled in the doorway. It's hard not to. They're scolding the half-empty bottle of Jim Beam whiskey Makayla procured from the kitchen like it's a toddler. One is tall, gangly, and has a snapback sitting crookedly on a bed of brown curls. The other is short with shockingly red hair and ghostly pale skin, and is wearing what can only be described as a grandma-knitted sweater. They're like something out of a bad, drunken dream.

Aleah stands between the two new space invaders and the bottle.

"Who the hell are y'all?"

A clumsy, giggly explanation ensues. They're Jamari, the tall Black boy, and Courtney, grandma-sweater wearer. Freshmen. High as hot-air balloons, thanks to the baggie of gummy bear edibles

Jamari's clutching. As it turns out, to elevate their current euphoria, they'd been sneaking shots from the very bottle they're now staring adoringly at.

"We've been looking everywhere for her," Jamari says, his eyes soft and reddening by the second.

"Him," Courtney corrects.

"Them," chirps River, smiling anxiously.

That alone sends Jamari and Courtney into another fit of loud, gasping laughter. Whatever is in those gummies could mellow out an army of Aleah Birds.

"We're also looking for a place to finish off these babies," Jamari announces, shaking the baggie like a set of keys to a brand-new Bugatti.

Luca's face wrinkles. "Aren't you only supposed to eat one of those?"

Jamari says, "Technicalities are a scam."

"More like medically proven facts to keep you from, I don't know, overdosing," Makayla says, bundling her hair up into a loosely knotted bun. "I'm not *Pulp Fiction*–ing anyone tonight."

"What?" Jamari and Luca say in unison.

Before Makayla can launch into a rant, Courtney ambles into the room, smiling weirdly. She has huge, green-gold eyes and a pug nose. "Would you consider bargaining for the return of our new friend?"

"No," Aleah snaps just as Makayla says, "What're the terms of your negotiation?"

I rub impatiently at my eyes. Once again, *my*—technically River's—sacred space is being overtaken by unwanted interlopers.

"A few of these . . ." Courtney jerks her head toward the baggie. She drops her voice into a creepy, raspy tone, rubbing her hands together. "In exchange for the *precious*."

Aleah cautiously steps back, clearly missing the Gollum reference.

(Thank you, Jacobs family, for inviting me to suffer through a marathon of the Lord of the Rings trilogy.)

"Wait!" Jamari shouts, gauchely spinning to face Aleah. "I know you!"

River says, "She's Aleah Bird, star point guard for the Brook-Oak Ballers" with the kind of pride a parent has when discussing their child's achievements with the neighbors.

"Former," whispers Aleah so quietly and dejectedly, I don't think anyone else hears it. But I do.

"No, no, no." I'm shocked Jamari's snapback doesn't fly off with the aggressiveness of his head shake. "That's not it. I don't do sportsball."

"I play soccer," Courtney chimes, for no reason at all.

"You're the girl who broke up Delexi," says Jamari, snapping his fingers while smirking. His ability to multitask is respectable considering his current state.

Also, I'm not a fan of the whole ship-names thing. These are real people I go to school with. Not characters from a fanfic on the internet.

Courtney shoots Jamari a puzzled expression. "Aren't we calling them Lerek?"

"*You* called them Lerek," corrects Jamari. "The rest of the school named them Delexi. She's the—"

"The nobody," Aleah spits, her jaw tense. "Nobody to you or anyone else who doesn't mind their own damn business."

A *yikes* expression pinches Luca's face, but Jamari giggles and nods, looking more impressed than frightened.

"Yo, I love that about you," he says as if he's known Aleah for more than five seconds. "The way you low-key choose violence all the time. Respect. I heard you whooped Derek's ass for telling Lexi about the hookup."

"No shit, I heard the same thing!" Courtney says excitedly. "Aleah, girl, is all the hot goss true? What happened with Lexi?"

You know that feeling before a thunderstorm? The way the gray starts to devour the blue from the sky. The silence before the first crackle. The metallic taste at the back of your throat. Everything smells fresh and alive.

This is that moment.

Aleah's eyes widen. Her head slowly tilts sideways like a possessed child in a horror movie. Hands curling into fists. Her chest expands. Tiny exhales exit her flared nostrils.

I contemplate stopping her, then remember I have no desire to be on the receiving end of her wrath.

"Actually," Makayla says loudly as Aleah's left foot scoots forward.

Her dad used to box. Taught her to spar before she learned to write in cursive.

"How about we take these," Makayla continues, swiping the baggie from Jamari. "And you two can return to the hellish corner you spawned from without me informing Chloe two *freshmen* are at her party, uninvited. Okay?"

"But—!" Courtney starts to say.

Jamari hooks an arm around her waist, easing them backward. "Message received," he says, chin cocked defensively. "If you want to play the narc card, go 'head. We'll find other friends."

They're halfway into the hall when River scrambles to their feet, calling out, "Hey!"

Courtney and Jamari freeze.

"Do you two have a ride home?" River wonders. "Do you need a sober buddy's number? In case you . . ."

I recognize the hiccup in River's speech. Their nervous tics like fidgeting with their bracelets.

Courtney and Jamari share a calculated look. It lasts about three seconds before they crack up. Their laughter echoes down the hall as they leave.

Makayla kicks the door closed. "Assholes." She lets out a long sigh. It's almost as if she's exhaling the breath we've been collectively holding all night. A smile splits her lips. She jiggles the baggie above her head.

"Who's down for some real fun?"

It doesn't take long for us to return to our circle on the floor. River tries their hand at mixing drinks. Aleah immediately chugs whatever they've concocted. Either it's good or she's looking for a quick mind wipe of the last ten minutes. Maybe the entire night.

I can't say I blame her.

Makayla distributes the edibles among us. I decline. Luca does too, which gives me this fuzzy, loopy feeling in my stomach. For all I know he's allergic to THC. Still, my heart adds another checkmark in the Reasons Luca and Me Are Compatible list.

Hell, I didn't realize I started a list.

Aleah's two drinks in, clearly out to escape the earlier tension, when she suggests we play Never Have I Ever. We're all buzzing in some way, growing exceedingly comfortable in our hideaway. Luca's giggling between sips. Makayla, shoes off, hair down again, leans against River, who's vibing to the playlist streaming from my phone. I'm on a sugar high, reaching for another cookie when Aleah throws out the first statement.

"Never have I ever deleted a social media post because it didn't get enough likes."

"No fair!" groans Makayla, tipping up her cup.

"Basic, party of one," teases Aleah.

We all explode with laughter.

"Fine." Makayla shakes out her hair. "Never have I ever been late to class . . ."

Everyone begins to raise their cups, grinning.

". . . for an emergency poop."

Aleah flashes Makayla a middle finger as she slurps loudly. Luca and I join her, avoiding eye contact. I know he's smiling embarrassedly just like I am.

"Taco Tuesday in the cafeteria is no joke," grumbles Aleah.

We trade off like that for a few rounds, laughing and drinking and gasping at the quiet revelations. Anything goes. From school stuff—*"Never have I ever faked an illness to get out of a test"*—to the spicy—*"Never have I given or received oral"*—to the questionable—*"Never have I ever gone forty-eight hours without showering."*

River hiccup-giggles after I take a nonchalant sip of my OJ. It was only *once*. Away meets while having to pull all-nighters for bonus-point quizzes lead to some very suspect hygiene choices.

"Never have I ever . . ." River taps their chin, thinking. "Never have I ever done any landscaping *down there* to impress someone!"

*Fuckfuckfuck.*

So maybe—a big maybe—I thought something was going to happen between me and Runner Boy at one of those track-meet rendezvous. Other than the usual spit exchanging before he went ghost again. Preparation is key, right?

Thankfully, as I raise my cup, three others join me. Makayla shrugs it off. Aleah keeps her eyes lowered. Luca's cheeks are brighter than the fairy lights above us.

He shoots me a wry smile. "Never have I ever serenaded anyone."

I moan, gulping more juice. My bladder might not survive another round.

"To be fair," he whispers to me as Aleah interrogates Makayla drinking too, "you did Mariah proud."

I wish I could blame my lightheadedness on alcohol, but I'm completely sober. Yet everything inside me feels wasted. In a not-Jell-O-shots-related, good way.

I clear my throat. "Never have I ever kissed a friend!"

Luca takes a long swig.

My eyes scan around. River frowns down at their cup, their fingers squeezing so tightly, the edges crunch loudly. I'm only distracted from them when Makayla pinches Aleah as she discreetly swallows.

"What? Who? When?"

Makayla throws out questions like a red-carpet reporter trying to find out what designer Aleah's wearing.

"It doesn't concern you," Aleah mumbles.

"Is it—?"

"Ugh, fuck this," Aleah interrupts her. "Never have I ever broken a friend's heart."

Silence wraps an iron grip on the room. Even my phone has decided to stop playing music. Every breath I hear is my own. Swallowing hurts as I register the entire group's staring at me.

In my dreams, sometimes, I imagine this day. When I'd be sitting across from Aleah. No one else around. I've thought of a hundred different ways to phrase "I'm sorry" that didn't sound weak or pathetic or excusatory. And in every dream, she'd forgive me.

But the longer she glares at me, I realize nothing I say will fix what I did.

At the very least, I owe her the truth.

"I fucked up our friendship," I admit. My heavy frown makes it impossible to hold my chin high. "My pops was hurting so bad when your uncle left."

Arms crossed over her chest, she waits. She wants more.

Sighing, I say, "We were at Kroger. Two weeks after the breakup. You were there too. With your dad, I think." My breaths are shallow, painful inside my lungs. "The look on his face when he saw you— it was like he was looking at a ghost. He had tears in his eyes. I couldn't handle it. *He* couldn't handle it."

"So . . . you tossed me aside." It's not a question.

"No." I hesitate, rubbing the back of my neck. "Yes, but not like that."

"Like what, then, Theo?" Aleah snaps. "How do you call a *friend* who did nothing wrong to tell them you don't want to see them anymore? That you'd moved on."

"I—"

"And then you ignore their existence. Never look their way. How is that not tossing them in the trash?"

Luca shifts next to me when I plead loudly, "My pops is all I had!"

"You had a fucking friend!"

It's true. I had Aleah. I had Jay. By then, Darren was in the picture too. But Granny was gone. Every day I went home, the only person waiting for me was Dad. I never felt less important to him. Like I had to compete with Mario in the picture. But after Granny died and Mario left, I don't know. I became his *everything*.

I just wanted him to know he was mine too.

"You don't understand," I whisper.

Fuck. I never wanted to do this in front of an audience. Never wanted six pairs of eyes watching me sniff and stutter over words as I explain what a total asshole I've been.

"No," Aleah argues. "This isn't about your dad. Or just you. A friendship has two people."

"I know, I know."

"You clearly don't."

The hairs on my forearms stand up. My body knows the next question before she asks it.

"Was your dad and Uncle Mario's relationship the only reason we were friends?" Her voice catches, but there are no cracks in her stiff expression. No tears brimming in her eyes like mine.

"N-no!" I swallow. "It wasn't."

But was it? Is that all my closest relationships are? An extension of one of Dad's relationships? Aleah and I met because of Dad and Mario. Mrs. Scott and Dad's friendship created the one I have with Jay. Every piece of who I am in this city is because of Miles Wright.

Maybe it really is time to leave.

Maybe I should be like Makayla—ready to start over somewhere free of the things Dad broke and ended and left me to carry on with.

"You believe me, right?" I ask Aleah.

A hard eye roll is the only answer I receive.

In every one of those dreams, I'd tell her what I did wrong. The things I told my pops so he'd stop asking where she was. Not having the guts to talk about what was going on with Dad in person. She'd think it over. Nod along, like she understood. Like she'd never want Mario to hurt the way Dad did. We wouldn't hug, but she'd forgive me.

She wouldn't look at me like she does right now.

Like I'm not even worth hating.

I'm nothing to her.

"You two couldn't be friends at school?" asks River.

"We were twelve," I say, almost exasperated. "We didn't even go to the same school."

We saw each other whenever Mario came over or at church. But she stopped attending. The breakup was barely cold before Mario left. He was Aleah's ride everywhere. Her dad's schedule was too hectic, and he was never close enough with my pops for Dad to reach out.

It's what's made parts of the past five years easy. I never had to see Aleah after ending our friendship. Not until freshman year at Brook-Oak.

"Besides," I say to River, "I didn't want to feel like we had to hide our friendship from my pops."

River's eyebrows slant like they don't believe me.

Thing is, as much as I want, I'm not sure that's the truth either.

This has been my dirty secret for years:

When Dad finally asked why I stopped spending hours on the phone with Aleah, I lied.

*She's busy with new friends. She's moved on.*

It was the first time in weeks Dad hadn't spent his nights crying after he thought I went to bed. I didn't want to bring up Mario's name. Didn't want to admit I ditched Aleah for him. For both of us. I didn't want to tell him I was still confused about whether I'd done the right thing.

Because, at the time, it *had to be* the right thing. Dad was getting better every day. I couldn't put him through all of that again.

*Oh, baby boy.* He'd kissed my forehead. *I know how that feels.*

I knew he was talking about Mario.

*I have Jay. And Darren,* I told him. *And you.*

It was enough to make him smile and drop the subject. He ordered pizza. We watched the Transformers movies. He kept me tucked under his arm the whole time. Never once did we acknowledge the other one sniffling at the funniest scenes.

Now I roll and unroll my T-shirt sleeves, trying to buy myself time. The right words are so far out of reach, they might as well exist in another galaxy.

"I'm sorry, Aleah," I finally say, voice cracking. "I'm really, really sorry."

"No, you're not," she disputes, recoiling when my hand reaches out. "Sorry would've came the day after you stopped talking to me. Sorry would've came the first day of school at Brook-Oak. The first time you saw me in the halls. Anytime before tonight."

When I glance around, River avoids eye contact. Makayla's mouth is pulled sideways like she's disappointed. Luca chews on his lip.

"Sorry shouldn't come *after* you've been called out," Aleah adds. "That's not an apology. It's guilt."

She's right. I am guilty. For five years, guilt has walked next to me like a replacement best friend. A hologram of the person who would've never made the choices I made.

How can I be hurt by any offense Jay's ever committed when I've done all of this to Aleah?

"Wow," says Makayla softly. "That got . . ."

"Heavy?" Luca offers.

She nods. "Anyone else want to drink to that?"

Out the corner of my eye, I see River take a sip. Luca's mouth opens like he's about to ask them who's heart they broke, but I'm hit with a thought.

"You didn't drink," I tell Aleah.

"What?"

"'Never have I ever broken a friend's heart.'" I repeat her statement. "What happened with Lexi? Wasn't she *your* best friend?"

Aleah blinks for a beat. She's processing how to answer the question. Finally, she flops back onto the floor, shoulders slouched.

I recognize this pose. The weight of something finally bringing you to your knees.

She whispers, "We hooked up."

"You and Derek?" Luca asks, scandalized.

"No." She grimaces. "Me and Lexi."

"Oh." Luca says the word while my lips can only form the letter.

Another fact about Aleah Bird I didn't know—she's queer. Like me.

I wonder if, back when we were two kids sitting in the pews, she was figuring things out like I was. Maybe she already knew.

What would my life have been like if I had a queer best friend instead of two straight friends? Someone who faced the same issues I did. Who knew exactly what I was thinking when Jay and Darren didn't.

Aleah's brow wrinkles. She picks at already chipped blue nail polish on her thumb. "I don't know when it started. The flirting. I'd kind of liked her for forever, but . . . I didn't think she noticed."

Even though she's not looking, I nod.

"She'd joke around about kissing sometimes." Aleah laughs hollowly. "We were always wasted, so I never let anything go down."

Makayla slips an arm around her shoulders. "It happened on the tourney trip, didn't it?"

Aleah tips her head toward the ceiling, fighting tears. They come. Slow at first. A winding trail on her left cheek, then right.

"She kissed me. Then I kissed her. And we kept . . . We weren't even drunk!" A choked noise breaks free. "The next morning, she denied everything. Said, 'I'm not like you! I have a boyfriend! I'm not supposed to do this.' We argued and screamed for a while.

Next thing I know, her and Derek are over, we lose the game, and everyone blamed me."

As quick as it came, Aleah shrugs off Makayla's arm. Scoots away. "Even my *friends* decided I was at fault."

Makayla sheepishly drops her chin.

"And you took it because you didn't want to out her," I say quietly.

More tears dribble down Aleah's chin. She doesn't wipe them away. Her hands are shaking in her lap.

"Why couldn't she just admit she felt the same?" She inhales sharply. "Why do the people I love keep rejecting me?"

It's the first time our eyes meet. There's no wrath behind hers. Only sadness. Someone tired of being repeatedly broken.

"My mom. Lexi." Her bottom lip trembles. "You."

"I—"

The *I'm sorry* almost kisses my lips again. I hold it in. I know she doesn't want it.

"Aleah," Makayla tries, cautiously inching a hand forward. "It's all talk. What happened with Lexi isn't a big deal. People at Brook-Oak are like goldfish. They'll move on to the next thing soon."

The vexation returns to Aleah's face. "No, they won't. You of all people know that!"

"It's different with you."

"Ha!" I'm startled by the noise coming from my own throat. I can't believe what I'm hearing. "You think it's easier for her? For *us*?"

Makayla looks confused.

"No disrespect to your sitch at school, but it's not like that for us," I say, wiggling a finger between Aleah and me.

Aleah nods. Despite what's happened, we still share more commonalities than differences. One of them being Black teens from poor-to-average families at a school trying to be woke, but constantly failing.

"Black students at Brook-Oak have to be twice as good at everything just to get by," Aleah says patiently. She's clearly given this speech to every white friend she's ever had. "We need to be star athletes *and* the top of our classes. Kind *and* accepting. The moment we step out of line, it's a wrap. We don't get second chances."

"No matter how good we are, we're still 'lucky' to be there," I add, fighting off the wobble in my voice. "It's never enough for—"

I stop short. Would they even understand what I want to say?

"My pops," I finally whisper. "I love him so much, but he has goals for me. So many . . ."

"Expectations?" offers Luca.

I nod slowly. That's what it is, isn't it? An expectation. Something I have to live up to.

"I can't let him down after he's worked so hard to give me a future," I admit. "How am I supposed to function if I disappoint him?"

It's wholly self-pressure, I know. Dad's never explicitly said he'd disown me if I don't get into Duke. He's not the type of parent to hang something over your head for long. Not like the Scotts do to Jay. But the look in his eyes whenever I win a race. Ace a test. Accomplish anything on The Plan's checklist.

A twinkling, enthusiastic *I'm so proud* gleam appears. As if I'm the son he's always dreamed of. I'm everything he never got to be.

"We'll never be the flawless kids our parents imagine," says River.

Luca stretches his legs out, crosses an ankle over mine. I let it rest there comfortably.

"Disappointing the adults in our lives is part of being a teen," says Makayla, winking.

I chomp on a cookie. Nothing they say absolves what I'm feeling about Dad. But at least I'm not alone.

Aleah lifts her cup. "Never have I ever cried so much in one night." She takes a huge gulp, then wipes snot on her shirtsleeve. "Sorry."

We all laugh, toasting and chugging.

Again, it's Aleah who makes the next suggestion: "Let's get out of here. This room. This damn party. I need *real* food, less drama."

"Same," I say.

Immediately, Makayla offers her car keys to me. The DD title lives on. I don't mind. Any reason to keep our little crew together.

We clean up the snacks. Gather up the Monopoly pieces. Put Maddie's bedroom back together as best we can.

At the door, we all hesitate at the idea of facing the party again.

I step into the hallway first.

Thankfully, I'm still not alone.

# 15

# THIS IS OUR NIGHT

**When I was** younger, I had a minor candy obsession. Light emphasis on *minor*. I couldn't resist those individually wrapped Jolly Ranchers. Specifically, the green apple ones. Granny, with her bottomless tote bag always in her lap, was my enabler.

She had an infinite supply of Jolly Ranchers swimming beneath Kleenex and cosmetics and loose change.

She also had one strict rule: *Never before dinner, TJ.*

It was fine by me. It meant she'd tuck a piece in my palm at least twice during church services on Sundays or on long car rides with her and Dad. Under no circumstances did I break her rule.

Except that one time.

We were at a corner store, Granny and me. Dad was busy grocery shopping for dinner. Granny needed a brand of spice she could only find at Warner's Stop & Stock.

Since Granny was his favorite customer, the hairy, brawny clerk behind the counter always happily escorted her around, showing off all the new products while filling her tiny cart with supplies we definitely hadn't planned to get. I stayed near the front, impatiently biting my nails, counting down until I was back home with a TV and something delicious to eat.

Then my eyes spotted a treasure on the front counter.

A plastic jar stuffed to the brim with Jolly Ranchers. A euphoric rainbow within reach. Allowance was scarce those days. There was no way Granny was going to buy me candy so close to dinner.

The clerk was talking his head off between aisles. It was just the three of us in the store. All I had to do was stand on my tiptoes and swipe a piece.

No one noticed.

Not Granny while purchasing her special spices—and a few additional items.

Not Dad when I spent extra minutes in the bathroom as he cooked, savoring the tartness of the candy.

I'd gotten away with it . . . until bedtime.

Granny sat down on my bed, like always, ready to tuck me in. Her expression was tight. She didn't sing to me that night. Instead, she huffed and shook her head and lectured me.

The next day, we walked back to the corner store. The scene of the crime. She paid for what I stole, then made me apologize. Through tears and snot, I stuttered out words. All I remember is Granny's humiliated expression. The *hurt*.

I'd broken her trust.

That day, I learned clean getaways don't exist. There's always someone or something waiting on the other side.

I'd almost forgotten that lesson. But tonight?

Tonight refuses to let me walk away from *anything* without consequence.

The party's still raging as I nudge through the crowd. Luca's right behind me. River, Aleah, and Makayla follow closely. Early-aughts hip-hop booms through the rooms. The smell of tequila and chlorine and sweat coats the air.

We're almost to the front door.

It's my own fault we don't make it, though. Peeking down at my phone, I scroll through my messages. Where the hell is Darren? I've texted. Even dropped a **wtf D???** in the WhatsApp group chat. Nothing. I'm okay with leaving Jay behind to clear my head for a few hours—I'll be back to make sure he gets home safely—but I don't want Darren to think I abandoned him.

Not like he did to me hours ago.

Eyes on my screen, I don't notice the body in the doorway until I nearly collide with it.

With Jay.

I freeze, jaw tight, fingers curling to fists. I'm not going to hit him. But the desire to is bubbling to the surface.

"Theoooooo!" he says like yesterday in the quad, this time with a giddy, slurring voice. "Bro, where've you been? You went all Pac-Man on me?"

I flex an eyebrow.

He giggles. "Ghost! Like Pac-Man. You went . . . uh, ghost." He even adds the corny video game sound effects.

Now I want to punch him.

Laying out my best friend for failing to inform me my crush

has a boyfriend is one thing. Me, a Black boy, throttling Jay, a financially secure and connected white boy, in a public setting is another thing. The risk isn't worth it. *He's drunk*, I tell myself. A half-assed excuse, but it's enough to keep my fists at my sides.

I'm unresponsive to his joke, keeping a manageable distance between us.

Jay rears back with an affronted expression. Message received. Good. His dark brown eyebrows lower. Threads of blond hair fall from his topknot into his eyes. His round jaw works in a small circle like he's chewing on words.

"What's wrong?"

*You.* I almost say it. "Nothing," I grit out.

"Then let's go find D and—"

I don't budge when his hand touches my shoulder, then falls away. "I'm actually gonna head out."

He peers past me. I can tell when he clocks Luca and River. His left eyebrow arches, then curiosity pulls at his cheeks, which means he's probably seen Makayla with us. The wrinkles around his eyes deepen and he sniffs, looking unnerved when he finds the final face in our group.

"What's the deal, bro?" Jay says. "You're making some questionable choices tonight."

I'm not sure if it's the alcohol, Jayla's influence, or the real Jay talking.

"Could definitely make some better ones," I comment.

He blinks, confused again.

It's the same way he looked outside by the pool.

The dam that's been threatening to break all night finally

reaches capacity. Anger races uncontrollably under my skin. How can he pretend to not know what I'm talking about? I never thought I'd get to this point with Jay. We've always pissed each other off over the smallest things, then got over it. It's the cycle of friend-ships. But none of this feels small anymore.

"Theo, what the h—"

"Save it," I interrupt. "I'm not gonna stand by while you shit-talk people who don't deserve it. Not like you did earlier."

"Wh-what?" His face flushes a deep pink. "What're you—"

I cut him off again. "Cole. I heard him at SpeedEx, *bro*. The whole thing. You didn't say shit to defend me."

His silence is another cut down the center of my chest.

"It's bad enough I let all the microaggressions pass. All the toxic bullshit." I shiver thinking about the things I let go unchecked in the locker rooms. On the bus rides to and from meets. "But I'm not letting you slick drag Aleah just 'cause you're Jayson fucking Scott, some untouchable commodity at Brook-Oak."

"Where is all this coming from?" Jay's voice breaks a little. He's surprised. He leans closer, dropping his voice to ask, "Is this about the dare?"

Eyes are falling on us from everywhere. In my periphery, a crowd's forming. I think someone's phone is out. We'll be a hashtag in no time.

"You knew damn well Christian had a boyfriend, didn't you?" I hiss. My gaze bounces around the room. God, I hope Christian's not watching.

Jay's Adam's apple bobs. "No." He shakes his head. "I didn't know."

I squint at him. "I saw you two talking."

"I was making conversation." He laughs shakily. "You know me! I'm friendly!"

No. I *thought* I knew him. I thought Jay would always have my back. He'd never hide something hurtful from me. He'd never be what I was to Aleah—a coward.

"We were just . . . chatting," he continues. "Swear I didn't know before tonight."

The air flees my lungs. My mind replays the end of his sentence. "What do you mean 'before tonight'?"

Jay's lips are a thin line, unmoving.

"*When* did you know?"

He stays quiet. Whispers around us are gaining volume. Crimson floods his skin, from his hairline to his collarbones.

"Fuck, Theo," he exhales, trying to scoot closer. I step back. He holds up pleading hands. "I wouldn't do that to you." He runs a hand down his sweaty face. "I want you to be happy!"

I study him for a moment. Something's not adding up. I don't even care if he's being honest at this point. This isn't just about the dare.

Through my teeth, I ask, "Do you?"

"Bro." He sighs, eyes on the ceiling. "Yes."

When he stares at me, it's the Jay from that throwback Instagram post. From freshman year. From more than a decade of friendship.

"And I *did* stand up for you to Cole. You heard me, right?"

Yeah, I heard him. *Theo's chill, I swear.* But was that enough? It doesn't feel like it.

I chew the inside of my cheek.

"You've been my bro all my life," he continues. "I wouldn't let someone talk shit about you being gay. When you came out, who was right there? Taking you out for pizza. Shouting about it all on Insta."

*Jay and Darren. TNT. My boys.*

The fists at my sides tremble. My muscles are fighting against each other. The anger currently living inside me is battling the tug of nostalgia.

"You've never said anything before now," Jay points out.

Now I stand silently.

"Just . . . come back to the party with me and D." He reaches for me. "We can talk it out. Or chill. Namaste and all that shit. We came here for a good time, remember?"

I do. We came here to unwind. The Nameless Trio being ourselves. At least, that's how it should've been. Instead, I came here to complete a dare. To ask a boy to prom. Prove to everyone I could get the W.

Prove it to Jay.

"Nah," I say hoarsely.

"Nah?" Jay snaps back, sudden annoyance tightening his expression.

I shake my head. I don't want to pretend this is okay. What he's done is okay. Over my shoulder, I smile at the four anxious people waiting on me. The ones I have nothing to prove to.

To Jay, I say, "I'm gonna take a break."

"A break from what?"

"You," I say, unbothered by his large, infuriated eyes. "TNT. Everything."

I don't hear whatever Jay spews as I brush by him. Only the erratic rhythm of my heart. The pulse of dance-pop drowning out my anger. It's one thing to have the spotlight in the middle of the quad for a ridiculous dare. I don't want any added attention for walking away from my best friend.

Halfway down the stone walkway, a chorus of "Mack! Mack! Mack!" catches up to us.

Outside the Campbells' residence isn't as bad as I thought it'd be. Empty White Claws decorate the lawn. Sporadic groups take selfies. Someone's underwear hangs on a bush. A flush-faced, curly-haired kid is busy talking to a rock.

Nothing too out of the ordinary other than the mini-squad of cheerleaders who've stopped us.

Jayla struts forward like a queen bee emerging from the hive. She gently squeezes Makayla's shoulder. "Hey." Her smile is honey-sweet, her tongue poison-tipped. "Are you leaving?"

Makayla's eyes bounce from us to them. She half shrugs.

"Come on, Mack." Jayla's pouty face has been frequently effective when used against Jay in the past. Makayla seems equally susceptible. "We were gonna team up for a game of flip cup. Girls versus boys." Jayla's eyes flicker to Makayla's name tag, then River's. The crinkle between her brows is a blink-and-you'll-miss-it moment, but I spot it. "We need your steadiness. Your leadership."

All of Jayla's drones nod in unison.

Makayla chews her lip. Out here, the air's damp and warm, but her arms curl around her midsection like it's freezing. Her gaze wanders over Luca.

He frowns.

"We have to stick together, Mack." Jayla's attention is aimed at Aleah. Lexi's nowhere in sight, but the aftereffects of their fallout are still felt.

It takes extreme restraint not to unload on her like I did on Jay. But this isn't my fight.

When Aleah turns away, Jayla smirks. "You're staying, right," she says to Makayla.

It's not a question. More like an ultimatum disguised as a request.

Makayla's mouth opens like she might say something. Truthfully? Her silence earlier said it all. She's not going anywhere.

"Let's go," I mumble.

A second later, Luca's at my side. River's anxious, quick steps are loud behind us. Aleah's annoyed sigh reaches me before we're at the end of the walkway. I don't glance back to see if Makayla's followed. Being disappointed by others has become tonight's theme.

"What now?" Aleah asks while we stand in the street.

Cars and SUVs line the road. A young moon sits like a hook ready to catch all the stars in the blue obsidian sky. River walks a straight line, one foot shakily in front of the other like an intoxicated gymnast practicing a balance beam routine. Luca keeps glancing back to Chloe's house. Like Makayla's going to spontaneously appear.

*Sorry, buddy, there are no K-pop duets in your future.*

"How are we getting grub?" Aleah inquires. "How are we getting *anywhere*?"

"My sister's car's too small to fit all of us," laments River.

Aleah's phone lights up. "I can't call my . . . uncle." She gives me a look. We pretend her brief pause meant nothing.

For now, we've called a truce. At least, I have.

"Makayla was my ride," whispers Luca. His fingers pull at the ends of his hair. I catch his wrist to stop him, grinning.

"We'll figure it out."

Makayla's keys bite into my palm. Grand theft auto wouldn't make a positive impression on my Duke application. With my other hand, I swipe until I find the rarely used rideshare app on my phone. Dad made me download it. He keeps an emergency credit card on file. *In case you're ever stuck somewhere and I'm unavailable*, he'd said.

This constitutes an emergency, right? I'm stuck. Sort of. Dad's incapacitated. Okay, *sleeping*, but it counts.

Three cars are in the area. I almost hit Request, but my thumb slips as the sky catches on fire.

*Pow! Pow! BOOM!*

Crackling thunder echoes above our heads. Bursts of blues and reds and oranges. Stars combusting, turning to thin clouds of smoke. Down the road, fireworks streak over a house that rivals the Campbells' property in size.

"Wow," River says in a long, awed breath.

The four of us stand shoulder to shoulder to watch. *Go big or go home*, Prospect's unofficial motto. I'm impressed.

"I need to get closer," Aleah insists, phone in hand.

She jogs downhill before I can comment. River chases her. I don't budge. The view's decent from here.

Luca's shoulder is still pressed to mine. Our hands orbit each other by our sides. We watch River and Aleah film each other. Whoop loudly like they're at Thunder Over Louisville. Like this display is all for them.

"Hey," Luca whispers. His index finger curls around mine. I don't pull away. Flashes of lightning shine off his eyes as I pivot to face him. A smile dances from the corner of my lips when he stammers, "Um, I'm really trying to act chill, but tonight's been a lot and—"

He cuts himself off.

I lean up on my tiptoes, anxious for him to finish. Yes, tonight is a lot. Has it all been bad, though?

Have *we* been bad?

(Is there even a "we" on the table? Do I want a "we"?)

Luca's eyes scan my face in a wild pattern. His breaths come faster. Mine do too. He bites, then releases, his lip, like he thought better of it. Like he's overthinking everything the same way I am.

Our fingers intertwine. I trace the smoothness of his knuckles.

*Pop! Pop!* is the soundtrack around us. Red lights streak over our faces. He leans forward first. I tilt my head. Hesitation fades like the dying glow of a firework before another explodes.

I taste the smoke in the air before the flavor of his kiss: sour-sugar and lemony vodka and *wow*.

No other word.

It's far from urgent and desperate like making out behind the bleachers with Ghost Boy. More like clumsy on my end and patient on his. He knows what he's doing. His lips are velvety, his tongue teasing.

It's everything I wish all those previous kisses had been: Unforgettably perfect.

He leans away first. I spend two seconds kissing the air, eyes closed, undoubtedly looking like a horny teen virgin. If the Jordans fit, right?

Our fingers unknot as we shift back on our heels. Words fly out of my mouth before my brain has an opportunity to filter them.

"What was that for?"

For a moment, he doesn't react. I think he's processing. Then the softest grin pushes his cheeks up. "Never have I ever kissed a boy just because," he replies.

"Just because?"

He nods, no explanations offered. Only a flicker in his eyes. Blush rising in his cheeks.

I consider leaning in for another kiss.

*Should I give him a reason?*

But a voice shrieking over the explosions in the sky makes me jolt backward.

"Wait! Don't leave me!"

I blink twice. It's Makayla, sprinting toward us like she's poised to replace Darren on the track team. Alcohol clearly has no effect on her coordination. From our other side, I can hear Aleah and River jogging up.

"You're back?" River says excitedly, sidling up to Luca's side.

"Yeah," Makayla replies breathlessly. "This party's dead anyway."

Aleah narrows her eyes, hands on her hips. I share her doubt of Makayla's sudden change of heart. Just not as aggressively.

"Are we still going to get real food?" Makayla asks as if *she* hadn't abandoned us fifteen minutes ago. "I'm starved."

Aleah juts her chin like she's still waiting on a very loud, very public apology.

Luca combs fingers through his hair with an unsteady hand. I wonder if he's thinking about the kiss.

I wonder if anyone saw.

River holds up their phone. "There's six different restaurants open late. Most of them are bars, so I doubt we get in." They tap on one location. "Ooh, a Waffle House not too far away!"

Aleah's next words come out shyly, something I've rarely heard from her. "Perfect. Uh, if that's okay with everyone? I don't have a lot of money."

No one speaks. We don't give her pitying eyes either. I get it. Dad always makes sure I have enough money for *reasonable* things. But I know the cost. The days he'll have a sandwich or microwavable Japanese noodles for dinner to stay in budget.

"I'm down," Makayla chimes in.

Behind their glasses, River's eyes brighten like a new cascade of fireworks.

Luca waits for my response.

If I'm being honest, I want to go home and crawl under my sheets. Stay there until graduation. Forget I just had a falling-out with my best friend. That my *other* best friend is ghosting my texts. That I might've thrown a major wrench in The Plan since, if Jay and I aren't talking, there's no chance Mr. Scott will write me a recommendation letter for Duke.

On top of the fact that prom is a lost cause.

But even after everything, I don't want the night to end.

I *like* being around this group. Weird, but true.

"Fine," I groan, unable to sell the fake annoyance in my voice when my mouth keeps ticking upward. "But I don't want to hear a peep when I add ketchup to my hash browns."

# 16

# LEAN ON YOUR FRIENDS

**The second I** start up Makayla's SUV, the Bluetooth syncs with her phone and the interior is flooded with a stripped-down, emo-lite pop song. It's just . . . sad. My eyes widen at Makayla in the rearview.

"What the in T. Swiftie nonsense is this?" Aleah groans from behind me, clicking her seat belt.

"Fucking Luca," Makayla grumbles, rapidly scrolling through her phone to change the song. She leans forward, head popping between me and Luca. "*He* made that playlist." She jabs him in the shoulder.

"Ow!" Luca flinches away. "¡Basta! You like that song too."

Makayla flops back into the middle back seat as I ease onto the road.

I chance a glimpse at Luca. He's pouting but blushing too. The urge to once again question his musical taste is abandoned once the GPS starts calling out directions. I'm in a foreign neighborhood, at night, and don't want to risk ending up in Indiana or something.

"You're dying to dunk on me, aren't you?" Luca asks when I stop at a red light.

A laugh leaps from my mouth. He pokes my shoulder playfully.

I almost miss the light turning green, too captivated by Luca's stare.

I want to kiss him again.

Luckily, I'm saved from accidentally blurting that out loud by the crooning coming from behind us.

A throwback Lady Gaga song is playing. Makayla and Aleah's voices are a perfect mismatch. I've heard Makayla sing in school plays. She has a nice, made-for-musicals tone that could easily transition into a pop music career. But I haven't listened to Aleah in forever. Her voice is confident. It doesn't crack on the high notes like when she was younger. It's this rich, full alto.

I think she's holding back. Like she could do more.

In the rearview, Aleah leans into Makayla. Their laughter interrupts the cacophony of their harmony. I want to ask Aleah if she's going to pursue singing after high school.

Would she be mad if I wanted her to?

We come to a four-way stop. Flashing blue lights ahead bounce off the windshield, forcing me to squint. Instinctively, my hands move into the proper positioning on the wheel. I confirm my seat belt is fastened. Sit taller, perfect posture. I have a smile at the ready if needed. In the mirror, Aleah does the same. I wonder if her heart is thumping like mine.

*Never give them a reason to look at you the wrong way. To think you've done something*, Dad's said to me since I was old enough to ride in the passenger seat. *They'll find a reason, but never give them one.*

*Them.* The police.

As I cruise by, staying just under the speed limit, uniformed officers circle two vehicles on the side of the road. There's been an accident. One car crashed into a brick mailbox. The other slammed into a sugar maple tree, the front end crushed.

"Oof. That's brutal," comments Luca. He cranes his neck. "Hope everyone's okay."

Red and white lights are approaching from behind. The first blare of the ambulance's siren is matched by a sharp inhale from the back seat. I almost swerve at the noise.

It's River.

They're doubled over, head between their knees, hands cupped over their ears.

"Uh, Riv? You okay?" Aleah says.

Makayla hovers over River as if she's unsure what to do.

"Oh. I'm fi-fine," says River after a beat, gradually straightening up. "Thought I saw . . . a spider."

"A spider!" Luca shrieks, knees banging against the dashboard as he pulls his feet onto his seat.

"Chill, Alge-bro." Aleah shakes her head. "They *thought* they saw a spider. Not an axe murderer."

Luca grumbles something back, but I'm too busy staring at River in the mirror to catch it. Even with their broad smile, I clock the thin layer of sweat on River's forehead. Their chest has barely slowed to a steady rhythm. Every few seconds, their head turns to glance behind us.

I do too.

But I think we're watching those dim, winking blue lights for different reasons.

For almost midnight on a Saturday, Waffle House is relatively dead.

I haven't made a habit of visiting twenty-four-hour restaurants specializing in speedy service and decent grub in the middle of the night, but, from our corner booth, this place looks like a graveyard. A final stop after a night of drinking, a late shift, or pure boredom.

Random solo diners sit at the bar. In another booth is a girl with reddish-brown skin who looks slightly older than us, her tablespace crowded with a laptop, two mugs of coffee, a forgotten omelet, and a mound of textbooks. Three college bros swap loud stories over waffle stacks on the other side of the restaurant. Online delivery drivers occasionally pop in to grab plastic bags of food.

We spend more time on our phones than talking after we've ordered. I'm distracted by movie-trailer reaction videos. Anything to keep from scrolling through the WhatsApp chat. Luca's next to me. We're pressed together, shoulders to elbows. Knees and ankles too. Something about this feels oddly cozy. Like we've done it a dozen times before.

Like we could keep doing this in the future, if . . .

I startle, face hot, when Makayla groans, "Oh my God, stop doing that right now!"

Her accusing tone attracts eyes from the Bro Squad, along with Study Girl, but it's not aimed at me. Makayla reaches over to snatch

Luca's phone away. He almost knocks over a tray of sugar alternatives trying to escape.

I mistakenly look at his screen.

It's a pic collage of him and Devya on Instagram.

"You're torturing yourself," Makayla asserts.

"I'm preserving memories," he argues.

Their squabbling is muted by my own thoughts. Did that kiss mean anything to him? Was it merely spontaneous? Or was he experimenting with someone who's not Devya? I stop my spiraling at *Am I just a rebound?* because, frankly, the last thing I need to do is overthink one more thing.

The kiss was a one-off. Two boys having a little fun. That's it . . . right?

"Luca, seriously," Aleah says while sipping her sweet tea. "Untag, delete, unfollow, block if needed, start fresh. In that order."

Makayla nods with pursed lips. River appears on the verge of agreeing too.

Would it be appropriate for me to say anything considering what happened less than an hour ago?

Luca sighs heavily. His eyes are fixated on his screen. Devya smiles back from behind a stuffed teddy bear. The caption is all kissy and flaming heart emojis. Sickeningly cute.

"I lied earlier about Aja and the beer," he explains, idly scrolling through his grid. "I saw Dev. She was alone. I had a chance to talk to her and, I don't know. It hit me."

His finger stops on a photo of the Ramírez brood, matching round chins and eye-crinkling smiles on every face.

"I was doing all this"—he waves a hand above his head as

if that'll fill in the rest—"the promposal, fake dating Makayla"—Aleah and River share a look at him finally saying it out loud—"all because my parents found out she dumped me."

Makayla builds a tower out of the individual jam cups as if she's heard this already. I angle toward him, biting on my thumbnail cuticle.

"Shit," Luca hisses. "They say if I wasn't so open about being bi, if I kept it on the low, then Dev would've stayed with me. My sexuality had *nothing* to do with our breakup."

Damn.

I try not to imagine every discussion at the Ramírez dinner table pivoting from TV shows and homework to Luca's dating life. His sexuality. Why being himself has left him alone.

Our server passes with menus and water glasses for a couple that's settled into the booth in front of us.

Luca slouches lower. "It's hard enough when other queer people erase my bi-ness or brownness whenever it's convenient for them. I don't need to be shut down by my family for being me too."

Aleah rests her temple on her knuckles. "It's one hell of a thing being Black or brown *and* queer."

Luca nods, grimacing.

"One community loves you for your melanin but denies you because of your queerness." Aleah smiles sadly. "The other claims to fight oppression because 'love is love' but is quick to forget the added struggle we face because of our Blackness."

"Or brownness."

There's no arguing with them. It's facts.

"I walked into Aja on purpose," Luca admits. "I needed an

excuse to get away. Figure shit out. Did I really want to win Dev back because I still have feelings for her? Or am I trying to make my parents happy?"

I bite a little too roughly into my thumb's skin wondering which conclusion he came to.

"Sorry," whispers Luca. "Didn't mean to make things awkward."

"*Psst.*" River flicks the back of his hand. "That's what we do in this crew."

Luca snorts.

The discussion shifts to a plotline in a TV series I haven't seen. It's the perfect cue for a brief respite. I excuse myself. My brain needs another break. Talking about all these things—being queer and the way it can alter relationships and how it's hard to balance it all—has me thinking about Jay and what he said at Chloe's.

Have I ever called him out before? Looked him in the eye and said what was on my mind? Or am I the guy Makayla says I am? Someone who lets shit fly because it's easier that way. Because confrontation can lead to self-examination none of us want to face.

In the corner, near Study Girl's booth, is a TouchTunes jukebox. The winking blue and white lights call to me. Since we've arrived, it's rotated from Cardi B to Justin Bieber to something vaguely disco and too old for even Dad to know. When I walk up, the digital screen flashes JUKEBOX CLASSICS. Ah, that explains it.

I fish out a few dollars left over from the bag of chips I bought at SpeedEx. Fortunately the song library is current enough that I don't instantly want a refund.

I'm halfway through the TOP PLAYS when another body sidles up.

"Oh no. Adele?" Luca smiles. "Are you okay? Should we have an intervention?"

My own grin is automatic.

"This coming from *you*?" I say teasingly. "Tell me, Luca, how many Billie Eilish songs are on your playlists? Ten? Fifty?"

He clutches his chest, feigning hurt on a level Makayla wishes she could achieve.

I lick at my ever-growing smirk. It's hard to miss the way Luca's eyes track that one motion. Or the way my chest warms. The small dip in my stomach.

*Was it just a kiss?*

"Maybe," I suggest lowly, "this is more your speed?" My index finger hovers over the BOY BAND HITS playlist.

Luca's puckered mouth twists sideways. "Asshole."

I hold his gaze. How could five seconds feel like an eternity? We're not having a staring contest like Aleah and me. It's something else. Like we hope the other doesn't blink. Like, if we close our eyes, even briefly, this all goes away.

Whatever *this* is.

He blinks first. "Let me guess . . ." His fingers bump mine away from the screen. He scrolls before grinning. "This is what you call romantic?" The smug bastard's stopped on a black-and-white album cover I know very well.

I gasp. Heat spreads from the bridge of my nose outward as I say, "Mariah's iconic! Timeless."

Study Girl peeks her head from behind her laptop. Her *Dude, really?* glare sends an itchy, embarrassed feeling crawling over my skin.

"That's certainly a hot take," counters Luca.

I shrug.

"So . . . if you could prompose to anyone," he begins, waiting until I'm focused on him again. "Not, like, you know . . ."

*Christian*, I think he wants to say.

"No one we know," he quickly corrects. "An imaginary person. Hypothetical date." He's stumbling, face rapidly turning maroon, and I'm helpless to how quickly my mouth curves upward. "*Someone*. Would you go with Mariah?"

I purse my lips. Pretend to consider my options. Even back in Maddie's bedroom, I never really thought about what song I'd use to prompose to Christian. Whether I'd even go that route. If given the chance, how far would I lean into my own corniness?

My stomach flips the other way.

It's a shame I'm almost too scared to let myself think that big. My dream prom night. *Dream promposal.* All of it. Like expecting these simple but enormous things is too dangerous for people like me.

Luca's soft, curious eyes watch me.

It can't hurt to dream big for a second, right?

My fingers slip under his to touch the screen. I swipe and swipe. His hand never leaves. Silver rings kiss my knuckles as I find what I'm looking for. Press play.

Suddenly, the Waffle House is filled with, you guessed it, One Direction.

Luca groans obnoxiously.

"What can I say?" I rub the pad of my thumb along his grand-father's ring. "Sometimes it's not about the song, but *how* you prompose."

As if on cue, Makayla appears in front of us. Her smirk says she knows what I'm going for.

Everything happens so quickly. Makayla drags me to the middle of the restaurant. She tosses her hair over one shoulder, smoothly falling into the role of Devya. I drop to bended knee, pretending to be Luca, heart-eyes and all. Aleah hops into a kneeling position in the booth, singing gleefully. It's a crime against humanity that she knows every lyric to this song. At least she nails the Rolling Tones cheesiness.

The true scene-stealer is River, who hip-checks me out of the way to kiss the back of Makayla's hand midway through our performance. A true Peter Vasquez understudy. I fall dramatically, devastated expression cranked to level eleven. That's when Aleah loses it.

At the last second, as I'm standing, Luca swoops in. Phone in hand. He blinks up with doe-ish eyes. *Oh.* He's me.

I roll my eyes. "Ha, ha."

After helping him up, our hands stay clasped. For the longest moment, I finally let myself picture it: Luca and me. Dancing to played-out music. Posing for silly photos. Kissing as he fixes the lapels on my rented tux.

My heart tightens then expands.

After an echoing applause from the diners and staff, the air around our table is supercharged. We're all smiling over our plates. Strips of bacon are exchanged for toast slices. Heady scents of thick maple syrup and melting butter and the Tabasco sauce Luca drenches his eggs with fills my nose. He even passes me the ketchup bottle for my hash browns, no judgmental eyebrows included.

No one discusses what just happened. We all know it was badass.

Out of nowhere, River slams a hand on the table, cracking up. They're red-faced. Tears stream down their cheeks.

"Hmm, those edibles finally kicked in," says Aleah, smirking.

But River isn't laughing anymore. They're sobbing.

"S-sorry," they stutter, dabbing their face with a napkin.

Makayla rubs their back.

"Sorry," they repeat, breathing hard. "I haven't felt this silly— felt so much like myself since . . ."

Their silence hangs for a full minute. An uncomfortable heaviness sits on my shoulders as River trembles and sniffs hard, wiping away snot. I rest a hand near theirs on the table.

"Since when?"

River exhales hard, leveling me with a bleary but certain stare.

"Since I killed my best friend."

# 17

# NEW SQUAD RULES

**The quiet at** our table stretches forever.

Bacon sizzles on the flat top griddle. The Bro Squad argues about Marvel movies. Silverware drops and clatters. Food orders are barked out from behind the bar. The jukebox is now rotating through nineties ballads thanks to Study Girl.

But we're caught in a noiseless bubble, huddled around River as they steady their breathing.

"Devaughn Ameen," River says slowly to the fresh glass of water our server dropped off. "My best friend. My whole heart."

I never interacted with Devaughn. He was a year behind me. Keeping up with over a thousand students at one school is impossible. But something in the newborn streaks falling across River's heartbroken smile makes me wish I would've known him.

River swipes through photos. Their cheek mashed against a slim-faced boy with rich, dark-brown skin and a shadow fade that makes his ears stick out. His grin is infectious in every pic.

"He died last year." The hand holding River's phone trembles. "Car accident."

Everyone at Brook-Oak heard about it. But none of us know the full story.

"Was he . . . ?" Luca doesn't finish the question. I think he's scared to ask. We all are.

"No, no." River bites their lip. "He didn't drink. He was fifteen."

I try not to look doubtful. Jay was sneaking Darren and me alcohol during sleepovers when we were fourteen.

"I'm serious," says River. "The only rule he ever broke was meeting up with me down at the Vogue once a month for the late showing of *The Rocky Horror Picture Show*."

"Okay. Sorry."

River barely steadies the water glass as they sip. I look past them to the jukebox. Boyz II Men comes on. "End of the Road," which is way too ironic, but fitting when River explains what happened.

Devaughn didn't have a ride that night. His parents were early-shift hospital workers. Always in bed before nine p.m. River was dressed in full costume, waiting nervously for him at the Vogue. They suggested Devaughn "borrow" his parents' car.

"He crashed into a tree." Fresh tears spill across River's cheeks. "I'm the reason he died. Because I wanted my best friend with me. It was our thing. Being queer and campy and free with the audience. He was the only person who knew I was enby. The only one who loved me for me. Other than Katie, I guess. Definitely not my parents or anyone at school."

"Riv." Aleah can barely speak. She's smearing tears from her own face. "It's not your—"

"It *is*."

The music fades. Luca scrubs at a water ring, not making eye contact. My fingers inch closer to River's but never touch. I want them to know I'm here.

"How do you keep going when the only person pushing you along is gone?"

None of us have an answer to River's question.

It's my turn to stare idly at the table. My throat is dry. All I can think about is what my world would look like without Jay's and Darren's jokes or endless text threads or random FaceTime calls during the night.

What would life be like without Dad standing over me while I studied? Without his hugs or temple kisses. Without his *I'm proud of you* smiles.

"He's gone. Because of me. And I'm too scared to even visit his grave," River says into Makayla's shoulder.

My stomach tightens. Losing Granny was hard. I still struggle going to the cemetery to visit her.

"Sorry for stealing your spotlight, Luca," sniffs River, laughing weakly before blowing their nose.

Luca grins back.

"What if you did?" I ask impulsively. When more than a few eyes look my way, I quickly clarify, "Visit his grave."

River's eyebrows shoot up like I hadn't heard a word they just said. Thing is, I did. I've been terrified to do things before.

But there was one thing that always finally pushed me to finally commit to something: TNT's dares.

"I dare you to go visit Devaughn's grave," I say, smiling. "With all of us."

"This isn't a game," hisses Aleah.

"I'm serious." Maybe it's the adrenaline from the promposal reenactment. Or the exhaustion of the night hitting its peak. Maybe I'm tired of these dares being a requirement to maintain a friendship rather than something I *want* to do. Something that makes you jump headfirst into a pool knowing your friends will be right there when you emerge.

I tell them as much, beaming helplessly.

"New rules," I declare. "Everyone dares someone else to do something that'll, I don't know, make a difference. Aren't you tired of feeling like we're damned if we do or damned if we don't?"

Almost vibrating out of my seat with excitement, I turn back to River: "I dare you to visit Devaughn's grave with us . . . tonight. Tell him how you feel. Say goodbye."

River still looks doubtful.

Luca bumps my shoulder, half smirking. Aleah stares me down, but what's new? Makayla whispers something to River.

"Okay," croaks River.

"Okay?"

River turns to Luca. "I dare you to prompose again. Someone new. Go to prom with whomever you want. Let your family be mad AF."

"Wow, Riv." Aleah nods her approval. "Put him on the spot."

A fire circles the brown of Luca's eyes. It's ridiculously sexy.

"Fine." He points at Makayla. "I dare you to share the *real* Makayla on social media. One post. Introduce your followers to your book-ish side or whatever."

"Oh my God, you little shit." Makayla flips him off, giggling. "Only if Aleah tries out for the Rolling Tones."

"Fuck you, no," Aleah says, cackling into her tea. "Never happening."

"Aleah!" Makayla smacks her shoulder. "You have to. I dare you."

"I don't have to do nothin' but stay Black and die."

I hold back a grin. It's one of Mario's favorite quotes from *Lean on Me*, an essential Black film he and Dad made sure we watched at least three times.

"We sink, we swim, we rise, we fall," I say quietly, another quote from the movie. The smallest twitch pokes at the corner of her lips. The littlest of smiles.

"Not gonna lie," says Luca. "I wouldn't mind seeing you put Amanda Cox in her place if she tries to voice-correct you."

Makayla claps enthusiastically. "Spring auditions are soon. It won't kill you to try out. Something to separate you from the Ballers."

Aleah stares at her nearly empty cup for a moment.

"I guess," she finally says. "I know my dad would love it. My uncle too."

This time, neither of us runs from what the acknowledgment of Mario's existence means.

"Who knows." Her eyes lower, jaw tensing. "I might not even go back to the Ballers anyway."

I want to tell her she can't quit the basketball team. It's her ticket to an athletic scholarship. Breaking out of Louisville. Any D1 school would be *lucky* to have her. But who am I to say that out loud?

Aleah squints my way. "So, that means I have to dare you."

"Er. You don't . . . have to?"

She leans on her elbows, dragging out her contemplating. It's the longest, most painful sixty-five seconds of the whole night. Maybe my life.

"I dare you to—"

*Go to hell?* I think, but never say.

"—do one thing for yourself."

I lean back. Is that concern in her eyes? I can't tell. But when she says, "It doesn't matter what, as long as it makes you and *only you* happy," I know she means it.

We're not Birdie and TJ anymore. But this isn't bad either.

After a quiet beat, I agree. "Okay."

Aleah leaves it at that.

I fold my hands behind my head. It hasn't been a perfect day by a long shot. But I don't know. With Makayla already waving down our server for the checks, River demolishing the rest of their waffles, Aleah scrolling through the official Rolling Tones TikTok, Luca's hip and knee and ankle pressed to mine as he crunches on cold bacon—maybe the night's just beginning.

Maybe our lives are too.

"Got it!" Makayla announces, flashing us her phone screen.

Pinned on the map is the cemetery where Devaughn's grave is. Thirty minutes away. River exhales shakily, but Aleah grabs their hand.

We're doing this. Together.

"I need to run back by the party first," I say, feeling the shape of Jay's keys digging into my thigh. "One last stop."

## 18

# GOODBYES ARE NEVER GOOD

**The walk to** Jay's SUV is endless.

Maybe that's my nerves talking. Our group chat is still a dead zone, which only heightens the buzzing in my system. I texted Jay before leaving Waffle House. Told him I was coming back to give him his keys. He's left me on read.

Part of me wants to get in and get out. Leave the keys with Jayla or someone. But I can't.

While driving back to Chloe's, all I thought about was Aleah's dare.

One thing for myself. I don't know what that is. Maybe talking to Jay, telling him what I should've countless times before, will help.

Or maybe it won't.

I parked Makayla's vehicle almost a block away. There weren't any spots closer. Despite it being past one a.m., the party's still jumping. Before walking away, I caught a glimpse of Luca through the passenger window. Even the shadows couldn't hide the flush of his cheeks when I mouthed, *I'll be right back.*

My phone vibrates in my palm. I quickly unlock it, anticipating some sign of life from Darren. But it's only an Instagram notification.

I scroll through my cluttered activity screen.

A handful of likes on a post I made yesterday. Ten new followers after I'm tagged in a live video dancing with Kendra. The last notification is a *your post from 1 year ago* reminder. I make the mistake of clicking on it.

It's me and Dad.

Our arms are around each other's shoulders. We're cheesing for a selfie after a big meet. I'm still in my track gear. A first-place medal hangs from Dad's neck. He's also wearing a Duke T-shirt with a matching fitted baseball cap. It was one of his rare weekday evenings off. He drove an hour in traffic to come see me run.

His caption is as loud as his voice that day:

**Duke-bound, baby!**

An abyss opens in my stomach. Guilt has been quietly gnawing at my insides since I walked away from Jay in front of everyone. Now I can't decide if it's because of how I acted toward him or because of what our complicated situation means for Dad's dreams.

"Mom! No. I'm fine."

I jolt at the sound of Jay's voice. He's leaning against his SUV. Well, it looks more like the SUV is holding him up. Blond strands have come loose from his topknot. They hang messy and greasy over his face as he groans into his phone.

"No, I haven't been drinking!"

I stop short.

Jay swallows hard when his eyes raise. He doesn't verbally acknowledge me. Whatever Mrs. Scott is yelling distracts him.

"No, I'm not using the Jules tone with you. Don't say that."

His shoulders fall. Whether it's from frustration or exhaustion, I can't tell. But I don't inch any closer.

"I'll be home soon," he says through his teeth. "Yes, I'm still with D and . . ."

His eyes flit back to me. His nostrils flare widely when he adds, "And your golden boy."

The nickname, his voice sharp, claws at my flesh. Rips away my own fatigue. Leaves behind exposed nerves and weakened bones.

"I swear, I'm not gonna fu—I won't *mess up* anything by doing something stupid. I know better." Jay sizes me up again. I tighten all my muscles, fighting the flinch threatening to break free. His frown deepens. "Love you too. Gotta go."

He hangs up before Mrs. Scott finishes. If that were Dad, my phone would be lighting up instantly. Hell, he'd probably be pulling up right now with a stern lecture.

"Mom says hi." Jay laughs hoarsely. "Like always."

I don't try to interpret the look in his eyes.

Instead, I ask, "Are you okay?"

He waves a sloppy, dismissive hand at me. "All good." The slur in his voice says otherwise.

"Okay." I draw out the word as I approach. "Give me your phone. I'm ordering a rideshare. You can't drive."

"Can't drive 'cause you have, uh, my key-thingy."

Really? Key-thingy? I cross my arms. "I have your keys because—"

"You left us." He *pffts* until the hair in his eyes moves. "Left me."

It's hard to pretend his wounded voice doesn't bother me.

I kick loose rocks from the street. "You were being an ass."

He doesn't have a comeback for that. Only rubs at the back of his neck in that shy way he does when his mom's scolding him for something Jules did and has nowhere else to place the blame.

After a beat, he says, "Give me my keys, Theo."

"No."

"Fine. Then drive us home."

"I . . . can't."

He makes an annoyed face. "You can't?"

I look over my shoulder. Makayla's SUV isn't visible this close to Chloe's. Still, it's like I can feel their eyes on me.

"I just . . ." I say, softer, before realizing I don't owe Jay an explanation. Shifting back, I say, "There's no way in hell I'm letting you drive like this. I can't have that on my conscience."

Jay snorts. "Your conscience," he scoffs, stumbling away from the car. He throws his hands in the air. "Theo, the guy who suddenly thinks I'm not a good friend. Theo, the golden boy my mom's—"

He cuts himself off. I arch an eyebrow, but he continues staggering from side to side.

"Looks like we've got a problem." He wipes a hand down his shiny face. "What are we gonna do about it?"

I have no idea.

Why did I think this would be easier? Nothing about me and Jay has ever been simple. Not lately.

My brain is screaming, *Just tell him how you feel.*

"How about this," Jay says, smirking. Under the orange

streetlights, his eyes are thundercloud gray. He pushes his hair back, then finishes: "A dare."

"Um, what?"

"A new dare. Since you've already lost the last one—"

"Because you didn't tell me Christian had a boyfriend!"

The boom of my voice doesn't faze him. For the first time, he doesn't deny knowing either. "An L is an L in the record books, bro. No asterisks."

I bite my cheek to stop from going off on him.

"Same stakes as before: a win for you means the prom night of your dreams," he offers like it's a favor.

From the edge of my vision, a couple of cars down, I see two boys. One is hidden by the shadows. But the other boy—I'd recognize Christian Harris in the middle of a hailstorm. Of all the people who could be exiting the party right now, it's him.

His eyes lock with mine. An anxious smile creeps across his mouth. It doesn't last long. I don't bother grinning back. I realize he's not even in my daydreams of the perfect prom night anymore.

Someone else is.

I turn back to Jay. "And if I lose?"

"Same thing," he says with a haphazard shrug.

I can't believe I'm even contemplating this. Letting Jay goad me into another dare. Pretending like I owe him anything.

I don't. But I owe *myself* something. A lot of things.

"Double or nothing," I eventually say, chin lifted. I have no idea what Jay's dare is going to be. But I have to take a chance. "If you win, I'll show up in Mountainview gear when we get back from spring break. Hell, I'll even wear a crop top." I don't know where this sudden burst of boldness is coming from, but I try my hardest to keep it at max level.

"And if you complete the dare?"

"Prom," I say, pursing my lips, "and a favor."

"What kind of favor?"

"You'll find out," I reply. I don't mention his dad or the Duke letter. We're already stumbling on the thinnest sheet of ice. I repeat, "Prom and a favor."

"Favor." Jay smacks the word around his mouth like he's just eaten a gas station burrito. He reclines against his SUV, cheeks less flushed. Taking his time with a response, he exhales, then says, "Fine. But if you fail, *you* have to drive us home. ASAP."

Guess I should've seen that coming.

I fight the urge to glance over my shoulder again. Back to where Luca and the others are waiting.

"Are we good?" Jay asks loudly.

My heartbeat speeds up like a rollercoaster soaring downhill. Sweat tickles the back of my neck. I can't abandon this new group yet. Jay hasn't revealed what his dare is, but he's sloshed, so his brain function is limited. It can't be that bad. There's still a chance I can get both the things I want.

"Ayyooooo!"

Darren jogs into the street. He's not as clumsy or disheveled as Jay appears. In fact, there's a bounce in his step. He's exceptionally . . . euphoric?

"D," I say as he comes to a stop. "Where the hell have you been?"

"My bad." He's panting, hands on his knees.

I reel back with an affronted expression. "Your bad?"

Is he high right now? I've been wondering if my best friend had been kidnapped, left for dead in rich suburbia like in a horror movie, and he's been getting baked? The audacity.

He quiets a burst of laughter with his hand. "I'm so . . ." More giggling. "I just had the night of my life!"

When I can't do more than blink, confused, Darren rambles about hanging out with Bree, one of the two girls from Yearbook. South Asian, I think, with terra-cotta skin and curly hair. Turns out the other girl—Kelsey—was Bree's wingman, promptly abandoning them once she got the conversation rolling.

Bree and Darren talked video games. Similar tastes in food. Laughed at memes and videos until his phone died.

"She kissed me by the pool!" he shouts to the neighborhood.

The half-asleep streets are almost too quiet. It makes all the thoughts in my head echo louder. I'm happy for him. As far as I know, it's his first real kiss. Clearly, he and Bree have a connection.

So . . . why am I so focused on Darren having the night I wanted for myself?

And why isn't what I had with Luca—even if it was more private—just as good?

"D, that's great." I offer him the sincerest smile I can manage.

"What's going on here?" Darren motions between me and Jay. "Something up?"

Before I can reply, Jay staggers forward. "Nah!" He drops a hand on my forearm. "We good, Theo?"

Every time I look at Jay, I remind myself this isn't the best friend who brings me Gatorades on Fridays. Who's stayed up late helping me study for an exam.

It's the alcohol.

It's whatever pressure his mom laid on him during their phone call.

Darren watches me closely.

I slide my hands into my pockets. I should tell Darren what's happening. What I'm considering doing. All of it. Would he try to convince me otherwise like he did back at the ramen bar? Could he get me to walk away from this opportunity?

"We're good," I confirm through my teeth.

Darren squints. There's no time to assuage his suspicions because Jay says, "I dare you to find Jayla in the next twenty minutes. Bring her back here. I want to make sure she gets home safely."

"That's it?"

Jay stretches onto his toes, yawning. "Yup! Convince my girl and prom's yours, bro."

"And the favor."

He shrugs. "Yeah. That too."

On paper, it appears easy. Go back to the party. Find Jayla. Plead with her to leave behind the cheer squad to catch a ride-share home with her boyfriend. But this is Jayla, not my biggest fan.

Even if this feels like a trap, I still say, "You're on."

Jay brandishes his phone, snorting. A few taps later, he flashes the stopwatch app we use to measure our run times during the off-season. "Time's ticking, Golden Boy."

19:55. 19:54.

I watch the numbers change with every heart-aching inhale.

This is my second shot at . . . *everything.*

I take off, arms pumping. Legs catching a familiar fire like when I'm really pushing myself on the track. I haul my proverbial ass in what I'm sure Jay thinks is the wrong direction.

But it's not. Finding Jayla can't be that hard.

I have somewhere else to go first.

Everyone's gathered outside Makayla's SUV. Luca sits on the hood, phone in hand. He's recording Aleah teaching Makayla a new dance even I haven't mastered yet. River's parked on the ground near a front tire, mimicking their every move.

The road crunches under my soles as I skid to a stop in front of them.

"Ready to go?" Aleah asks.

"A-almost . . ." I heave out. "Just a small deviation in our original plan."

Makayla's brow wrinkles. Then River stands, their head tilted curiously.

"Gimme like twenty minutes. Twenty-five, tops."

"For what?" Aleah asks.

"It's just." I try to catch my breath. Sweat dribbles from my hairline to my eyebrows. I've never been this exhausted from running before. "I promise I'll explain when I get back."

"No," Aleah asserts, "tell us now, Theo. What's going on?"

"You won't understand." I manage to keep my voice on the edge of calm, even though that's quickly slipping away. "I need time."

Something I have very little of and explaining things to Aleah won't help.

Luca slides off the hood. Confusion shadows his face. "Time for what?"

Ugh. This isn't what I imagined when I decided to run all the way back here. Then again, I don't know what I was thinking. That I'd tell Luca how much unexpected fun I've had with him tonight? That I think I like him? And there are potentially worse prom dates around every corner at Brook-Oak, but I hope he's feeling the same thing I am?

That we'd look pretty good holding hands at prom?

This is the problem with giving yourself permission to dream big. It makes room for all the what-ifs. The endless spiraling. All the *no*s we don't want to hear but know might come.

*I'm going to prom*, I tell myself. *I'm getting that letter.*

"Uh." I avert my eyes from Aleah's stiff gaze. Force myself to focus only on the tiny crease between Luca's furrowed eyebrows. "I have to do something."

He blinks three times. "What? I thought you came here to—"

"Jay," Aleah says before he can finish.

"Jay?" Makayla falls in next to Luca, hands on her hips. "What *about* him?"

Prickling heat attacks my face. Swallowing hurts. My brain scrambles for anything but the truth.

"Funny thing is—" *Shit*. I have nothing. There's a growing knot between my shoulder blades. I finally say, "I agreed to a dare from Jay."

My phone buzzes in my pocket. The screen barely lights up. My battery is at 8 percent. Power save mode has already kicked in, thankfully. I don't answer Jay's call, checking the time instead.

I've already lost three minutes standing here.

"So, you're in the middle of *another* dare?" Makayla shakes her head in disbelief. "From Jay? *The* Jayson Scott who royally screwed you over on the last dare? The same guy who—"

"That's not him," I interrupt, unable to soften the defensiveness in my tone.

"Oh? Who is he, then?"

I don't have an immediate answer for Makayla. *It's complicated* doesn't sound like enough. So many different versions of Jay occupy my head, but it's the Jay from over ten minutes ago who stands out the most. The defeated one who reminds me of the boy from sleepovers at his house where he'd whisper about carrying around all his parents' expectations. Never wanting to let them down.

I know what that's like.

In fact, we *all* do.

Isn't that enough to overlook the other versions? Maybe that's selfish. Maybe that's what I hope Aleah sees when she looks at me. The Theo who broke her heart hoping it would mend his dad's.

She huffs noisily. I guess not.

"I don't have time for this." Aleah holds up her phone. "Uncle Mario or not, my dad will kill me for being out until two a.m."

"Okay," I agree. "Then let me—"

"No, Theo," she nearly shouts. "It's a wrap. I'm done with the bullshit. Are you really going to choose Jay over us?"

"I'm not choosing."

The sharp look in her eyes says otherwise.

"I'm not," I repeat to Luca, my voice scratchy and low and foreign to my own ears. He doesn't respond. Barely holds my gaze.

River clears their throat. "Maybe Aleah's right." Pale fingers pull at their bracelets. "It's late. We should head to the cemetery before—"

"What's the rush?" I groan, tugging at my hair.

But time is an issue. It's ticking in my head. Bright descending numbers all headed toward zero. I need to go find Jayla.

You know that second before you say the wrong thing? When your brain intervenes, finally gaining control over your motor skills, and whatever fucked-up thing you were thinking never makes it out. It lives inside you forever, but at least no one heard you say something awful?

That doesn't happen this time.

I say, "It's not like Devaughn's going anywhere" before my systems have a chance to shut my mouth down.

The change is instant. River flinches hard, like my words have slapped them in the face. Luca's jaw drops. Makayla says, "Theo, what the fuck is wrong with you?" while Aleah pinches the bridge of her nose. My insides freefall all the way to my feet.

I turn to River. "I'm sorry." Those two words, three syllables, seven letters aren't enough. My voice trembles when I add, "I didn't mean—"

"No, you did," Aleah interjects. "It's so on brand for Theo Wright to say something like that."

A million and one thoughts crash in my head. Test the firmness of my skull with their impact. But the one that gets through is: *She's wrong about me.*

I hope it's not another lie.

"We still have time to go to the cemetery," I tell River. "Let me finish this—"

"Aleah has a curfew," River interrupts. "I do too. We should go home."

"You can't leave without me," I say in a desperate attempt to hold them here. To keep this little world we created together. Even if I'm the reason it's crumbling. I jiggle Makayla's keys. "I'm the sober driver, remember?"

"Really?" Makayla hisses. "You're holding sobriety over our heads now?"

"No," I rush out. "I meant—"

"Meant what?" Luca asks lowly.

"I—" My attempt at something that doesn't sound selfish and manipulative fails. What can I say? All I can follow up with is "Here."

I toss Makayla's keys into the air. Aleah expertly snatches them from the sky like the future WNBA star she is.

"I'm calling my sister." River marches around Makayla's SUV. Even hidden in the shadows, I can see their shoulders shaking like when they were crying at Waffle House.

That haunting image is replaced by Aleah, hip cocked, arms folded.

"I gave you a simple dare. How've you already failed?"

"I didn't—"

"You did. All of this is about Jay. Or someone else. None of it is about you."

"It is! I'm doing this for—" I pause.

Two cars drive by. The air is still fragrant with the burnt smell of fireworks. In the distance, a chorus of Rolling Tones' voices serenades the night. They harmonize a creepy version of "Hide and Seek," a song Darren obsessed over after watching *The O.C.* last summer.

I stare into the harsh orange light from a streetlamp.

I'm doing all of this for . . . me?

It shouldn't be one of those fill-in-the-blank test questions I never get right. Yet, it is. And I don't have an answer.

"Have you ever known what you wanted, Theo?" Aleah says.

*Yeah*, I want to tell her. A long time ago. It's nothing but faded, discolored imagery in my head now. A memory so blurred, I can only make out the edges. I wish it was enough.

Truth is, it never has been.

"I'd say I'm surprised, but I'm not." She laughs hollowly. "I'm not disappointed either."

"Aleah," I attempt, but she cuts me off immediately.

"Thanks, everyone! Tonight was *swell*," she says dryly, her glare pointed directly at me. "So much better than you pretending I don't exist."

She walks in the opposite direction River went.

"I'm gonna call us an Uber," Makayla tells Luca. She swaps her keys for her phone. "Someone can bring me out here tomorrow to get my car."

Before she's too far, I call, "Makayla!"

She stops, back stiff, sparing the barest glance over her shoulder.

"You get it, right? This is who we are." I pat my chest. "We chose these friends. And they chose *us*."

It's a gamble. Reasoning with the side of her who, not two hours ago, abandoned us for the cheer squad. Because of obligation. Because that's how this works.

Right?

"We can't just change everything in one night."

Makayla chews her lip, as if she's envisioning the right way to reply. I hold my breath. With a lazy shrug and in the least convincing voice, she says, "Sure, Theo. That's exactly who we are," before walking away.

Then it's Luca and me.

His expression is new. *Disenchantment*, one of those SAT words I learned from my app. I try to smile. He doesn't react. What was I expecting?

We blinked and whatever magic we had back at the Waffle House fizzled out like an open can of soda sitting untouched on the counter for too long.

After our silence lingers for a beat, I say, "I gotta do this."

My resolve to win this dare hasn't diminished. If not for prom, at least I can get the recommendation letter. One less thing to deal with.

Luca's teeth pick at a corner of his lower lip.

I wait quietly, chest tightening with every second.

He finally says, "Aleah's right, isn't she? You're choosing him over us?"

"It's not a him or you. It's a dare. I'm choosing what's *best*." I grip my phone tighter. "Isn't that what you do with your family?"

His face wrinkles.

"At the end of the day"—I pause to glance down at his nails—"we do what's best for them and us."

He laughs harshly. "What? So, one night of me talking about my family and you think you know everything? That's it?"

"Am I wrong?"

All of Luca's features sharpen. Anger darkens his eyes. He shoves his hands into his pockets. His pants are dry. Of all things, I notice *that* before he speaks again.

"You're clueless. Don't compare my family sitch to your friendship with a proven dickbag." He exhales. "It's not the same. *We're* not the same."

I swallow and blink.

"You can twist it any way you want," he continues, "but this is you picking." He laughs again. It sounds like a balloon bursting. "All night people have been telling me to move past Dev. Get over it. Stop holding on. But look at you . . ."

I begrudgingly wait for him to finish. Time's running out. I should go. The window to find Jayla, to fix my future, is closing fast. But I can't convince my feet to move.

"I'm more than what happens with my family. With my ex-girlfriend. I'm done running." Luca shakes his head. "I thought you were too."

Frustration rips through me. Why can't I have both? My old friendships and new ones? The night of my dreams and the future my pops is trying to create?

Luca stares at me expectantly. He wants a response.

I scowl, then shrug. "Guess not."

His shoulders fall. It's the first crack. The crunch of Luca's sneakers as he turns away sounds a lot like my heart shattering behind my ribs.

I spin on my heel. I can't watch him huddle with Makayla, whispering furiously, both regretting spending even a single second of their night with me. I do one last phone check—eight minutes left—before sprinting back toward Chloe's house like a gold medal is on the line.

Like *everything's* on the line.

Jayla's nowhere. If I were a cheerleader who loathed my boyfriend's best friend, where would I hide?

Clearly, I didn't think through this search-and-rescue plan.

When I got back inside the Campbells' pad, I checked all the obvious places: couches in the main room. The dance floor. Sparkling water station in the kitchen. Downstairs where the STEM nerds had officially taken over the ping-pong table for a complex game of drunken Scrabble.

Nothing.

On paper, this dare was simple. In execution? Far from it.

As I cross through the kitchen again, careful not to bump into anyone who wants to talk or needs me to hold their hair while they barf, I swipe through Instagram stories on my phone. Maybe someone tagged her. But I barely make it through two before my screen goes black.

*Shit.*

My battery is officially dead.

I turn a corner and decide there's one final spot to investigate: the pool.

Jayla can't swim. An almost fatal incident where Jay playfully shoved her into the shallow end at a summer kickback last year led to a two-week breakup no one dare speaks of. She avoids all bodies of water.

"Jayla!" I shout the second the night's warm, muggy air hits me.

I'm met by wide-eyed, strange looks, but she's not here either.

"Theo?"

I swing around. Kendra's lounging on a wicker chair, legs folded under her. I sprint over. "Have you seen Jayla?"

"Like an hour ago? She and Jay had another one of their fallouts."

Everything at the party fades. My brain fails to upload Kendra's words. Nothing processes.

"Wh-what?"

Kendra unlocks her phone, taps away, then shows me the screen. It's a video of Jay and Jayla arguing in Chloe's front yard. Whoever's recording is too far away to capture quality sound. Jayla's gesticulating with her hands. And Jay's having a tantrum before *groveling*, only for Jayla to stomp away.

The video ends.

"She peaced out after that." Kendra says it so matter-of-factly, I barely put everything together.

Jayla's gone. And Jay knew. I walked right into the dare. Never questioned why *I* would be the one to convince her to meet him.

I assumed it was because Jay knew it'd be a hard, but not impossible, thing to pull off.

"Theo? You okay?"

Kendra's voice is a fuzzy noise in the background of my thoughts.

I let Jay play me. Again. I left behind a group of people who wanted nothing from me but honesty and authenticity, for someone who couldn't define either of those words if they were bolded, highlighted, and font size 72.

Now I've ruined a chance with them and failed another dare.

"Hey. Theo?"

I stare off to the pool. The water's surface is still. It's an almost perfect reflection of the sky—shadowy and endless and full of possibility. I want to fall headfirst into it. Smash that image. Sink to the bottom. Feel the burn in my lungs. I want the pressure to dull the noise and empty out my thoughts.

Until I don't remember what it's like to feel wanted like I was by Luca and the others.

# 19

# WRIGHT OR WRONG

**My alarm goes** off at 7:00 a.m. Then at 7:05. Again at 7:10.

I forgot to turn off my weekend wake-up call. After the last twenty-four hours, I wish that weren't the only thing I forgot about my life.

At the screech of the 7:15 alarm, I finally roll over, staring at my ceiling. My eyeballs are dry, throat cottony. I ignore the urge to pee. There's a heaviness pinning me down. I know what it is, but admitting it is pointless.

It won't change what happened.

When I finally peel the sheets back and drag myself out of bed, everything feels sideways. Like I'm navigating through one of those carnival fun houses. Except, it's never-ending. I can't find the exit. Even in the bathroom, it's like I'm staring at a doppelgänger in the mirror instead of myself.

Was that the real me last night? The boy I was with the crew from Maddie's bedroom. Or was he who I could've been—*should've been*—but now it's too late.

While walking downstairs, I waffle between going on my morning run or crawling back into bed until spring break is over. I'm dressed in shorts and an old T-shirt, earbuds in hand. But I can't persuade myself to face the world. The emptiness is overwhelming. I could barely stand up in the shower.

Something's missing. Not Darren or Jay, who I haven't heard from since dropping them off at the Scotts' around three a.m. No, it's the others.

I . . . miss them.

*It was just one night*, I remind myself. One moment in a bedroom with four people I hadn't planned on keeping contact with once we got back to Brook-Oak. Excluding Luca, obviously. But it's more than him.

It's River's geeking out over Monopoly. It's Makayla saving me by the pool. It's the way I made Aleah laugh after so many years of living without that noise.

In the kitchen, I find Dad at the table. He's hunched over his phone. No weekend crime drama is playing. No plate of cold bacon by his elbow. Instead, he's rubbing his temples.

"Uh, good morning?" I say on the way to the fridge.

He doesn't answer.

Poor posture aside, there's an obvious stiffness to every one of Dad's muscles. His jaw and shoulders, down to the tendons of his forearms. He exhales long, even breaths.

"Everything okay, Dad?"

His head snaps up. Noticeable bags sit under his eyes. Slowly drooping eyebrows and his mouth hardening are the first real signs. Next is when his gaze lowers.

I track his eye movements to his phone. *Shit.* The rideshare app probably emailed him an invoice. Usually, when I stay over at Jay's, Mrs. Scott drives me home early on Sunday mornings before their family goes to church. I knew Dad wouldn't be alarmed if he saw me in my own bed when he woke up. But I couldn't bother Mrs. Scott in the middle of the night for a ride home without her or Dad finding out what happened, so I used the app.

"Sit down," he says in a cool, scratchy voice.

"Dad, I can explain—"

"You lied to me," he interrupts. His index finger stabs his phone screen. "I got a call from Jess Scott at six this morning. My son's best friend's mom—one of *my* closest friends—who I thought my son was safe with."

"Dad—"

"No one's parent ever calls another parent at *six in the damn morning* just to chat," he snaps. "To my surprise, Jess was calling to see if you, the son I trusted, were okay. She hadn't seen you like I *thought*. You hadn't stepped foot in her house yesterday. And on her way to get coffee, she found Jay vomiting in the kitchen sink."

*Oh.* So . . . he knows everything, then.

I lean against the fridge, swallowing. What am I supposed to say?

"Do you know what it's like to apologize to Jess and Justin fu—" He catches himself, shaking his head. The tension in his jaw could snap a tree in half. "I had to talk soft and gentle, TJ. In a tone that Mr. Scott wouldn't find *offensive* because God forbid a Black parent speak through their concern and fear in a voice that someone doesn't like. Then we're angry. Uncivilized. Abusive."

"No one thinks that about you, Dad," I say quietly.

But it's loud enough for his eyes to widen, fury rising.

"I've worked so damn hard to be a respectable parent in their eyes," he hisses. "To make sure they never have a reason to think I'm not on their level."

My chin drops. He's right. Everyone loves Miles Wright. He makes sure of it.

"I was okay," I say to my feet. "I'm fi—"

"SIT. DOWN," Dad roars.

I flinch hard against the fridge, knocking a pizza delivery magnet off the door.

The only time I've ever seen Dad this enraged was when he found out about me stealing candy from the corner store. He raised his voice for about two minutes. Lectured and grounded me. But he's never screamed. Never slammed his hand against a table like he does now.

After that incident, I've never given Dad a reason to lose his cool. I was the good son. But it's like years of fury is finally unleashed from its cage.

"Anything could've happened to you!" yells Dad.

I ease into the chair across from him, heart racing.

"You're a Black boy out late doing God knows what with no one to look out for you," Dad continues, chest heaving. "No one's gonna spare your life because you're with Jay. Do you think proximity to his whiteness will save you?"

"No." I sigh.

"They don't care who your friends are. What kind of student you are. How nice you appear. You're *always* a threat."

It's a speech I've heard from him or Granny at least three times a year since I could talk.

"Trayvon. Eric. Tamir. Sandra. Alton. Antwon."

Dad's voice cracks. He only says their first names. As if he's known each one of them. As if instead of being a segment on the news or a memorial on a street corner, those were his children. But that's how it feels each time a new T-shirt comes out with another name added to the list. With every new hashtag.

Like I'm losing more blood. Family. More faces that look like mine.

Dad's eyes are glassy. He shivers before adding, "Breonna Taylor."

I can't help wincing. There are murals all over Louisville, even in the upscale neighborhoods where they probably wouldn't have acknowledged her existence if she were still here.

"Daunte Wright."

It's not even half the names. But it's enough.

"Yes, times have changed," says Dad, exhaling shakily. "But this hasn't." He reaches across the table to jab a finger against the skin on the back of my hand. "This is what they see while you're out *lying* to have a good time."

"I didn't," I say, barely managing to swallow the hot spit in my mouth. I don't tell him what happened. Why last night was far from a good time. I insist, "I didn't drink. Didn't do drugs. I didn't have sex or do anything risky. I was—"

*Safe? With people who wouldn't let anything happen to me?*

It's irrelevant information to Dad. He says, "You lied to me about where you were going." A sadness coats his face. "How do I know you're not lying now?"

I don't have a counterargument. Picking at the broken skin around my thumbnail, I shrug.

Dad's wrinkled T-shirt has a hot sauce stain near the collar. His jaw is unshaven. He probably hasn't showered.

All because of me.

Behind him, I eye the whiteboard. The Plan glares judgingly back.

"I'm sorry," I whisper.

Dad lets out another sigh. "How do you think our family looks to the Scotts?" he asks in a low voice.

I bite my lip so hard I almost taste blood. Anything not to answer.

"Did you at least ask for the recommendation letter?"

It's one question in the dozen or so Dad's already asked. But it's a lit match dropped on the kerosine in my blood. The fire climbs up my throat.

"I don't give a damn what the Scotts think about us!" I yell.

Dad's pupils dilate to the size of Mars, but I'm unaffected.

"Why do *you* care so much?" I ask.

He pauses. It's like he's thinking over his next words. How to manipulate them to sound perfect, as if the Scotts were sitting across from him and not me. "Jess has been my friend for a long time and—"

"And shouldn't that be the reason you're allowed to make mistakes around her?" I offer.

He's quiet for a moment. "Our friendship has nothing to do with you wrecking your future," he finally says.

"You have no idea what I deal with," I growl, finding some of my own Wright ire. "What I've been putting up with from Jay and every other privileged dickhead just to impress them."

Dad's shoulders coil around his ears, but he doesn't interrupt.

"None of this is easy for me," I add, laughing emptily. My eyes sting. I think my chest is going to collapse.

Dad's Adam's apple bobs, but he stays quiet.

"I work hard every second. Follow every step. And guess what? It's never enough." I close my eyes, willing the tears back. "Now I have to rely on a real d-bag to write me a letter to get somewhere."

Dad leans on his elbows, his face a calm that unnerves me. "If that's the heaviest of your burdens, then that means all my tireless efforts are paying off."

"You think I'm ungrateful?" I ask, slumping in my chair.

His mouth doesn't say yes. His eyes do, though.

"Every day I'm reminded of what you've sacrificed to get me here," I say, shaking my head in disbelief. "Missing my track meets to pick up extra shifts. When you look too tired to eat dinner. Days off researching college app fees. Scholarships. Never upgrading your wardrobe so I have new cleats. Never . . . dating."

This time, Dad squirms.

"I see it all the time." I up-nod at the whiteboard. "It doesn't make being successful any less stressful. It makes it worse."

As hard as I fight, my voice falters when I say, "I'm terrified to fail because you'll think we both failed."

Finally, Dad's resolve splinters. His shoulders fall. He stares at a scratch on the table.

"God," I whisper, "Aleah was right. I'm always doing things for everyone but me."

Dad's head jerks back up. "Wait. Aleah-*Aleah*?"

Fuck. I didn't mean to say that out loud.

"Yes. Aleah."

"When did you two start talking again? I thought you said she wanted nothing to do with you."

I say, "I lied."

It's what I am, right? A liar. A horrible friend. A thoughtless asshole out to please the world at the cost of himself.

I wasn't sure this day would ever come. When I called Aleah to end things, I waited until Dad was asleep. Unlike Aleah, I didn't have a phone back then. I had to use his. For days after, I'd lie awake at night worrying she'd call him. Tell him what I did. Or scream about how Dad and Mario's relationship broke our friendship.

But she never did.

So now I do. I tell him about the Kroger incident. How hard it was watching him walk around like he had nothing left. How all I wanted was for him to be himself again. And ditching Aleah did that. It fixed his broken heart.

Or I thought it did.

Dad's pale. His mouth opens and closes like a fish ripped from the water. He's barely inhaling. The sting behind my eyes increases.

We're both quiet for a long time.

Dad's hands tremble. "You're going to apologize to Jay's

parents," he eventually says. "Then you'll ask for that letter. Focus on track. Your grades."

"Dad," I attempt.

His eyes finally meet mine. "Get the hell out of this place so you don't repeat the same cycle our family's been living in for generations."

I flex my fingers on the table. Count backward from five. Anything to cool the frustration I feel bubbling up again. Nothing works. I need to tell him what I've always been too scared to admit.

"I've never hated our life here," I say. "I'm not embarrassed to be a Wright. I'm proud, unlike you."

My eyes fall on The Plan again and I spit out, "The only reason I'd want to leave here is to escape the shadow of being Miles Wright's perfect son!"

Regret immediately hits me. I guess I don't know how to get anyone to hear me without being hurtful.

Dad looks past me like I'm a clone and he's trying to find the real Theo.

Maybe Jay and I aren't that different.

After a long beat, Dad's chair scrapes against the floor. He pushes back from the table. Purposefully, he avoids my gaze. In one long swipe of the eraser, half the blue marker from the whiteboard is gone. Dad slouches as if he doesn't have the energy to finish.

"You're grounded. For all of spring break. Starting now," he whispers.

"Dad, I—"

"No phone. No leaving the house unless it's for a run. No Wi-Fi. Use my laptop for all your assignments that require internet," he continues as if I never opened my mouth. "No friends either."

Not a problem. I don't have any left.

"I won't force you to apologize to the Scotts," he starts. "I'll fix it. And this Aleah thing . . ."

He trails off, grabbing his phone. The back door squeaks open. Unfiltered sunlight pours in. The glow highlights the exhaustion in Dad's face. He looks so much older. Defeated too.

"Decide who you want to be," he croaks. "Or you'll end up like me—alone."

The door closes with a heavy thud.

Out of everything we've said, that last word hurts the most.

It's true. There's no TNT. No new friends from Maddie's bedroom. No prom. No real future to look forward to.

Only loneliness.

It takes a minute before I leave the table. Exit the kitchen. In the living room, I catch a glimpse of one photo on the wall. Granny and me at Pride. Our ginormous smiles brighter than the blue sky and rainbow flags in the background.

I remember Dad hoisting me up on his shoulders afterward. Our laughter flying all the way into the clouds. Granny holding his hand as we marched through summer heat.

I wanted nothing more than for Dad to feel the same way I did about him that day: *proud*.

Today's not that day.

I can't stomach my own reflection in the photo's glass. Dad's disappointed voice echoing in my head. I'm barely halfway up the stairs before the onslaught of tears rips an achingly loud sob from my throat.

# 20

# RUNNING NOWHERE

**School breaks are** always way too short. But spring break without a phone, unrestricted internet, or a change of scenery from the four walls of my bedroom is the longest, most painful time away from school ever. I'm looking forward to returning to Mr. Kumar and Algebra 2. Me, excited about *math*.

Ugh.

But a six thirty a.m. track practice awaits me first.

Waking up two hours early on a Monday to catch the public bus to Brook-Oak wasn't terrible. Definitely not something I want to repeat on a daily basis. Today's forty-minute journey was necessary.

With no phone all break, I haven't talked to Darren. Not so much as an email could be sent on Dad's laptop without his authorization. It felt absurd for our first communication after eight days to be me asking Darren for a ride to school. Plus, I'm not certain where we stand. Where *I* stand with him.

How much does he know about what happened at the party?

Darren's always been the chill one in our group. The mediator. Is this the one time he chooses Jay's side over mine?

I couldn't ask Dad to drop me off either. We're still not talking. Not like normal. We've resorted to brief sentences. Sometimes only single words. Small nods and head shakes. There haven't been any discussions about what we said that day. No apologies. We haven't eaten dinner together. Shared popcorn while judging the Transformers movies.

We're two drone bees buzzing around a hive with no queen.

Sad thing is, it makes me miss Granny even more.

So, public transportation it is. No biggie. Just your average Black student in a cerulean BOHS hoodie, JanSport in his lap, munching on brown sugar cinnamon Pop-Tarts, and wondering what fresh hell awaits me once I get to school.

The locker room is empty. A few familiar cars littered the parking lot when I arrived, including Jay's. Despite how I feel about what's happened with him, I'm staying true to my word. Something I learned from Granny.

After a thorough search, I don't find Jay or any of my teammates hanging around. Perfect. I need at least ten minutes of peace before I do this.

Unfortunately, I'm only given six.

As I'm pulling on my cleats, open gym bag on the floor, folded joggers on the bench next to my leg, a "Hey" echoes nearby.

I eye Darren cautiously, replying, "Sup."

Friend or enemy?

After a brief inspection of his attire, the answer is immediate: *friend*.

Darren's dressed in a forest green and cardinal tracksuit. They match the shorts I have on. His unzipped jacket reveals a loose-fit white T-shirt with an ugly cartoon tree on it.

Mountainview High's mascot.

It's hard to ignore the ache in my cheeks from grinning so hard.

"Uh, you look tight," I comment.

He rolls his eyes. "I look *sick*, bro." He then hits a few quick poses, modeling our rival's wardrobe like he's stepped onto a runway in Milan. My best friend is straight out of a low-budget comedy movie.

My smile widens. Darren *is* my best friend. Through and through, he's always been there for me, including right now, dressed like he's the one who lost the dare.

"So . . ." I begin, fiddling with my laces, "how much do you know?" After his brow furrows, I add, "About what happened at the party?"

"All of it."

"All of it?"

He nods. "At least Jay's POV." His bicep nearly bursts through the Mountainview jacket as he brushes a hand over his hair. "Most of it I put together on my own."

"Uh-huh."

A smirk pulls at my mouth watching his arrogant expression. Darren Holmes, true detective. He and Dad would make a great crime-solving duo.

"But if you want to fill in some of the blanks . . ." He leans against a pair of lockers behind him, timid eyes surveying me. "By all means."

I hunch forward, elbows on my knees, digging fingers into my hair. The room is fairly quiet. The occasional drip from a showerhead in the distance. That one halogen light that needs to be replaced buzzing like a fly. Anxiously, I tap my spikes on the cement floor. Anything to dim the noisy replay from Saturday night in my head.

"What's there to tell?" I ask, launching into an abridged version of what occurred before Darren can respond.

He listens intently, his face remaining neutral.

After I finish, he says, "I figured as much" with a frown.

"Are you mad at me?" I ask after a long pause.

"Mad at you?"

"Yeah, you know." I toss my hands up. "For not speaking to you on the ride back to Jay's. Or explaining things then. I dunno . . ." I rub the back of my neck, unable to look him in the eye. "For being an asshole about your great night when—"

"When you were having such a shitty one?"

*Well, yeah.* Not that I say it to him.

Guilt rattles me, though. How did I ever think Darren would intentionally ghost me? That his heart hasn't always been in the right place, even if he wasn't? That he was *anything* like . . . Jay? I couldn't help myself.

"Theo, bro." His hand rests on my shoulder. "I'm not mad you iced me out."

"Technically, my pops grounded me. No phone. No internet."

"Wow. Bet that was rough." Darren snorts, then quickly collects himself. "The only person I've been mad at is myself for not pulling you aside to talk more. Speaking up when I knew Jay was in the wrong."

He squeezes my tendons until I raise my eyes. "I should've done better."

My nose wrinkles. It's the same thing Makayla called me out about—being quiet when I should use my voice to check others. The same thing I wanted Jay to do for me at SpeedEx.

"I won't hold it against you," I say with a half-hearted laugh.

"You *should*." He grins crookedly. "Best friends have a lot of jobs. Speaking up, even if it makes others uncomfortable, is a priority."

I return his grin.

"Even when I'm not there-*there*," he starts, patting my shoulder now. "I've always got your back." He puffs his chest, showing off his Mountainview clothes once more. He's a total dork, but the honesty in his voice is indisputable.

Clearing my throat, I say, "Thanks."

Everyone's allowed a selfish. Self-care too. But knowing your friends can do both and still be there for you matters.

I stand and stretch. "Since we've been mutually terrible friends lately . . ."

Darren squawks, feigning offense as I unzip my hoodie before hanging it in my locker. I sigh, continuing, "Tell me all about—"

"Whoa, whoa!" Darren staggers back, eyes wide. His stare lands on my midsection.

Right. Almost forgot.

I spent my last chunk of money saved for a prom haircut,

plus bow tie and matching socks, ordering Mountainview apparel during the break. A pair of kitchen shears turned the T-shirt into a bonified stomach-revealing crop top. Man of my word and all.

Wearing it to school this morning required way too much courage, but I couldn't stop thinking about Luca. It's been happening more than I care to admit. I remember his black nails. The way we're tired of accepting this role of masculinity Black and brown boys are obligated to uphold. His frankly "fuck your rules" mentality. Despite what I said outside the party, that's what I really got from our conversation in the bathroom.

We're both working toward being who we want to be.

"Yeah, so." I stand taller, chin raised. "Is this a problem?"

"Uh, no. Why would it be?"

I shrug.

"But if you're starting an OnlyFans to pay for prom," Darren says, eyebrows wiggling, "one, you're underage. Two, I support your thirst-trap behavior, but not in the name of formal wear and slow-dancing to Adele."

It's the first genuine laugh I've let out in more than a week.

"Shut up." I wrench an arm around his neck, dragging him toward the track. "Tell me all about Bree, you sycophant."

"Sure! But first tell me where these abs came from? Daaaamn, Theo."

The team is stretching on the green field our track surrounds when Darren and I arrive. Guys go through their pre-practice routines, earbuds in, finding their zone. Some goof off. Two seniors, Abel and Julio, pass a soccer ball back and forth instead of warming up. Typical benchwarmer fodder.

Tingles spread through my belly. I'm shoulder to shoulder with Darren as half our teammates stop to look.

"Jealous wannabes," says Darren. "Flex those abdominals."

"*Not* helping," I mumble.

The second Jay sees us, he freezes. His large eyes narrow. He whispers something to Grant, an underclassman. Even from a distance, his smirk is electric. If everyone hasn't caught a glimpse of us yet, Jay's sharp whistle certainly fixes that.

"Nice quads, Wright!"

Stifled laughter follows. Three upperclassmen give me a standing ovation. Kavon shrugs before returning to his heel-toe drills.

By the time our spikes touch the polyurethane track surface, Jay's waiting near the starting lines. Arms crossed, eyebrows knit, annoyed expression fully loaded. He's paler than usual. His topknot is crooked, clothes wrinkled. He looks like he's barely surviving a weeklong hangover.

*Good.*

"Why're you dressed like that, D?" he asks. "You didn't fail the dare."

"I know." Darren beams. Then, as casual as ever, he says, "Solidarity. You know all about that, right, Jayson?"

Jay's jaw flexes at the betrayal. He levels me with an even stare. "Proud of you for not punking out."

The impulse to punch him returns. But it won't solve anything. Only add to my growing list of problems.

"Why would I?"

My cool response turns Jay's face maroon. "Whatever." He extends a fist bump. "We good? TNT, yeah?"

I blink hard. "What?"

"Come on, Theo. Let it go."

"Let it . . . *go*?" Absently, my voice rises. Several eyes are on us. By now, I'm sure half the school's heard about what went down between me and Jay at the party.

"It was a dare," he says. "It's what we always do."

I can feel every bone and tendon in my fingers ache. Carelessly bitten nails dig into my palms. Resistance is waning.

"You're a dick, Jay," I hiss. "The shit you pulled is much bigger than a—"

"Wright! Jacobs!"

The morning skies are that nice blend of blue and rose. A ripe spring day is imminent. But the thunder in the air is Coach Devers's no-bullshit voice as she stomps onto the track.

At first glance, Coach Devers comes off as one of those former athletes turned motivational speakers. In the halls, she grins widely. Tosses out random uplifting quotes to students. Always wearing some bright, neon workout clothes. The only time she raises her voice is when students are late to class, because she values educa-tion as much as sports.

But here? Coach Devers is an unpredictable hurricane between the white lane lines.

Right now, she looks as if Darren and I are trying her patience. To be fair, we kind of are.

"What the actual hell are you two wearing?"

"Practice gear?" Darren tries, smiling impishly.

His charm works on almost every teacher, librarian, and adult he comes into contact with. But not Coach. She's immune.

"*Mountainview* practice gear," Jay notes like a true snitch. "Our rivals."

Coach turns her stone-faced look on him. She obviously doesn't need his help.

"Why are you on *my* track wearing that?" Coach asks Darren and me.

"Uh."

"You know what? I don't care."

She promptly lays into us about breaking team rules. The sacred competition between Brook-Oak and Mountainview. Respecting our school, our teammates. Threatening to keep us out of finals for not taking any of this seriously. It's a raging tempest of shouting and pacing and spittle.

I haven't been on the receiving end of one of these since missing a practice my first year with the team.

When she's done, Coach is breathing heavily. It's the quiet after the storm. My knees almost give out. Darren looks ready to throw up. Jay's satisfied grin stands out among all the faces surrounding us.

"But I'm not benching you," Coach finally says.

The pressure against my lungs finally releases.

"Wait, what?" Jay screeches like a fire alarm.

Coach's head snaps in his direction, forcing him to startle backward. "I'm not benching them," she repeats to everyone.

No one speaks. But eyes are moving. Silent conversations happen within the circle.

"Whatever this is . . ." She waves a hand at Darren and me. "Don't do it again. We need all the help we can get to win conference finals. That means having a strong hurdler and the best relay team we can put out there."

"Yup," Kavon agrees. He's another senior, well respected for his work ethic and kindness off the track. Like clockwork, others begin to concede.

"Coach, no," Jay objects. His stance wobbles a little when Coach glares. "You laid down the rules from day one. We need to respect them. There's consequences if we break them."

Our eyes lock over Coach's shoulder.

"As an alternate for the relay team," Jay starts, beaming, "I can replace Wright. We can still win."

"Bullshit," Abel coughs into his fist, then hastily ducks behind Kavon.

Another rule: no swearing at practices.

"I can perform just as well as Theo," Jay notes. "Probably better."

I ignore the *ooohs* from the guys. My heart thuds loudly. I'm back to walking through a fun house version of my life. Upside down and sideways. Reality crashes into me: *This* is what Jay wanted all along. Why he added the Mountainview consequence for failing the dare. Why he didn't speak up after finding out about KD and Christian.

He wants my spot.

But for what?

"Know your role, Scott," Coach says, pointing at the whistle and stopwatch hanging from her neck. "I'm in charge. I choose the lineups. I make the final calls."

"But—"

"If you want Wright's spot so bad," Coach continues, interrupting Jay's whiny protesting, "then respect the laws of the track. Prove yourself. Race him for it."

Another series of crowing is quickly silenced by Coach's lethal glare. Jay scowls, undeterred. Me? I'm shaking. But not from nerves or embarrassment.

It's frustration and indignation and resolve.

"Fine," Jay grunts, stepping out of the circle.

Coach glances my way.

Wordlessly, I follow Jay to the starting line. Before I reach him, Darren yells, "Theo!" Over my shoulder, he gives me a determined nod.

We have our own secret conversation: *You've got this.*

"On my whistle," Coach says when she's in place.

I don't spare Jay the glance I can feel him giving me. I ease my body into position. Slide my right foot back. I focus on the red surface. The white lane lines. Slow my breathing. Tune out all the noise from our teammates.

*Find your zone*, Coach has told us repeatedly in the past. *Don't just focus on winning. Where do you want running to take you?*

I've never been able to answer her question.

I ran to win. To impress and help my teammates. To chase Dad's dreams.

But when the whistle blows, I know.

I'm running from the Theo I was supposed to be toward the Theo I want to be.

Around the first turn, Jay is ahead. My start was sluggish. I haven't stretched. The burn is already racing up my legs. During spring break, I did the bare minimum, too distracted by everything else.

Now my failures are catching up. Outstretched claws desperate to sink into my skin and snatch me back. Yank me away from my own goals.

I fight against them to close the gap.

Things is, I've always loved track. Being good at something. But somewhere in the back of my mind, I knew running was also part of The Plan. An endgame. It kept me ahead of anyone to my right or left.

On those last one hundred meters? With Jay inching closer to the finish line, his own self-centered goal meaning an end to mine? I mentally add another bullet point to the whiteboard that has controlled so much of my destiny:

*Show Jayson Scott who I really am.*

That's all it takes. I dust him.

At the finish line, I double over. Gasp for air. Sweat drips in my eye as Darren hugs my neck, whooping in my ear. A booming "Theo! Theo!" chant breaks out. I catch some of the team trying to console Jay, but he shakes them off, only making eye contact with me.

I don't blink.

I don't let him win this either.

Coach ends the celebration. She barks at everyone to finish their warm-ups. Get ready for practice. Then her steely eyes locate Darren and me. At the very corners of her mouth, I spot movement.

She's repressing a smirk I unabashedly show off for both of us.

That is, until she reminds Darren and me we still violated team rules. While the others work out, we have to run three miles, which feels like a death sentence after just expending my best efforts defeating Jay. She's not finished, though.

"You'll be cleaning the team's locker room too," she adds, finally smiling. "For the next month."

The groan Darren lets out is almost as loud as Coach's warning whistle.

We're barely starting our jog before Jay's by our side.

He's breathless like me, but still manages to spit, "Congrats! Once again, you're the golden boy. Everyone's fave."

"Chill, bro," Darren says.

Jay ignores him. "You have no idea what it's like, do you?" He shakes his head at me. "The pressure I'm constantly under from my parents. To be perfect. To fix everything Jules fucks up. To *earn* my way into a school they approve of. They won't even pay my tuition until I show them I'm exactly the kid they expected Jules to be."

Frustrated tears sit on his blond eyelashes.

"All they see is a mess-up waiting to happen," he heaves out. "All my mom talks about is how I'm not Theo, the golden child."

"Stop calling me that."

"Why? It's true!" He laughs wildly, wet trails streaking his cheeks. "You win at everything, and it doesn't even matter to you. But I *need* this, Theo. You don't."

A rebuttal waits in my throat. I want to remind him my pops is the same way. Of the conversations we've had over the years about this. The things that will never be handed to me like they are for him. Jay's rich, white, a boy, and straight. He always has the advantage. He'll never have to work as hard as me.

But what's the point? He's never seen the imbalance in our friendship. In who I am versus who he is. All the things Jay gave me were so he could take more later. We weren't fully honest with each other about anything.

Jay wipes at his eyes, bottom lip trembling. "I always lose with you, Theo. Even when I win, I lose." He sniffs hard.

The feeling's mutual, then. I don't hurl that at him like he does me. Instead, I whisper, "I'm done, Jay," before jogging away.

Behind me, I hear some of the team mouthing off at Jay. Kavon leads the charge. The tiniest wave of relief rolls down my spine.

Maybe Darren's not the only one who has my back.

Darren and I run in silence. Our forms are similar. Breaths synchronized. I wonder if our thoughts are too. I doubt it.

My brain keeps returning to Jay. Our friendship was never like Darren's and mine. It wasn't homegrown, the roots planted by common interests and shared experiences. Our friendship stood on a foundation others built for us. Lived in a house we didn't craft.

It belonged to our parents, not us.

"Hey," Darren says between pants, "you never told me where you were during the party."

I look at him questioningly.

"I *know* you didn't spend the whole night chasing Jay or . . ." He hesitates. "Christian."

I should probably tell him I'm over that. There's another boy I'm kind of stuck on, who most likely hates me by now.

"You really want to know?" I ask as we finish our second mile.

"Duh!" He rolls his eyes. "Best friend. Doing better. Remember?"

I snort, though it takes more effort than I'm willing to admit. My legs feel like jelly. A sharp ache I haven't felt since my early days on the team moves through my calves.

Turns out one last lap is the perfect amount of time to unload my night with the others.

I spare no detail, especially when it comes to Luca. By the time I'm done, we cross the finish line. Darren falls into the grass, groaning. I join him. We're soaked in sweat, heaving.

"Damn. Sorry about the Luca thing," he eventually puffs out. "I mean, you did say some pretty messed-up things. Even for you."

Blush flares against my cheeks. Thankfully, my wince goes unnoticed.

"But it sucks for him, mostly."

"What do you mean?" I ask between gasps for air.

"Coming in second place twice in twenty-four hours?" he replies with a lethargic shrug. "And then the guy he *kissed* throws the things he's dealing with at home in his face? Brutal."

"I wasn't his first pick either!" I complain. "I was his *rebound*."

Saying it out loud hurts a lot more than letting it bounce around my head all week. It was the only way to not feel like the Luca thing was a total loss. Even though it is.

"And you know that because . . . ?"

"Because he—" I stop myself.

*Because his first choice wasn't his from the start. It was his parents'. And all I did was remind him of that.*

I obviously do a poor job of disguising my thoughts since

Darren says, "Don't you just love when those epiphanies hit you. It's like . . . *magic*. Or a slap in the face."

"Shut up," I moan, too exhausted to punch his shoulder.

He goes quiet for a second, and I turn my head to eye him.

"What?"

"This is the most you've ever told me about a guy." There's no weirdness is his voice or side-eye. Nothing about being gay or having a crush on a guy affects Darren. They're simply indisputable facts to him.

To Darren, I've always been just Theo.

"I just—" My heart rate spikes like I'm still on those last fifty meters of a race. "I wanted prom so bad. Everyone else gets this . . . *big* high school dream."

Tears burn against my eyelashes. I blink them back.

"It's like the universe keeps telling me no." Quietly, I add, "Because I'm me."

Darren remains quiet. My chest tightens. I don't know why I keep expecting him to be like Cole. Like Jay. But I'm so glad Darren keeps proving me wrong.

"You know," he begins, "I want that for you too. I'll never walk in your shoes. As much garbage as we both constantly face, I can't say I'll ever experience it at the same level as you do."

I blink and blink.

"You deserve your big gay-as-F prom night." He elbows me. "For reals. I understand why you did what you did."

I smile at the clouds. "Thanks, D."

"Anyway," he says, rolling onto his side. "Sounds like you have a handful of dares to make up for. And soon."

The grass itches the dip in my spine. It's official: wearing a crop top certainly has its negatives.

"You think I should . . . try to fix things?"

"Yes, asshole!" He laughs softly. "They're your friends."

"You are too," I whisper.

"I know." He yanks blades of grass up. I wonder if he's upset I took one of our traditions to another group. That there are others who know a side of me I didn't show him. Darren eventually says, "You can have both, Theo. No one's gonna question your loyalty. Friendships shouldn't have limitations. The only rule is don't be a dick to people you care about."

I chuckle. "Like Jay."

"Like Jay."

After another pause, the wind mercifully brushing over us, he says, "They're your friends, so fix it."

I get the sense Darren doesn't need me to reply.

He rolls onto his back, smirking at the slow-drifting white clouds like he's never been wrong about anything in his entire life.

# 21

# OUR GHOSTS NEVER LEAVE

**"To the left.** Not there. To the *left*."

"Okay, Beyoncé, I hear you," I mumble, re-centering a standing ring light that's almost taller than me for the fourth time.

Makayla glares from in front of an all-white bookshelf that *is* taller than me.

"Choosing violence today, I see," I whisper.

Snark probably isn't wise considering Makayla's the only one from our little group currently speaking to me. Luckily, I didn't have to resort to pleading with Jayla to get Makayla's attention. Nope. Good old-fashioned social media begging did the trick. Although, she left my DM on read for forty hours before agreeing to meet up.

Let the record show I didn't creep on Luca's account just to see his crinkle-eyed smile. All I've been receiving in the hallways now are glimpses at the back of his head as he pointedly walks in the opposite direction. I also didn't create and quickly delete a finsta in hopes of sending a follow request to Aleah's private account.

I have some dignity left.

(Barely.)

"Here?" I sigh, repositioning the ring light.

"Perfect," she replies while checking the glow intensity in her phone's camera. "Was that so difficult?"

Instead of complaining that, yes, setting up the light—along with helping her detangle fairy lights as well as reorganizing her books so the spines formed a rainbow palette—was indeed grueling, I flop on her bed, wincing when she throws me another stink eye for messing up her pillow collection.

"Sorry."

She sighs dismissively, turning away to study her shelves. I predict an inevitable headache in my future.

I let my gaze roam around her bedroom.

Hardwood floors stained dark. Hanging shelves stuffed with trophies and awards—cheerleading, gymnastics, drama camp. Sheer curtains let in enough late afternoon glow to make everything appear sharper. Her throw blanket feels hand-quilted with the kind of care an elderly relative puts into crafts. On the wall behind her desk is a framed poster for *Wicked*, which I'm guessing is her favorite musical since there are at least two photos of her dressed as Glinda for Halloween.

The rest of the room is all Brook-Oak Cheer Squad swag and . . .

"Um. You have a lot of—"

"Books?" Makayla follows my eyes, lips pursed. "Wow, you really think I'm nothing but a stereotypical cheerleader? Mean girl philosophies, ponytails, and a weakness for rumors, huh?"

"No." I wrinkle my nose. "I mean, I *probably* did. I've made a lot of unfair judgment calls in the past."

Neither one of us mentions Jay's name. I'm sure we're both thinking it.

"Thrilled I was the one to change your opinion," says Makayla without any real heat in her tone. A half-hearted smile dances across her lips.

"Anyway," I say, plucking a stuffed penguin off her bedside table that Makayla quickly snatches back, "that's why I'm here, right? For your dare. Help everyone—myself included—get to know the *real* Makayla."

Hugging the penguin close to her chest, she says, "You don't have to do this."

"Yes, I do," I reply firmly. "For the group."

"But we're not . . ."

"Friends?" I raise my eyebrows.

She nods into the penguin's head.

"I know." I pick at a loose thread on her blanket. "But I fucked up that night for everyone. I want to make things right."

"You know," Makayla says, laying the penguin on her desk before sitting next to me. "This doesn't count as accomplishing your own dare. Selfless sacrifices aren't a personal goal."

"Oh, trust me," I say, beaming, "my motives are completely selfish."

She snorts. "Let me guess: Luca?"

"No."

"Math obsession aside, Luca's a snack." She waggles her eyebrows.

Rubbing my suddenly damp palms across the knees of my joggers, I say, "I want to help him finish his dare too. Another promposal." As much as that's going to suck considering it won't be *me* he's promposing to. "I could use some help with date suggestions, though."

"Wait, you're not—"

I shake my head before she can finish her question.

"He doesn't want anything to do with me," I comment.

*Not after what I said*, I almost tell her. I'm sure Luca already has. My green Luigi- and Yoshi-sock-covered feet slide across the hardwood.

"Plus," I add with a defeated sigh, "since Jay's not paying anymore, I can't exactly afford the big, magically gay prom night I wanted. Luca deserves better than a chicken finger dinner and a date rocking one of his pops' old suits."

Thankfully, Makayla doesn't react once I finish word vomiting on her bed.

"You really care that much about what others think of you?"

I laugh. "Like you don't?"

She shrugs. It's almost believable, considering her appearance. Hair bundled up in a chaotic bun on top of her head. An off-the-shoulder peach top with white shorts. Barely any makeup on.

For a long moment, she openly studies me. It's like she's trying to unlock a door. Unearth a hidden treasure.

*Sorry, Makayla, nothing special here.*

"Should we, uh . . ." I signal to the ring light. "The video."

We're recording content for her YouTube channel. A get-to-know-me tag thingy. I don't know.

"Yeah." She grabs her phone from the bed. But she doesn't mount it on the ring light. Instead, she taps opens a file. "Would you mind watching this first?"

"What is it?"

She wobbles a little, passing her phone to me.

"A video I made this weekend about reputations. The harassment me and other girls have had to deal with." She wrings her hands. "And the people that call themselves friends when you're going through this."

"Oh." I delicately cradle her phone in my hands. "Okay."

"I haven't posted it yet," she admits.

I press play.

Makayla's in the same setting: her bedroom. Most of the background accessories are stripped away. No fairy lights. Books out of view. Early morning sunlight washes over her bare face. She sits cross-legged, smiling in the beginning of the video while introducing herself and what she's about to discuss.

I can feel her nerves through the screen, but I keep watching.

Two minutes in, she's crying but still laying it all out there.

The messages and comments on her posts. Social gatherings she's avoided unless she knew she'd have at least three other girls with her the whole time. The whispers at school. Adults who've spent more time commenting on what she wears than what's happened to her. Friend after friend who preferred to low-key slut-shame her in the name of a joke rather than stand up for her when it mattered.

Four minutes and ten seconds in, the sting against my eyes is unbearable.

She mentions the guys who swore they were "the good ones" but never bothered to check other boys who targeted her or anyone else.

I'm shaking.

By the end, Makayla's listing resources. Help lines. Web pages. She's smiling again, even with a red nose and tear tracks on her cheeks.

When the screen goes black, I can barely swallow. Listening to her tell the story at the party was rough. But this . . . it aches in a brand-new way.

"Makayla," I say, choked. "I'm sorry."

"Pro tip, Theo," she says, taking back her phone. "If you want to apologize to someone, tell them exactly what you're sorry for. Name it. Own it. Or don't say it at all."

I nod, hands trembling against my thighs.

I feel shitty about not being able to name it like she said. But I regret so much. One day, I hope I can give her the real apology she deserves.

She smiles sadly. "Thank you anyway."

"I can't tell you whether to post it or not," I begin, gesturing to her phone, "but I'll support you either way."

The corners of her lips wiggle. She exhales, a genuine Makayla Lawrence grin appearing in the aftermath.

"Enough of that." She finally hooks her phone into the ring light. Grabs a small remote. "You're here to help me with this Book Boyfriend tag. Can't believe I'm going on main so everyone can see the . . . um."

"Real you?"

She wrinkles her nose, nodding.

"I've seen worse versions of you."

After punching my shoulder, she drops a stack of books in my lap. "Sit there and look pretty while we talk about books."

Before she starts recording, Makayla twists to face me. "Hey. I'll help with the Luca thing," she says sincerely. "But I need you to help with someone else's dare first."

I squint curiously.

"River."

I don't even hesitate to reply: "Bet."

"I can't believe I've never tried this!"

"Dope, right?" I say, dunking a red straw into my white Styrofoam cup.

River nods eagerly before powering through a brain freeze from slurping down too much of their cherry limeade slush.

I have my signature blue raspberry one.

We're outside a Sonic Drive-In not too far from Brook-Oak. Katie, River's sister, dropped us off, promising to return after her eight o'clock Intro to Film class. She goes to the University of Louisville. I almost asked her opinion about the school. If she likes being close to home.

But today's not about me. I'm here for River.

"It's so good," exclaims River as we walk through the parking lot.

I laugh. "How have you never had a Sonic slush before?"

"Bad Yelp reviews?" River offers. "I try not to eat at places with less than three-point-five stars."

I almost choke on another slurp. "No one comes to Sonic for their food or service." Proudly, I lift my cup into the air like it's Excalibur. "Only for the glory that is their slushes."

"That's fair."

"They're one of my fave ways to come down after a meet," I tell them. "Minus the brain freezes."

On cue, River winces through another frozen headache.

I manage to keep my cackle in check.

Part of me wants to mention how TNT used to come here. Trading off who bought the round of slushes. Sitting in the back of Jay's open trunk. Watching the sunset with our cleats kicked off, legs swinging as we talked about nothing at all. But I'm not ready to go there.

The Jay-shaped wound in my chest is still fresh, taking far too long to heal.

We follow the sidewalk along the main road in a comfortable silence. When did we get to this point? Where the quiet isn't awkward? I'm used to the way River flicks hair out of their face every five minutes. And they don't mind my humming as we walk.

Just two kids moving through the world.

Two friends?

My eyes are drawn to River. They chew on their red straw. Their pace slows to match mine.

"I'm really sorry about what I said the other night. For—" I pause, scrambling for what to insert here.

"Being a prick?" River offers. "A jerk?"

"Well—"

"An asshat? Douchebag? Complete—"

"Geez. Point taken!" I hold a hand up. "How many more nouns did you have ready?"

"At least five."

River grins, chin tilted so high their glasses unsettle on their face.

"I was . . . all of that," I say, sighing. "And I shouldn't have been. I said messed-up shit. Ditched everyone. I acted like our group wasn't important when it really was. I'm sorry."

River shrugs. "I understand."

"You do?"

"When Devau—" They stop, breathing deeply. I give them as much time as they need. "After everything happened with him, Katie kept trying to encourage me to do things. Go to counseling. Hiking. Painting. Join a queer support group."

Ahead of us, the sun kisses the green hills in the distance. Buildings are blurred by the light. Trees dance with a rare breeze.

"My parents insisted I visit his grave. Process things," River continues. "All I wanted was to stay in bed. Be alone."

Our arms brush as we turn a corner.

"I was the biggest asshole to them," says River, pushing fringe out of their eyes. "I thought I knew what was best for . . . me."

I stir around my melting slush.

"Anyway, sometimes we're jerks to the people who actually care. I don't think those moments define us or them."

They pause again, but this time to snap a panoramic photo of the slow-bruising sky. I stand away from the camera's lens.

"I'm also sorry I didn't invite the others along," I say.

Because, other than Makayla, they're still not acknowledging my existence at school.

"It's cool," says River nonchalantly.

"You sure?"

Even with the red straw between their lips, their smile is ever present. "Mmhmm." Their face scrunches after another rush of too much cold slush.

"Slow down," I say around a laugh. "Savor it."

"There's a lot less pressure to do this without . . ." River starts after a minute. "An audience."

We stop at a crosswalk. Across the street is a huge, rusted iron gate, open wide like a shark's mouth waiting to swallow anyone who passes. River doesn't seem bothered by how long it takes for the signal to change. I get it. This is an overwhelming step.

"To be honest," they say as we finally cross, "the night of the party? I didn't want to do it with everyone watching."

Guilt fills my chest.

I'm the one who dared River to visit the cemetery with all of us. I never thought of what that'd be like. To say goodbye to someone with strangers watching.

Dad wouldn't let me go to Granny's funeral. He said I was too young. He didn't want my last memories of her to be a closed casket sinking into the ground. I was so mad at him then. How could he take my choice away? The chance to see her one last time.

Now I realize he was right.

I'm glad my last memory is being curled with her in the hospital bed—even though I wasn't supposed to be—watching reruns of her favorite TV shows.

We dump our slush cups outside the gates. River pulls up a map on their phone. We follow it. The sun's still up, but there's a strangeness about being in the cemetery. It's not terrifying. More like an odd, sad comfort. Headstones everywhere. Bodies in the ground. It's almost as if a peace hovers overhead.

Nothing can hurt them now.

Devaughn's grave is covered in colorful flowers. Someone's recently cleared off the stone marker. The gold-scripted dates make me nauseous.

Fifteen years old.

River bends down to pick up an anime character plushie from the flowers.

"Goku from *DBZ*," they whisper with a short laugh. "God, he could be so unoriginal with his favorites." They grin. "Just like you."

"Hey!" I nudge their shoulder before wrapping an arm around them as they begin to tremble.

River quietly sobs. I blink at the petals swaying in the breeze. Sunlight skims over hundreds of headstones. The noiselessness is broken up by chirping birds.

River doesn't seem ready to speak, so I do.

"I can't imagine not having my pops around," I say to the sky.

We're still not really talking, but I know he's there. Always. When I wake up on the sofa after falling asleep studying, there's a blanket draped over me. On practice days, I find two Gatorades on the kitchen table before school. Freshly washed, folded clothes at the foot of my bed after school.

"I hate thinking about a world where he doesn't know the real me."

Every Pride, I ache for Granny. I wish she would've been around when I came out. I think she knew back then. But I couldn't tell her. She was sick and dealing with so much. Always worried about Dad and me. The last thing I wanted was to add another thing to the pile— the fear of what might happen to her gay, Black grandson if she wasn't around to protect me like she always had.

"Devaughn's the only reason I told my parents I'm enby," admits River.

I squeeze them tighter.

"I was nervous. He swore they'd get it, just like Katie would." River sighs wetly, bottom lip shivering. "My parents still struggle. Still get it wrong sometimes. They forget to correct relatives. But they try so hard to get it right. For me."

I hear the choked breath before the tears come.

Seconds later, my face is damp too.

"Losing a best friend sucks," they say, half laughing, half sniffling.

I shiver and listen.

"Why do I miss him all the time?" River stares down at the flowers. "I'm doing my best to move on. Hell, I spent a night hanging with the greatest group of people I've met since him."

Another stab of shame wrecks my chest.

"And I still felt so guilty afterward. Like I was replacing him," they whisper. "Is that how moving on is supposed to feel?"

"I don't know," I answer honestly.

I think about Darren. How he's *encouraged* this apology tour. He's okay with sharing our dares with others if it means I'll feel a little more like myself.

"Maybe you're not replacing him," I finally say. "Maybe we have room to share our real selves with more than one person. Maybe not every friendship is The One. When things don't end the way we hoped, maybe shutting ourselves off isn't the answer?"

River wipes under their glasses, snorting. "When did you become a philosopher?"

I laugh softly. "I wish there was a Wikipedia entry you could skim through for a solution."

"The TL;DR version."

The skyline begins to gray. The clouds are fuller too. A storm is in our future.

"We're all figuring this shit out, Riv. Devaughn was one step for you," I say after a minute. As hard as I fight, I think about Jay. "I'm pretty sure he doesn't want you to stop there."

River squeezes out more tears.

"You don't have to forget him," I whisper into their hair. "Let him know you miss him. You're trying. Going forward."

Birds take flight. The breeze changes directions. A small group in all white crosses the endless yellow-green grass toward another headstone. But time stands still for River and me. I hold them close. Ignore the dampness on my T-shirt as they cry. Pretend my own tears over Granny and Jay and the relationship Dad and I had before the party don't exist.

Eventually, we sit on the ground.

Together, we say goodbye to what was.

Maybe we say hello to what could be too.

As we walk out of the cemetery, dusting grass from our clothes and scrubbing tears off our cheeks, River asks, "Who's next on your

Sorry for Being Shitty, Help Me Be a Better Person tour?"

"Wow," I say, eyes wide. "Is that what they're calling it?"

"So, you're assuming you're cool enough to talk about?"

"Check and mate." I chuckle.

Katie's car waits across the street. She appears to be having her own moment to whatever song's playing. Thankfully the windows are up. I've heard one Zhao sibling sing already. The voice talent runs thin in that bloodline.

"Aleah," I eventually sigh out.

"Ouch."

My head whips in their direction. "It can't be *that* bad."

One of River's thin black eyebrows practically high-fives the darkening sky.

"Okay," I groan as thunder growls lowly in the distance. "It's gonna suck. Should probably get all my affairs in order. Notify my next of kin."

River smirks.

"Speaking of Aleah," I say as we cross the street. "I could use a little help getting her to, you know, be in the same place and time as me?"

River glares skeptically. I offer my most earnest, pleading grin.

With one hand on the passenger door handle, just as the sky shatters and the first angry drops of rain fall on us, River exhales, then says, "Why am I always the accomplice in your ridiculous meet-cutes?"

# 22

# UNREAD APOLOGIES ON THE NOTES APP

**Brook-Oak's state-of-the-art** gymnasium is a house of legends. From the ceilings to the innumerable gold banners announcing the school's sports achievements. Near the electronic scoreboard is a shrine of former championship-winning athletes, their jerseys embossed on cerulean tapestries. The bleachers are stacked accordion-like against the walls. HID lights reflect off the newly refurbished hardwood floors like colossal ivory stars. Painted in the middle of the floor is a fiery gold-and-cerulean bird.

That's right. We're the Brook-Oak Phoenixes. *We rise from the ashes of adversity!*

Or, for most students, the ashes of generational wealth and privilege.

That's not the case for the one student I find in the gym on a

Wednesday afternoon, dribbling a basketball twice before making a perfect three-pointer.

I watch from the shadows by the side entrance. An overdue apology awaits. I just need a few seconds to gather my words.

When Aleah breaks away to catch her own rebound, she spots me.

Oh well. No better time like the present, then.

"Hey!" I wave from the midcourt line.

She glowers. The ball's tucked under one arm. Instead of the standard-issue Ballers practice clothes, Aleah has on a vintage TLC tour shirt, loose joggers like mine, and gold-trimmed, white Curry 8s. They're fairly scuffed up but still sick.

Long seconds go by. My heart feels inside out. I break from our staring contest first.

"Aleah, listen. I just want to say I'm—"

"I don't want your apology."

I pause, grimacing.

Aleah passes the ball between her hands. Her pinched mouth wiggles back and forth in the same rhythm. She's thinking, her eyes fixed on the wall behind me.

Finally, she blinks. "I want the truth."

I nod.

"Sure you're up for that?" It's intentional, the way she ices me out with her sharp tone, the obvious distance.

I swallow, then reply, "Yes."

"When you said we weren't only friends because your dad and Uncle Mario were—" The hesitation returns. It's as if her wound has barely scabbed over, even after all this time. "Were you being honest?"

It's the one question I've never wanted to answer.

This time, I look beyond her. To the rafters. Into one of the bright lights until it hurts more than the truth I've been terrified to confront.

If someone had asked me five years ago, I know what I would've said: "No." It's why I ended things. In that moment, it was clear.

At least, I thought it was.

Now all I think about is my friendship with Jay. That foundation others built for us. A paper-thin house we grew too big for. Isn't it the same with Aleah? Dad and Miles introduced us, provided the ground we stood on.

But it never felt like Jay and me.

I used to lie in bed, hands folded behind my head, watching my ceiling. I'd imagine a million different scenarios where Aleah and I meet other than at church. On a playground. In a community pool during the summer. Dancing to the same song at a party.

I never saw those things with Jay. I couldn't imagine it happening any other way than through our parents.

"Yes," I finally say, my voice thick. "You were my best friend. They didn't matter."

"Obviously they did."

"But it's not why we *stayed* friends."

"Are you sure about that?"

"Yes," I say earnestly. "Aleah, our connection was real. You saw me like—" I pause the same way she did minutes ago, face pinched. I won't say his name. "Like a lot of people haven't seen me."

It aches from my toes to temples knowing I walked away from that.

That I might not ever have it again.

She spins the basketball on her index finger, one eyebrow raised. I think she's telling me the ball is in my court or something metaphorical.

"I'm sorry I—"

She groans, dribbling the ball loudly like she doesn't want to hear it. I don't care. Makayla's right. If I'm going to apologize, I'm going to name it. Own it.

"I'm sorry I chose my pops over you!" I shout. "I'm sorry I ever thought I had to choose between you two when Mario left!"

When the echo of her dribbling softens, I add, "I'm sorry I thought there were sides. I shouldn't have let their relationship change ours."

She watches the ball rather than me.

"And I'm sorry I abandoned you. I was an asshole."

Aleah bounces the ball high one last time before catching it.

"You were young."

"No, I don't want any excuses for what I did."

"Oh, I'm not giving you any," she says pragmatically. "Simply pointing out facts. You were young. Undeveloped. I'm not saying you're mentally capable of handling a real, honest friendship now." I wince, hand to my chest, but she continues. "You're trying, I guess. Y'know, with age hopefully comes growth."

I smile. "Did you just drag me while low-key encouraging me?"

Her eye roll is instant. "I contain multitudes."

She really does. Always has. Who wouldn't want a friend like her?

"I heard about the Jay thing," she says out of nowhere.

Of course she did. Nothing happens around this school with-out it either being a hashtag, a meme, or the hottest distraction from an assignment.

"I'm glad you ditched him," she notes. "Sorry, not sorry."

A small grin tickles my mouth. "I don't hate him," I quietly admit. It's another hard truth I'm learning to live with.

"I get that." She scrunches her nose. "I don't hate Lexi. Or my mom." Her hands are less coordinated as she bounces the ball. "I don't hate you either, Theo."

We stare at each other. Her eyes aren't as loaded with venom as before. They're soft. Something like twelve-year-old Aleah. Eventually, we smile in a way that feels like we're okay.

Not fixed. But okay.

"Anyway." She nails another flawless three-pointer. No back-board, all swish. When she recovers the ball, she says, "I know you're here for my dare. River warned me."

Sold out by my mutual anime buddy. Figures.

"And?" I ask.

She makes another shot, this one swirling around the rim before dropping in.

"It's already done." She says it so casual. But there's some-thing in her stuttered footsteps as she lines up for a shot she never takes. A beat before her face is lit brighter than those fireworks in Prospect.

"I'm in." I'm not sure if it's her voice or a sneaker against the hardwood that squeaks. "I'm going to be a freaking Rolling Tone!"

*Definitely voice.*

"Really?" I can barely contain my own excitement.

I want to hug her. Swing her around. Scream victoriously. But I manage to find my chill—and my desire to avoid bodily harm—to say, "That's huge. Right?"

Aleah shrugs. "It's aight."

She's such a liar. I'm not gonna call her out. Amanda Cox will do enough of that for both of us.

"Well, then." I pace around her, hands behind my back. "Guess that means I need to give you a new dare."

"Uh, that's not how it works," she argues.

Another pair of sneakers squeal on the hardwoods. Darren's hustling over to us, grinning. It's a good thing I didn't let River in on my backup plan in case this all went to hell.

Darren snatches the ball from Aleah, goes for a layup, and . . . misses badly, crashing bodily into the wall.

With age clearly doesn't come better friend choices.

After recovering, Darren asks, "Was that awful? On a scale from one to ten?"

"Negative five," I reply. Aleah's too busy doubled over with laughter to answer.

Darren brushes himself off, cheeks a burnt red, before turning to Aleah. "Theo's right. A new dare must be instituted."

"Because . . . ?" Aleah says.

"In order for it to count, you have to have at least one witness from the crew," Darren explains diplomatically. "Cardinal rule of the dare system, duh."

I elbow him with a smile. Good old Darren Jacobs to the rescue.

Aleah pouts. "Sounds fake."

"Oh, it's very real," I counter, inflating my chest. "It's an automatic L if none of the dare committee is there to bear witness. Them's the rules."

I proudly accept Aleah's middle-fingered response as her admitting defeat.

"Fine," she grumbles. "What's the new dare?"

I tap my chin, thinking. There are a dozen different options. But every single one leads back to a dare that pushes her into being my friend again. That's not what I want. No more forcing things. No more situational relationships.

No more selfish dares.

My eyes fall on her left foot resting on the basketball.

"I dare you to stick it out with the Ballers," I say. "I dare you to chase your dreams no matter who's standing in the way."

Aleah puts her hands on her hips but doesn't respond.

That's my cue.

"And just to be sure there's an actual witness this time," I start, inhaling deeply before the next part, "I'll be there. Every game. Watching and cheering and embarrassing the shit out of you. I'm gonna tag you in sixty different videos for my measly one-point-one-thousand followers to see."

"You just had to throw that in," stage-whispers Darren, nudging me.

Aleah looks as if she's processing the gauntlet I've thrown down. I can tell she's searching for a counterargument by the way her lips part, but there isn't one.

"Okay," she relents in a whisper.

"Okay?!"

Aleah nods, then gently smiles.

"So . . . is this the new Nameless Trio? TNT-squared?" Darren tosses his arms around our shoulders, ridiculous biceps yanking us closer.

Aleah makes a face, trying to wiggle free. I share the same sentiment.

"No more trios," I groan, poking Darren's ribs until he staggers back. "And no more nicknames. The Nameless Trio? Who came up with that anyway?"

"Jay," Darren reminds me with a weak pout.

That's right. He thought we were nobodies the first day of school. Like we had to earn our place here. Make everyone love us. I coined TNT because I knew, as a group, we were explosive. Who knew fourteen-year-old Theo was so prophetic?

"We're not nameless," I declare. "We're not some collective hive-mind either. We have our own identities and goals."

I peek over at Aleah. "We're friends too."

She doesn't react other than hugging herself. I don't know why I hoped for something more. *I'm sorry* doesn't solve everything.

"Just so I'm clear," Darren says, "that's a veto on a squad name?"

"A hard no," Aleah confirms.

I nod in agreement. "I just want my friends to be friends with each other."

"Geez, what is this? Some Pixar wet dream?" Aleah's teasing smirk sets Darren off, his cackle echoing off the gym's walls.

I can't help my own chuckle. "Does this mean you accept my apology?" I ask her.

She's back to spinning the ball on one finger, but her response isn't as delayed: "Yes."

"And my friendship?"

"Pending," she says flatly, eyes narrowed.

I back away, hands up. I'm not going to push it.

This whole moment is enough.

Dad's leaning in the kitchen entryway when I arrive home. He looks as if he's been expecting me. I haven't even removed my backpack before he asks, "Can we talk?"

My heart catches as I nod.

Dumping my things on the sofa, I nervously follow him.

Nothing much has changed about our kitchen since we were last in here together. A few more dishes in the sink we've been ignoring. Dad's laptop on the table. The range light over the stove perpetually left on. An empty pizza box from Monday's we're-still-being-awkward dinner on the counter next to the Crock-Pot.

The whiteboard wiped completely clean.

*Oh.* Actually, that's new.

I blink at Dad. He smiles, then calmly says, "Sit down."

"Where's the, uh." I up-nod at the glossy, white surface while dragging out a chair. There isn't a trace of blue anywhere. As if Dad took the time to spray and scrub the board down. Remove every bullet point that's haunted me for years. "Where's The Plan?"

"Gone," he replies frankly. He flops down next to me.

That's new too. We've always sat across from each other at the table. Enough room to feel like we're together, in the same space, but still able to be in our own worlds on whatever electronic device we had nearby.

I frown. "But all your hard work."

"You mean all the things that overshadowed all *your* hard work?"

I don't answer. Dad doesn't look as if I need to. His smile remains Times Square–at–night bright while opening the laptop, tapping the screen awake.

The sun hasn't fully set. Through our back door, its orangey light bounces off Dad's smooth cheeks. Tangerine rings circle his animated brown eyes. He's shaved, got a haircut too. Nothing about his expression is the aged, weathered look from the other day that chases me in my nightmares.

He's himself again.

We sit in a dense silence. Dad's latest wallpaper—an old-school cartoon Optimus Prime—watches from behind the scattered icons on the screen. Let it be known, Dad doesn't delete anything. Ever.

Except maybe a plan that didn't work for either of us.

My eyes study the whiteboard one last time.

Simultaneously, we say, "I'm so sorry . . ." then stop, heads shaking in tandem as we laugh.

"Let me," he insists.

I lean back, allowing him to speak first.

"I'm sorry, TJ." He rests one hand on top of the other. "I never wanted you to feel like you had to be better than me. Better than . . . this place."

Scratching my temple, I wait. I know he has more to say.

"I've always loved my life—*our* life," he corrects, sighing. "But I wish it had been so much more."

He pauses, eyes closing. On the table, his hands shake. I rest one of mine on his, squeezing.

"I wasn't even twenty-three when your grandfather died." His eyes blink open. "Barely out of college. He was a *great* man. Worked hard. But he never told me he was proud of who I was. That he felt like I'd made it. That I was gonna keep making it."

I curl forward, needing to be closer to him.

"Your granny . . . God, I loved her," he whispers, head tilted back like he's speaking to her somewhere beyond our house. "I don't know if I became the man she wanted me to be either. Did I make her proud?"

Every muscle in my back tightens. I want to run into the living room. Snatch the photo of Granny and me from the wall. Remind him of that day. Of how proud I *know* Granny was of him.

Yet, the more I think about it, I don't know if I ever heard her *say* it.

Maybe it's one thing to show up for people. To mean things with our actions. But if we never say it too, how will they know?

"Dad . . ."

He shakes his head, smiling. "That's not the point." His hand turns over, grabbing mine. "Once you got into Brook-Oak, I became one-track-minded. Get you to the best colleges. Get you out of here."

He sighs. "I never went anywhere. I thought if you did, people would see I did something with my life. That you, as you so eloquently put it, wouldn't have to live in the shadow of Miles Wright."

I cringe. "I didn't mean—"

He waves me off. "No, it's true."

That doesn't make me feel any less like an asshole, though.

"You were right—about Jess and me," he admits. "Our friendship is . . . complicated."

I hold back a snort. There's that word again. It perfectly describes all my tangled thoughts about Jay.

"You don't know this, but after that first try with IVF, I made a long post on Facebook about the struggles. It's how Jess and I reconnected again. She hopped into my DMs—"

"Dad," I groan. "Rephrase that. It sounds . . . sketch."

He bumps my shoulder with a low chuckle. "Anyway. We started messaging. She helped me like she did at Brook-Oak. She planned ways to get the funds for another try. Cosigned on a loan. And *Justin*—" A familiar pained expression seizes his face when he says Mr. Scott's name. "He knew people. Helped me locate a better clinic."

I bite on my thumbnail.

Wow, Mr. Scott is one of the reasons I'm here?

"I've always felt like I owed them for that," he explains. "It also made me feel like I needed to be the perfect parent in their eyes. If I wasn't, would they think they made a mistake? That I wasn't the person they thought I was?"

"Dad, you're not—"

"I know!" He groans. "What you said was right—if someone's *truly* your friend, you shouldn't have to impress them. Shouldn't feel like you owe them anything other than being yourself. You're not obligated to them. Or vice versa. You should *want* the best for each other. Period."

My lips struggle to hold a smile.

"We're having lunch next week. Jess and me need to talk,"

he tells me. His index finger idly swipes the laptop's mouse pad, the cursor chasing nothing across the screen. "Maybe you and I can discuss what you're going through with Jay before then? Work things out . . . together?"

I nod.

"All this time, I thought I was doing what a parent is supposed to, TJ," says Dad. He holds my gaze. "But I failed."

"You didn't."

"Yes, I did! I forgot one of the most important parts of being a parent is to stop, *listen*, then ask questions. I need to pay attention to what you want for yourself."

His hand squeezes mine again. I cling to the heat. To Dad's voice.

"You're under a lot of pressure. A lot of bullshit . . ."

"Uh, *language*," I say, snorting.

"I want you to be happy with the choices you make, and . . . I need to apologize for something else."

With his other hand, he rubs his chin. In his face, I can see him piecing together the words, shifting the pieces, finding where and how they fit. Eventually, he gets there.

"I'm sorry I ever made you feel like you had to abandon Aleah because I was having a hard time."

"Dad, no. I didn't feel—"

He waves me off. "Yes. You did. Maybe not at the time. Maybe you were confused. But you did what you did because of me. And I'm sorry."

We both take a moment to breathe.

I stare at the table. I can't watch his eyes mist over. It's hard enough listening to the small tremble in his voice when he says, "My romantic relationships and your friendships are separate. They're *not* intertwined. If I'm struggling with something, you should never—*ever*—make the sacrifice so I can move on. That's not your job."

He clears his throat. I squeeze his hand.

"I'm sorry, son. I plan to tell Aleah this too."

My thoughts rewind to the ramen bar. Mario's face. How he hasn't changed much, other than his smile. It was a little less vibrant without Dad by his side. I know Dad doesn't owe me this, but I can't help my next question.

"Why did you two break up?"

Dad laughs sadly. It's his way of telling me he hoped I'd never ask.

"Mario's promotion relocated him to Houston," he begins.

I knew that much already.

"He wanted me to come with him," Dad continues. "Wanted *us* to come with him."

*Oh.* Me, living in Texas? Hundreds of miles away from Darren and Jay and Brook-Oak?

"Granny had died the year before. Your life, friends were here. Kentucky's all you—*we've* ever known. I kept thinking, 'How can I ask my son to start over?' "

"You told him?"

Dad nods. "We got into a big fight. He called me a coward. Said my decision was about me, not you. *I* was scared to break out of my shell."

I scowl, chewing my lower lip.

"Hold on." Dad chuckles. "He wasn't totally wrong. I was afraid. It's hard to step out of your comfort zone, no matter what age you are." He wipes at his eyes. "Mostly, I didn't want to be the reason you lost what you had here."

I think I know what he means. Me and Aleah.

"So, he called it quits. I let him leave."

*And then I walked away from Aleah.* I don't say it.

"He's back, y'know? Mario," I whisper.

Dad snorts. His expression says, *You're late to the party, kid.*

"Wait. You know?"

"Duh." He rolls his eyes. "News flash: You're not the only one with social media, TJ. I've seen photos. Location tags. We Gen-Xers know how to use technology too."

"Yeah, poorly," I retort under my breath. "You still have a Facebook, Dad. You're a narc for the government."

He exhales a "Boy, shut up" before turning the laptop toward me.

"Have you seen him? In person?" I ask.

"Mind your business."

"That a no, then?"

Dad elbows my arm. "This isn't about Mario or me." He pulls up his web browser. No less than ten tabs are open. I can't make out any of the titles. "This is about who it should've always been about: you."

Heat races through my cheeks. My belly squirms in anticipation of a lecture. Another Plan in the making.

But Dad only says, "Where do you want to go to school?" while clicking on the tabs.

Each is a different college. San Diego. Texas. Minnesota.

California. Florida, then Georgia. The last three tabs are all universities in Kentucky. Close to home.

Close to him.

Words turn to gum in my mouth, sticky and flavorless and hard to swallow. I turn my eyes on him.

"I don't know, Dad."

He doesn't yell. Not a speck of disappointment in his expression. Dad nods and smiles.

"Okay."

He opens a new search engine. "You have time to figure it out," he continues. "When you do, we'll move from there. We *might* still need a recommendation letter—"

I tense up.

"But I promise, we'll find the right person to write it. Together. No shortcuts," he finishes. "This is your future. Your plan."

My future. My plan.

Everything's about what's best for me. Not for me *and* Dad. It's no less pressure, but if I fail, I know Dad won't hate me.

He'll be right here, waiting for me to start again.

"Thanks, Dad," I say, a little choked, fully aware I haven't apologized yet for what I said that day. He doesn't seem anxious to jump into that conversation yet. It's for another time.

"I love you, TJ," he whispers, kissing my temple. "We're going to be fine."

And I believe him.

# 23

# THE THING ABOUT PROM IS . . .

**I wake up** to a text from Aleah. I almost forgot we exchanged numbers after we finished talking in the gym. We haven't reached dances-to-nineties-throwbacks-in-my-living-room friendship, but we're clearly on a level where she feels comfortable enough to message me at 6:42 in the morning with the worst news ever.

> **Aleah**
> **what up! plans in motion for luca to complete his dare.**
> **makayla found him a date!!! explain later**
> 6:42 A.M.

*Shit.*

My brain selectively forgot I so graciously reached out to Makayla for assistance with my final incomplete dare. Now Luca's going to have a date to prom not named Theodore Jamal Wright. Thanks, universe.

I consider not replying. Ignorance truly is a special form of bliss. But I accidentally left my read receipts on. Plus, I need to accept the Luca ship has sailed. I screwed up my chance.

He deserves the prom of his dreams.

After typing then deleting three different versions of the same "fuck my life" response, I settle on two words:

**I'm in!!!**

Then I scream into my pillow, hoping not to wake Dad.

The Marilyn Kensington Library is, quite frankly, stunning. Nothing like those dusty libraries in movies. Brook-Oak went all out for this sanctuary. Well lit, ideal temperatures year-round, limitless books, expensive computers and glass study rooms, and the perfect location to hide away from the world for hours. Another of this school's major selling points.

It's also one of the few places I've grown to love over the years.

For all the time I've spent here, I still have no clue who the donor is, despite the large plaque outside the double doors, but Marilyn Kensington must've been a *goddess*.

I have one hand on the brass door handle, finishing up a hilarious TikTok compilation of babies trying foods for the first time, when Darren catches me by the elbow.

"Wait! Let's go have lunch together."

I wrinkle my nose. "D, I need to study."

Even after a spring break full of books, I still feel behind. The extra track practices leading up to conference finals haven't helped.

"Bro, nourishment is a necessity," Darren asserts. "Your brain needs fuel."

"You need help," I joke back, yanking the door open.

"*Please*. Just today. Me and you, out in the quad."

At that, my hand goes numb. I lose my grip. The door almost swings closed on some poor underclassman's face as she exits. Fortunately, she palms it back at the last second. Darren compliments her freakish reflexes as she flings us the stink eye, stomping away.

I whisper, "The quad?"

Darren smiles sheepishly.

Studying isn't the only reason I've moved my lunchtime hangout to the library. I don't want to face Jay. Practices with him present are difficult enough. I jump at any instance to be somewhere he's not. The one course I'm acing is Avoidance 101.

"D, I'm not really—"

"Theo," he says, quiet but serious. His fingers tug on my T-shirt sleeve until our eyes meet. "I miss bonding with my best friend. You're always here. Then practices are, well, you know."

The team continues to tiptoe around the collapse of our little group. Plus, Coach wants us focused on being our best. That leaves no room for goofing off like Darren and I used to do.

"It's one lunch."

My sneakers squeak against the floor as I weigh my options. The weather's nice. A little sunshine might help me survive Mr. London's class after. Maybe Jay won't be outside. If he is, he'll probably be with Jayla's crowd. Word in the halls is they're "working on their relationship." Odds are they'll be swapping corsages and tongues by prom.

Darren's mouth has gone full pout mode, eyes ready to shed tears. Seriously, he's in the wrong program at school. YPT would suit him perfectly.

"Fine," I surrender. "But you're buying me *two* cups of pretzel bites."

He shoves me lightly as we fall in step. "I'll even throw in extra mustard packets!"

"Dude!" I yell, tossing a pretzel bite at Darren. "Are you on the run from the mob or something?"

He's been jumpy since we strolled into the quad, which is funny since I'm the one with more enemies than allies these days. Luckily, it's a Jay-less lunch break. No topknot or vicious glare in sight. That and the warm rays beaming on our stone table have made this a shockingly good time. But Darren's on obvious edge, looking around every corner like Ghostface from those Scream movies is coming for him.

"No!" Darren exclaims when I bounce another pretzel off his cheek.

"Bullshit." I laugh. "You owe Amanda Cox money or something?"

Speak the devil's name and she shall appear.

Through the sea of students enjoying the spring heat, Amanda marches forward with a couple of the Rolling Tones following. Hands behind her back, preppy style on level twelve, she smiles our way.

No. Amanda Cox is smirking *my way*.

She and the Tones stop five feet away. People are staring. Phones are trained on us like everyone's expecting a verbal throwdown worthy of social media notoriety. I swallow, then croak, "Uh, hello?"

With an unsubtle hair flip, Amanda raises three fingers, slowly lowering a digit at a time. It's a countdown. When the last finger drops, the Rolling Tones behind her—somehow doubled in number since their initial approach—burst into song.

Surprised laughter erupts from our audience, some cooing too. My heart lurches. Everything goes fuzzy. I barely make out the upbeat, poppy song they're belting out. The lyrics are mad corny and . . .

I gasp, eyes widening. *God, no.* It's "Live While We're Young" by One freaking Direction.

From all corners of the quad, the remaining Rolling Tones appear, falling into seamless harmony with Amanda. She's front and center, working through the robotic choreography that has won their a cappella group an assortment of first-place ribbons. Offbeat claps from the table next to ours encourage her to go all out.

That's when I notice something.

Darren's not beside me anymore. No, he's joined the Rolling Tones' line of rhythmless dancing. He's not the only one.

River's next to him. I clock Makayla jumping and shouting the lyrics off-key, earning a lethal stank face from Amanda. But the cherry on top. The most unbelievable thing is . . .

Aleah's here too.

She steals the lead from Amanda, hitting a dope slide-shoulder-shimmy combo while nailing her notes. I can't catch my breath from laughing. Tears stick to my eyelashes.

But it's not over.

Midway through the second chorus, the Tones and my friends reconfigure, forming a circle around me. Phones are aimed higher to capture every second. But I notice half the cameras are pointed somewhere else. Squeals arise. The volleyball team stands on tables to applaud.

Amanda plops a plastic crown on my head. It's almost like the one from Maddie's bedroom.

The Tones are humming a new, slower melody. I instantly recognize it: Mariah Carey's "Always Be My Baby." The song I serenaded this very quad with.

A cheek-aching, heart-in-my-throat smile engulfs my face.

The circle splits. With pink cheeks, impeccable hair, and a black T-shirt with a white *?* in the middle is Luca.

To his right, our friends form a line, all wearing white T-shirts with a black letter printed on them. Together, they spell out P-R-O-M-?

I can't breathe. New tears spring to my eyes. How is this happening? I'm having the moment I've wanted for so long but could never imagine transpiring. In front of all my peers, Luca Ramírez is promposing to me.

His crinkled-eye smile is twitching. He's nervous. After everything I said, how I acted, why is *he* worried?

"Well?"

There's not enough oxygen going to my brain. Wrinkles overwhelm my forehead. "I didn't think you wanted . . . I mean," I stammer. "You deserve a better date."

Luca rolls his eyes. "Hate to break it to you, but I get to decide what I want. Like going to prom with the people I *like*." He reaches up to fix the crown on my head. "And going with the boy who won't complain when I eat all the pink Starburst."

Despite myself, I snort.

He grabs my hand. His nails are still black. My fingertips brush against his rings.

"I don't care about impressing anyone," he says.

"Then what's all this?" I tease, acknowledging the phones recording us, the Tones' soft humming, our friends wearing promposal outfits.

"A dare," he whispers. "The rest I'll tell you later. Right now, I'm showing everyone the *real* me."

Laughter breaks through my lips. I grab his other hand.

"Well, when you put it that way," I say, and then do the other thing I never thought would happen.

I kiss a boy in front of the entire quad.

It's unquestionably *everything* I wanted it to be.

I'm delicately placing the plastic crown in my locker after school when Luca appears, leaning against the door next to mine.

He grins. "Hey."

"Hey," I whisper back, shouldering my locker closed.

All through my last two classes, my stomach's been a thick knot. The promposal had me higher than any edible ever could. But I kept hearing Luca's voice in my ears: *The rest I'll tell you later.*

*The rest*, as in why he's suddenly forgiven my shitty behavior at the party.

No such thing as a clean getaway, right?

"So, um." Luca twists his rings. The skin between his eyebrows tightens. He looks almost like he did when Devya chose Peter over him.

"I'm sorry," I blurt. "For how I acted. The fucked-up things I said. About you. Your family."

I didn't rehearse any of this. I never expected Luca to talk to me again, let alone prompose. But I lean into Makayla's advice. *Own it.*

"I'm sorry for making any of you think I was choosing Jay. That you and him or me were the same. We're not." I inhale unevenly. "I'm still unsure why you asked me to prom. You deserve better."

Luca tilts his head. "Theo, stop being so hard on yourself."

Seven words relieve the ache in my stomach.

"What changed?" I ask.

"Over break, I had a lot of time to think about you. Devya. My fam. Second chances."

I bite the inside of my lip.

"Not everyone deserves another shot," he tells me. "I didn't with Dev. I wasn't sure if *you* deserved one. Makayla's impassioned speech about why I should give you another try wasn't very convincing either."

Ugh. Figures, even though I technically never *asked* Makayla to interfere. Just to help Luca complete his dare.

"But," he says before I plead with the floor to swallow me whole, "Darren's speech did."

I do a double take. *"Darren?"*

Luca nods. "He practically tackled me after school. That guy's a talker. Told me everything about you, Jay, the crop top, the fall-out after the dare . . ."

I thunk my forehead against my locker.

Darren "TMZ" Jacobs and his mouth.

"Hey," Luca says again, softly, his fingers catching my chin. He rotates my face until our gazes meet. "All night, you let me go on and on about Dev. My fam. When we were alone, you never told me about your problems."

I shrug weakly. "Was kinda trying to figure it out on my own."

Other students shuffle through the hall. Locker doors slam. One of the Rolling Tones *aww*s at us.

"Yeah, Darren told me." He grins again. "It made me realize you're really far from perfect."

"Uh, thanks?"

He laughs loudly. His warm fingers trail down my neck. I shiver. He says, "I *like* being around someone I can be imperfect with. I didn't always feel that way around Dev. Or my fam. I can be messy sometimes."

The left side of my mouth pulls up.

"Come on." Fiery red blush flares against his cheeks. "You saw me fall on my ass trying to prompose. Grind on a fake girlfriend. Big wet stain on my groin. Lose a dance contest."

"Don't forget getting meme'd to Lorde."

He shakes his head. "Point is, you never made me feel like being me was a bad thing."

I lean into his hand. Beaming.

"And thanks to Darren," he says, shoulders relaxing, "I know what you did and said wasn't intentionally hurtful. He says you're growing. It takes time. But he's confident you really like me."

Now it's my turn to squirm as my cheeks burn. Huh. Darren's a good wingman after all.

"So my imperfectness makes me prom-worthy?" I chance.

Luca sucks in his lips, but he can't hide his smile, the rose in his cheeks. "Yes."

"Cool," I whisper, watching light dance around his dark eyes.

I signal behind him. "I'd talk about this longer, but, uh. Track practice." He looks embarrassed at keeping me here. I swallow before asking, "Do you maybe wanna walk with me?"

Once again, Luca surprises me. He doesn't hesitate. His hand falls from my neck to grab my hand. It takes two tries before we manage to find the right fit. Our fingers interlock like the hearts on his ring.

*Holy shit.*

I'm walking down the halls of Brook-Oak holding a boy's hand.

# 24

# WHAT ABOUT YOUR FRIENDS?

**Dreaming about and** finally saying yes to prom is vastly different from planning, preparing, and trying not to blow chunks everywhere two hours before the Big Event.

Currently, I'm a mess.

"Maybe we should've gone with the classic black one?" I suggest.

Dad makes a noncommittal noise as he fixes my bow tie.

"The midnight blue suit was fresh, right?"

Regret is stacking up like a Jenga tower. The blue tux was clean, stylish, and timeless. Nothing like what I'm wearing now. Why did I choose my prom attire based on the pair of socks I bought for tonight? Who wears Darth Vader on their feet to prom?

Dad hums again while rolling a lint brush across my shoulders.

"Or the ivory one?"

This time, Dad cocks an eyebrow. "With your clumsy genes? It's a *rented* tux. The insurance alone could've bought me a used car."

I know it's a joke. Thanks to Darren the Narc, Dad sat me down for another talk two weeks ago. This one about money.

"TJ, I work hard for a reason. To make sure you have what you need. To *occasionally* spoil you. Let me worry about what's happening in the bank account."

I promised I would, but all the price tags add up in my head. The tux, shoes, and haircut. Socks too. Thankfully, Luca bought the tickets, but still. Dad's time card is loaded with overtime.

When he steps back to admire me, I can see his heart tripling in size. He's happy. It leaves me flushed and less on edge.

"My clumsy genes are your clumsy genes," I remind him, smirking.

"God bless your G'Pa and the Wright blood flowing through our veins."

We laugh without getting caught up in the sad undertones of the moment. G'Pa and Granny might not be here, but I imagine them watching over us somewhere. Smiling at the ways we've kept going.

"Maybe . . ." Dad squints. "The black would've been a subtler option. This look is saying a lot for junior prom."

I gasp indignantly. The floor-length mirror in Dad's bedroom provides a perfect view of my fit. The scarlet red jacket over all-black shirt, vest, and slacks. My bow tie matches the jacket. Darth Vader socks. With my hair freshly sponged, I look older. A different Theo, even though I still feel like a huge dork internally.

"Just means we need to go bigger for senior year!" I announce, waggling my eyebrows at Dad's reflection.

He groans before fixing my lapels a final time.

I can tell he's eagerly anticipating me starting that part-time job at Crumbtious.

"Speaking of senior year," Dad begins, and suddenly my collar is one size too small. "Maybe it wouldn't be bad for you to take up a hobby? Something unrelated to school or track."

I fiddle with my cuff links.

Last week, we won conference finals. Dusted those Mountainview jerks. Yes, I'm still a little bitter about KD.

When Coach thought no one was watching, I saw her, hand over eyes, crying. It was amazing. It's all I could talk to Dad about on the drive home. Not the victory. Only Coach Devers's reaction.

He said "uh-huh" at all the key points, but I sensed something was off. Like he was reading between my words.

"You've set yourself up nicely for college apps," Dad continues as I tug on my crimson loafers. "Maybe you should give yourself something else to focus on? Something . . . fun."

"Track is fun."

"I know." He snickers. "Something solely for you, though. I'm giving you permission to be selfish here, TJ. Take advantage of it."

Who is this alien inhabiting my pops's body?

Through the floor, I hear a familiar, upbeat song. My left foot taps along. *Is that Montell Jordan?* I bite down on my grin.

"What about taking some hip-hop dance classes?"

Dad's head tilts so hard, I think his neck might snap.

"Yeah," I say. All the hours I've spent on my phone watching

YouTube videos. Mimicking TikToks. The adrenaline that exploded under my skin like Pop Rocks candies tossed in soda during the dance contest in Maddie's bedroom. "We'd have a lot of fun."

"*We?*"

"Come on, Dad!" I laugh. "Isn't it time you broke the Wright curse? Find your rhythm?"

"I have rhythm, thank you very much." His attempt at a stern voice gives way to his own sputtering guffaw.

We share twin smiles in the mirror.

"Dance class?" he asks.

"Dance class," I confirm.

"Fine. But if I break a hip before you head off to school . . ." He pauses, rubbing my shoulders. "Which reminds me—I know someone who's interested in writing you a recommendation letter."

"Da—"

"Not a friend from school or anything!" he preempts. "A business associate. You'll have to interview. Explain who you really are."

*Who I really am.* That's still a work in progress.

"So, no favors?" I say. "I have to earn this one?"

The amused look in Dad's eyes is contagious.

"It's all on you, TJ. If that's what you decide."

It's weird, the way he's letting me take the point on these big decisions. He only offers suggestions when prompted. Our dinners have been a lot more banter, less plan-oriented since Dad took down the whiteboard a week ago.

"I'll, uh, let you know," I reply while tugging at my collar.

"Cool." Dad smacks my hand away. "Let's get downstairs. You

know those two are dragging us to hell and back for taking so long."

"Those two," as Dad put it, were most certainly gossiping about us, though they try to play it off the second we're all in the living room together.

"Damn." Aleah leans back on the sofa to evaluate me. "Nice drip."

"Th-thanks," I stammer.

Tonight, Aleah is . . . *arresting*. It's the only word I can think of. She's wearing a chic black suit with sleek blue butterfly patterns. Curly hair pinned away from her face. Soft rose undertones along her cheeks. Her heels alone are made for a red-carpet step-and-repeat.

I don't know why I expected her in a dress, but I love her "F your traditions" power move. Only Aleah could pull it off.

"You're, uh . . ." I try.

She rolls her eyes while adjusting my bow tie. "Don't make this weird."

I grin.

"Who knew you'd look so fly in red?"

"I did!" Dad boasts.

The glare I send him is ignored as he pecks Mario on the lips. Yes, that's a Thing again. Turns out mutuals on social media leads to a lot of awkward DMs, flirting via likes, and a traumatizing amount of Dad taking weirdly angled selfies that require my approval before sending. They were all tasteful. No thirst traps. At least the ones I helped with.

Anyway, a few meetups later, they're a second-chance romance movie waiting to be written.

"While I'm happy for you two," Aleah comments, making a face that says quite the opposite, "all this unnecessary PDA is truly ruining my vibe."

"Hater," Mario says into Dad's cheek after another kiss.

I'm with Aleah. Vomit is churning in my stomach.

"Sorry we didn't take as long as you two to figure things out." Mario smirks.

Aleah and I share a brief look. We're not publicly using the "friend" title. But things have improved since our talk. We don't ignore each other in the halls. She was even at the conference finals, cheering on the team.

We're not rushing it. Like a deep cut, this wound needs sufficient time to heal. One day, we'll be TJ and Birdie again.

At least, I hope.

"Don't listen to him," says Dad, gently folding an arm around Aleah's shoulders.

Unlike with me, she's fallen right back into a comfortable relationship with him. It only took one long, clumsy call from Dad to her. The irony has been eating me alive.

"Mario's sarcastic and stubborn," Dad comments. "Big Capricorn energy."

"It's why you like me," Mario retorts.

Dad smiles sweetly. Watching him turn into a schoolboy around Mario as a kid was confusing but tolerable. Now, though? It's kind of cute. Sickening, yes, but it's as if Dad's getting his big moment too. I love that for him.

"My niece is right." Mario claps my shoulders. "You look . . . what do the kids say? Tight?"

"Jesus, Uncle Mario." Aleah laughs into Dad's shoulder.

The doorbell rings. It's River, Darren, and Bree arriving. We barely have time for hellos and twirling in our outfits before Dad and Mario corral us for photos.

"Look at all of you!" Dad cheers. "Future CW stars!"

"Dad!" I shake my head.

Darren has a laughter meltdown. Bree can't use his pocket square fast enough to clean the tears off his face. They make a sweet couple. Darren was already a teddy bear, but Bree brings out something new in him. He's a lot more fearless. I've also caught him checking more than one of our teammates when their jokes have gotten out of line.

"Okay, besties next!" Mario calls out.

It's weird standing shoulder to shoulder with Darren. A month ago, this would've been TNT. After HoCo, this is all Jay talked about. The three of us at prom. When did he change his mind? When did he decide winning his parents' approval meant more than our friendship?

"Can we hold off on more photos?" River requests.

They pull away from the traditional standing-sideways-in-front-of-your-date pose with Aleah to check their phone. It's cool River and Aleah are each other's "friend date" tonight. I don't know if Aleah would've come if River hadn't asked.

River's definitely going to steal more than a few looks in their fitted plum suit with a long, satin train.

I wish Makayla was here too.

She hasn't been around much. With only a month before graduation, Makayla deserves space to shed the bullshit she's dealt with for years. She quit the cheer squad. Distanced herself from some of the girls. I respect her choices.

She's skipping prom too.

"I don't want the attention," she told me last week when we ran into each other after school. "Time to work on me. Prepare for the future."

I wonder if it has to do with her posting that video.

The response was pretty big. I don't think Makayla expected it. The applause from strangers in the halls. Other students speaking up in the comments. During classes or in Brook-Oak's quad. Sharing their videos across social media.

She's started a mini revolution.

"We have to wait on Luca," River asserts, fingers flying across their phone.

"Yes," Dad agrees, eyeing me with a suspicious grin. "Let's wait on this boy that has my son texting at the table when he thinks I'm not looking. Staying up past curfew to FaceTime."

My mouth drops open. I want to self-combust.

Dad and Mario smile like it's a secret joke between them.

I'm officially no longer a fan of their rekindled connection.

Everyone laughs like they already know. Like Luca and I are so obvious when, I swear, we're not. Yes, we hold hands in the halls. Meet up between classes whenever possible. Chaste kisses in Sonic's parking lot. A handful of make-out seshes behind the bleachers too.

What can I say? Creature of habit.

We haven't made any formal commitments. Luca doesn't need to rush into another relationship. I just want to enjoy whatever this is.

The doorbell rings again.

Darren howls when I hurdle over the sofa. I reach the door before Dad. I need at least five minutes alone with Luca before the Meet the Parent thing happens.

"Wow." Luca almost steps off the porch, openly admiring me.

"Uh, same," I reply.

If Aleah's arresting, Luca's a word not yet invented for beautiful. We didn't coordinate outfits. A few texts here and there about what we wanted to wear. He's in a maroon three-piece suit, white shirt with a navy bow tie. His hair's styled exceptionally high.

I want to kiss him.

His tongue flicks across his lower lip like he wants the same thing.

We stand silently. Wide-eyed, smiling, words unnecessary. I've learned to like this about our time together. It uncoils the tension in my muscles.

"Oh, hey. Almost forgot." He lifts a clear, plastic container with a boutonniere inside. Two roses, red and black, twined by ribbon and ivy. "My sibs helped me pick it out."

"Nice" escapes my lips first. Then, "I got you one too. It's inside."

He grins bashfully. "My mamá helped too. She was *very direct* with the florist about her expectations." His chest puffs out. "She helped me get ready too."

Another downward glance reveals Luca's nails have been repainted. A subtle, clean matte black.

We haven't discussed what his family thought about him going to prom with a boy. I didn't know if he'd even told them. I almost ruined everything assuming things about him at the party. I'm not making the same mistake twice.

His free hand tugs on his collar. "About what you said outside Chloe's . . ."

My jaw clenches when he brings it up. I wish he wouldn't. I still feel nauseous thinking about that moment. But if we're going to be together, we need to be honest. I've ruined too many relationships with lies.

"You weren't totally wrong." He shuffles a little. "Families say the wrong things. Do awful shit. They can be there for you. They can also make you feel unloved for being yourself. I know I don't have to forgive mine. I'm not excusing them either. But they're still . . . blood."

I nod once.

"We don't choose our family," he asserts. "We choose friends. Relationships. What underwear to wear."

I avoid glancing down. This isn't the time to guess whether he's wearing those SpongeBob boxer briefs again.

I focus on the twitching corners of his mouth.

"My mamá is *trying*. My tías and tíos too," he continues. I don't mention him leaving out his dad. He shrugs. "If they fuck up again, I might feel differently. Maybe I'll move across the country to get away from them."

"Please don't."

His lips spread into a full, irresistible Luca smile that, yes, even in this very serious moment, I want to smash my mouth against.

"You're not forced to make the same choices, Theo." The hand not holding the boutonniere grabs mine, loosely tangling our fingers. "Do what's best for your own situation."

"*Finally*," I huff mockingly, "I was wondering when we were gonna make this about me."

Luca's lips pucker. Yup, kissing needs to happen soon. He says, "Arrogance isn't charming."

"I don't think you know what charming means."

We grin. My thumb strokes one of his rings. I know what he's saying. Dad and I had a similar conversation about Mrs. Scott. About Jay. About everyone we decide to let into our lives.

I haven't made a final decision on the matter.

However, I've concluded Luca and I have done far too much talking, not enough kissing, so I . . .

Jump and scream when Dad clears his throat behind me. Luca's eyes widen in instant fear. Our hands quickly separate.

A laugh stalls out in Dad's throat. "Can we maybe do this *inside,* you two?"

I grumble a "yeah" before leading Luca into the house.

From there, everything is painfully clumsy. Introductions between Dad and Luca. The "couples" photos that follow. Dad calling Luca out for looking stiff as a corpse as we pose face-to-face, foreheads nearly colliding. Is this what I was missing all those years of not having a boy to bring home to meet Dad?

Before we finish, Aleah wrangles Dad into a picture with Luca and me. He proudly stands in the middle, arms around our shoulders. Behind his back, Luca and I hold hands. I get to do this all night. Luca's thumb draws small circles on my skin like he's thinking the same thing.

Luca demands one final picture: Aleah and me.

Shutter sounds echo in the living room while we take center stage. At the last second, Aleah rests her head on my shoulder. The same way she used to in those worn-soft pews years ago.

Darren reminds us about the reservation his parents booked. A private room at our favorite ramen bar off Baxter Avenue.

"Just one more," Dad pleads, ushering Luca and me into another pose. He wants a picture of us pinning boutonnieres on each other.

And as cheesy-as-F it turns out, I love it.

We're standing in front of our wall of photos. Granny watches me pin a flower on a boy I'm falling for. She sees the real me.

# 25

# #ANEWFUTURE

**Tonight, the sky** is a sea of obsidian glittering with stars. Bass-heavy music pours out of the Gillespie, the venue Brook-Oak rents out annually for prom. Even from a distance, the fairy-tale magic of the lights and balloons and elegance sweeps you away. Gold, ivory, and cerulean banners welcome juniors and seniors. There's even an artificial gate erected outside. A bored teacher stands guard, checking tickets before admitting anyone inside. Students race to the entrance in heels and shiny shoes.

It's undeniably over-the-top, but I want in.

Our golden tickets are in my jacket pocket.

I can't wait to see the rest of the venue. Dance until my feet hurt. Take silly photos. Let Darren talk my ear off about all the gossip he's heard while eavesdropping by the punch table. Spin in an awkward circle while slow-dancing with Luca.

All the movie promises of nights like this being eternal and unforgettable are so close. But Luca stops short ten feet from the gate. I bump into his back, too caught up in watching Sage Chavez piggyback on Abel's back while taking a selfie.

"Sorry," I murmur, but Luca doesn't respond.

In fact, everyone has paused, eyes focused straight ahead.

It's Jay, blond hair sleeked back instead of in a topknot. He's in a stylish black tux with a gold pocket square. His freshly shaven face draws more attention to his stone-blue eyes.

He doesn't acknowledge the others. Only looks at me, lips downturned.

Darren interrupts our staring war. "Bro, not tonight." He rests a hand on my shoulder, trying to guide me past Jay and inside.

I don't budge.

As kids, Jay and I never mastered silent communication like I did with Aleah or Darren. We've always needed words. Big physical cues to interpret what the other's thinking.

However, tonight, I know what Jay wants.

To my left, Aleah grumbles something. River and Bree look undecided on what to do. Luca's fingers squeeze my wrist.

"Let's go," grunts Darren. "We're not here for him."

I stand my ground.

"I want to hear what he has to say."

"Theo," Darren groans like he's reaching his limit. "He's the reason you almost didn't get here. Ignore him."

I turn my eyes on Darren. "I've got this," I whisper. Then I nod at Luca, hoping he understands. He puts on his best grin, leading the others toward the venue.

Darren waits a beat. His face says he's holding back a hundred different choice words for me. Eventually, he follows the group, never saying a word to Jay.

"Bold of you to think I'd want to talk," I say once Jay approaches.

"Can't you tell?" He shrugs with a lighthearted smile. "I love to gamble."

"You're used to the odds being in your favor."

"Ouch." He fakes a wince. "When did you become so mean, Theo?"

I open my mouth, ready to unload on him, but he raises both hands, laughing.

"I'm kidding!" Once he takes in my expression, his smirk fades. "You're right. I'm used to winning. Having shit go my way. I'm sorry."

It catches me off guard. I almost stumble back. Then I hear Makayla's voice in my head. What she said about apologies.

"What for?"

Jay scrubs a hand across his forehead. He's thinking. A group of band nerds passes us, gawking. The implosion of TNT remains a hot topic in the outlier circles. My heart kicks when I search their group for Christian, but he's not there.

"I'm sorry about the dare. *Both dares*," he finally says once we're alone again. "I got so caught up in all the pressure from my family, I—it got to me, okay?"

"It got to you?" I squeeze out of my tight throat. "That's your explanation?"

"I've never felt good enough for them," he says, exasperated. "I've never felt good period, except when I was with TNT. Except when I was with you. You're my best friend. I miss that."

He blinks, eyes are wet, cheeks rosy.

"I fucked up." He cracks his knuckles. "Senior year's in a few months. I want to move past my family's expectations. Do better. Get back to normal."

*Back to normal.* Was anything ever normal about our friendship?

I struggle to look him in the eye. Not because he's on the verge of tears. Because nothing he's said acknowledged the hurt or stress he caused me. Nothing's about me. It's all about him.

It's *always* about people like him.

"That's not an apology," I say. "You haven't named a single thing you've done to me. For months. For *years*, Jay."

"I said—"

"Saying sorry and owning your fuck-ups are two different things."

His mouth snaps shut. Those tears slowly dry up too. His chest rises and falls rapidly. He's either going to explode or break down. I can't bring myself to comfort him.

It's all I've ever done, right? Comfort Jay. Excuse away his actions. Let him off the hook. Look past everything that's bothered me because he was nice and fun. Because everyone loved him. Because we shared a few similar struggles.

I hear Luca in the back of my head.

*We're not the same.*

"Jesus, Theo, what more do you want from me?" He flails his arms. "I helped you get all this. I helped you study to pass the entrance exam. I did whatever I could so we'd be together at Brook-Oak."

I shake my head, unsurprised Jay doesn't see how presumptuous it is to take credit for *my* extra effort to get here.

"What else do you want?" Jay exhales.

"I want you to *listen*," I snarl, trying my best to contain all the rage that's begun to outgrow my body. "Pay attention. Learn. Be empathetic. Stop doing the bare minimum when me or Darren aren't around. Quit waiting for me to teach you how to be better."

"I—"

"You what?" I interrupt. "Thought you did enough? With Cole? The guys on the team? Your dad?"

He swallows, blinking hard.

"You didn't," I whisper. "Maybe I should've said something sooner. But did you ever think about these things on your own?"

Jay's still quiet. I don't know what I was expecting. For him to agree? Admit he's thought about any of this? To do something other than stand there, breathing hard?

"Theo, I'm really sorry! I'm trying—"

I cut him off again. "I don't think you know what that word means, Jay."

His tears return. I can't tell if they're real or not. If they're because Jay knows what I'm about to say.

"I don't want to be around selfish people," I say. "Who take their personal shit out on others. I need friends who stand up for me. Not because it looks cool. Because it's what you *should* do."

I sneak a glance toward the castle. Where Darren is. And the crew from Maddie's bedroom. There's an uncomplicated tug to be around them. That's what I want from a friendship.

"Right now, I don't think you fit my definition of a friend," I say to Jay, shuffling around him. "Who knows? Maybe in the future, things'll be different. *You'll* be different. Maybe we'll be the kind of friends our parents wish they were."

"Th-Theo—"

I'm numb to his splotchy face and shaking limbs. There's no pity in me. Only four words I need to say:

"See you around, Jay."

Luca's the first person I see. He leans against a pillar outside the venue. I don't know how long he's been there. If he ever went inside. But I'm so happy it's him waiting for me.

He doesn't ask if I'm okay. Doesn't try to pull me into a hug or treat me like I'm made of glass. To him, I'm not fragile.

I'm my own version of strong.

Luca looks like he's perfectly fine with us standing here, gazing in each other's eyes, not saying a damn thing all night long.

I move in until we're practically nose-to-nose. "Dare completed," I finally say, biting my lip. "I did something that makes only me happy."

"I mean, technically, I'm happy for you too so . . ."

"Shut. Up," I say, kissing him. "Let me have this." Then I kiss him again.

"Hmm. Does the dare count, though?" He leans away, lips twisted sideways. "Are you sure anyone saw?"

I tip my head back, almost swearing at the sky. The rules of a dare truly need to be revamped in the future.

Luca cackles. His amusement is joined by River's snorty giggle and Darren's wheezing guffaw. Out of the shadows, my friends circle me and Luca, applauding.

"We all saw," says Darren, squeezing my shoulders.

"You did that!" Aleah shouts.

I roll my eyes, cheeks burning, but the grin tugging at my lips feels earned.

"Can we please go inside now?" begs River. "They have pizza rolls! It's all over Amanda Cox's Snapchat."

Overpriced gowns and pizza rolls? Well played, Brook-Oak.

"You becoming a Rolling Tones stan is not healthy for our friendship," notes Aleah, nudging River. They turn to walk in together.

Bree snatches Darren's hand, quickly following.

I'm on my first step to do the same when Luca says, smirking, "One more dare, Theo."

He yanks me into a quick kiss that doesn't go unnoticed by a passing librarian. I'm not even embarrassed about being caught.

Against my lips, Luca whispers, "I dare you to get on that dance floor with me and have the night of your life."

"You're gonna regret that dare," I warn, pecking him once more before guiding us in the direction of the ballroom.

I can't believe I'm here. I'm at prom with a boy, holding his hand. It's like the magic I've been chasing for so long is surrounding me. Tonight might not change my life. In hindsight, junior prom could be just another memory I forget until social media hits me with one of those flashback notifications.

I don't care. I'm finally getting my shot at what everyone else has.

And I know one more thing: this is the easiest dare I've ever been given.

So tonight, I'm making my own rules.

# ACKNOWLEDGMENTS

Creating this book was nothing short of magic. There were ups and downs, highs and lows, and so many lessons learned. But every second was worth it for this moment.

It also wouldn't be possible without so, so many wonderful people.

First, thank you, reader. I wrote this book for you. For the Theos and Aleahs and Rivers and Lucases and Makaylas. For the queer teens who need to know they deserve to be treated with respect. The ones who make mistakes, whether intentionally or accidentally. The ones who deserve apologies from the people who hurt them. The queer teens who dream of that big, unforgettable night they see in every movie or TV show. The QBIPOC teens who haven't found their people yet—it's going to happen. You will be loved and appreciated and valued.

Thanks to my incredible, wonderfully supportive agent, Thao Le, for continuing to believe in all the stories I want to tell—even the bad ones. To all the awesome people at Sandra Dijkstra Literary Agency for all their hard work uplifting the power of storytelling.

My amazing editor and the David to my Alexis, Dana Leydig. No one understands my corny sense of humor like you. My publicist, Lizzie Goodell, for creating so many opportunities for me to be weird and talk about books.

The phenomenal staff at Viking/Penguin Random House: managing editors Gaby Corzo and Ginny Dominguez; production editors Marinda Valenti and Krista Ahlberg; illustrator Cannaday Chapman, who gave me the most memorable cover; jacket designers Kaitlin Yang and Theresa Evangelista; interior designers Kate Renner and Monique Sterling; audio editor Emily Parliman, managing editor Kelly Atkinson, and the great staff at Listening Library; Brianna Lockhart and all the heroes in marketing and sales for fighting so hard for my books; the squad of my dreams: Shannon

Spann, Felicity Vallence, James Akinaka, and Bezi Yohannes in digital marketing—thanks for your endless support and love. Proud to be on your team.

This book wouldn't be possible without the tireless and enthusiastic help of Adib Khorram, Julie Murphy, Natalie C. Parker, Sierra Simone, and Tessa Gratton. Thank you for the giant Post-its, the daunting 9 Box, and for staying up extra late to help me unlock what this book was really about.

To every author who's lent their shoulder for me to cry on, especially but not limited to: Becky Albertalli, Nic Stone, Mark Oshiro, Roshani Chokshi, Dustin Thao, Kimberly Jones, Gilly Segal, Kelly Quindlen, Adam Silvera, Ayana Gray, Chloe Gong, Dhonielle Clayton, Leah Johnson, Karen Strong, Justin A. Reynolds, Claribel A. Ortega, Robbie Couch, Adam Sass, and Lana Wood Johnson.

To my family and friends for putting up with my cranky moods and the fact that I never have time to hang out, and for enabling my blueberry muffin and iced vanilla latte obsession.

To every bookseller, teacher, librarian, and educator who has put my books into the hands of the ones who needed them. Every indie bookstore that shelves my books for readers to grab. Special shout-out to my Atlanta bookstore family: Little Shop of Stories, Brave & Kind Books, Charis Books & More, and Read-It-Again.

To the book bloggers, BookTubers, BookTokers, bookstagrammers, artists, and anyone who has ever shared my books with their followers—you've kept this dream alive for me. I'll never be able to thank you enough.

And finally, another round of applause for . . . *you*. If this is the first, second, or fifth book of mine you've picked up to read: thanks for taking a chance on me. For knowing queer and BIPOC teens deserve stories that center them. We *all* deserve a win—I hope you get yours.